VENGEANCE
OF THE
PIRATE QUEEN

BOOKS BY TRICIA LEVENSELLER

Daughter of the Pirate King
Daughter of the Siren Queen

Vengeance of the Pirate Queen

Warrior of the Wild

The Shadows Between Us

Blade of Secrets
Master of Iron

VENGEANCE OF THE PIRATE QUEEN

TRICIA LEVENSELLER

FEIWEL AND FRIENDS

NEW YORK

A Feiwel and Friends Book
An imprint of Macmillan Publishing Group, LLC
120 Broadway, New York, NY 10271 • fiercereads.com

Our books may be purchased in bulk for promotional, educational, or business use. Please contact your local bookseller or the Macmillan Corporate and Premium Sales Department at (800) 221-7945 ext. 5442 or by email at MacmillanSpecialMarkets@macmillan.com.

Library of Congress Cataloging-in-Publication Data is available.

First edition, 2023
Book design by Samira Iravani
Feiwel and Friends logo designed by Filomena Tuosto
Printed in China

ISBN 978-1-250-86497-0 (hardcover)
10 9 8 7 6 5 4 3 2 1

ISBN 978-1-250-89194-5 (special edition)
10 9 8 7 6 5 4 3 2 1

ISBN 978-1-250-32472-6 (international edition)
10 9 8 7 6 5 4 3 2 1

For Jacob,
Because we shared a love of Pirates of the Caribbean
and writing stories. I miss you, bud.

"IF YOU WERE WAITING FOR THE OPPORTUNE
MOMENT, THAT WAS IT."

—CAPTAIN JACK SPARROW
Pirates of the Caribbean: The Curse of the Black Pearl

CHAPTER 1

YOU CAN'T BE AFRAID of the dark when you're the monster lurking in the shadows.

I've lived by these words since I was five years old. They've served me well through many cold nights spent alone. They're doubly useful when I find myself killing, which is more often than not. The pirate queen has many enemies, and I'm the one she sends to take care of them.

Tonight's target is the pirate lord Vordan Serad.

This is the first time in my career I've had to track down the same target twice. I don't like it. Would have been far better if we'd gutted Vordan the last time we caught him, but the late pirate king had wanted him alive.

Vordan's been busy since he escaped. He commissioned a ship under a false name, hired himself a new crew, and slowly began to grow his prestige, starting on the island of Butana. I have no doubt he hoped to raise enough forces to eventually usurp Alosa's throne.

He should have known better. He should have kept running after he managed to free himself during the scuffle between the land king and former pirate king. Might have had a nice, long life that way.

Instead, he has no idea that I'm curled up under his bed.

He prepares for the evening by lantern light. With my limited view from the ground, I watch him kick off his boots and throw them in the direction of the closet. A white bit of clothing joins them. His shirt, I think. Thankfully, he keeps his britches on. He riffles through one of his pockets, and a soft *chink* sounds a moment later. He must have pulled out that coin he likes to fiddle with and placed it on the bedside table.

Vordan seats himself on the floor, leaning his back against the edge of the bed, mere feet from where I hide. My heart pounds out a too-fast rhythm at the threat of discovery.

I could do it now, I suppose. Just roll over, grab my dagger from its sheath at my side, and slice his throat.

But Alosa wants him to know on whose orders he's being killed, and I'll be in a better position to keep him quiet if I can attack from above rather than below.

Killing is easy. The tricky part is being quiet. Being patient. Waiting for the right moment. That's what makes me good at my job. Being an assassin is not always about the easy kill. It's about the best kill.

I hold perfectly still and watch as Vordan stretches out his bad leg. Alosa once used her siren song to force him to jump from a two-story height. I'll bet he thinks about her every time it stiffens from the cold. He leans over to rub at the muscles near his knee before standing. He takes a drink from something at his nightstand, puts out the lantern, then sits on the bed.

I extend my arm until it is only inches from Vordan's left ankle. My fingers tiptoe ever closer, until my pointer finger is directly behind his heel. It would be so easy to slice his Achilles tendon. He'd never walk again. Instead, I draw circles against the wood slats on the floor, allowing Vordan to think the last thoughts he will ever have. Eventually, he sighs, pulls his legs onto the bed, and fidgets with the covers.

When he finally goes still, I listen to his breathing, waiting for it to slow. Then I wait some more. If I stay my hand until my marks are deeply asleep, they're less likely to rouse from any soft sounds I might make in the room. I don't want them to wake until I'm in position. Until it's too late to fight back. Not to mention, the longer I wait, the more likely it is that everyone else on the estate will be asleep.

I slide out from under the bed and stand, watching Vordan's sleeping form for any movement. When his breathing doesn't change, I draw a dagger and tread to the bed. Scant light from the moon slants through the window. I stand on the opposite side of the bed so my shadow isn't cast upon Vordan. He sleeps on his back, hands at his sides atop the covers, face pointed at the ceiling.

He's unremarkable in appearance, with a medium height and build. Brown hair and beard. No distinguishing features. It's how he stays hidden. Stays alive, really. We pirates don't typically have long life spans. At least not under the former king's rule.

As I let my dagger drift closer to his throat, I replace the face before me with one from my memories. One with lighter skin, a beauty mark on the left side of his forehead, a single gold hoop high up on one ear. Straw-colored hair and a clean-shaven face. A cleft in the middle of the chin.

My first kill.

I pretend they all are so I can savor it over and over again.

As instructed, I let my dagger rest on the skin of Vordan's neck. His eyelids twitch twice before shooting open. Without moving his neck, his eyes veer to the right so he can take me in. "You," he says. "You're one of hers."

"The pirate queen sends her best wishes. You'll need them where you're going."

"Wai—"

Before he can finish the request, I slice deeply, nicking the carotid artery. Blood drenches the sheets, drips quietly on the floor.

And I watch as the life leaves Samvin Carroter for the eighty-ninth time.

I clean my dagger on an unmarred section of blanket and sheathe it. Then I retrieve my rapier from under the bed and reattach it to my waist. Most pirates carry cutlasses, but I prefer the speed and dexterity of the rapier. Besides, I am noble-born, and I like to retain that remembrance of my family.

I exit Vordan's room, letting myself into one of the hallways of the exquisite mansion he'd been living in. He killed the family who owned it. Bribed or threatened all the staff. Set up what few men he had in the comfy rooms. It was the pattern I had to look for while tracking him down.

He learned the first time that if he stayed in one place, Alosa was sure to find him, so he'd take up residence in some fancy estate, stay there a month at most, frequenting the big cities and rallying supporters. Then he'd move to a new city on a new island within the Seventeen Isles and do it all over again.

Unfortunately for him, a discernible pattern is just as bad as staying in one place.

The door makes the softest of clicks as I shut it behind me before treading down the carpet-clad floor. I round the hallway and take the main staircase, stepping toward the outside of the steps, where they're less likely to creak. Three levels down and I reach the main floor. Thinking to leave the same way I entered, I pass through the kitchens.

"Hello?" a voice calls out, and I drop into a crouch.

Everyone is supposed to be asleep, but someone must have grown hungry in the night.

I might not be done killing. The thought sends a delightful shot of warmth to my sword arm, my fingers itching to reach for a weapon. As I crawl behind the nearest table, my heart races again. It's a wild percussion that I've grown used to, even crave at times. The thrill of the hunt.

"Did you hear something?" the same voice says.

"No, but it was probably Miss Nyles coming by the kitchens. Probably turned tail the second she spotted us."

The first man grunts. "We gave her a good beating last night, didn't we?"

"Not so good as the tupping we gave her the night before that."

Their laughter fills the corners of the room like a disease infecting a body. I peer over the edge of the table to get a look at them. Two brutes, mostly dark silhouettes next to the meager candle they have on the table between them. They're spearing cold meats with a knife before filling their gobs and passing a flask back and forth.

I could creep past them silently, leave the mansion with no one the wiser.

But I'm not about to do that after the conversation I just overheard.

It's a risk to attack with two of them fully alert, but it's one I'm willing to take.

I move under the table and push between two chairs. I am no more than a shadow as I waltz behind the pair and draw my sword. I strike the bigger one first, smacking him on the back of the head with the pommel of my rapier. The second turns and manages the first note of a yell as I slam his head down onto the counter. Both don't rise again after slumping to the floor, unconscious.

Footsteps pound above my head, roused by the short-lived sound, and I have a choice to make. I can still slip away, lose them in the winding city streets.

Or . . .

I stare at the duo on the floor.

Or I can see vengeance done.

It isn't really a choice.

I slip back into the dark entryway once I ascertain no one has reached this level yet. A banister lines the stairs, with rails connecting it to each step. I reach out to see if my hands will fit into the spaces between each rail.

They do.

As the men race down the winding stairs, lanterns held aloft, I climb them from the side with my arms, hauling myself up rail after rail. Reach, grip, pull. Repeat.

My legs are too high off the ground by the time the men hit the main floor for them to notice me. Four individuals cross underneath me to reach the kitchens. I let myself drop when the last one is in just the right position. He collapses to the ground under my weight, and I snap his neck before he can rise.

The first two men are already in the kitchens, but the third turns at the sound of his crewman falling. I slice his throat with the tip of my sword before he can make sense of the scene in front of him. I flick the blood from my rapier as I race for the doorway, placing my back against the wall just beside it. I sheathe my sword and draw my dagger.

"Two knocked out cold in here," one of the men says. "Sound the alarm."

The one following orders dashes out of the kitchens. I grip his arm, throw him against the wall, and rake the blade across his throat.

"Hello?" the remaining man calls out, likely having seen his crewman pulled out from his line of sight before the doors closed.

Why do people call out a greeting when something highly suspicious happens? Do they expect us monsters to announce ourselves?

He follows up with "Who's there?"

I adjust the grip on my dagger as I wait to see what he'll do.

He shouts for help, cluing me in to his approximate location in the kitchens.

I throw the doors open wide, sight my mark, and fling my blade. The dagger lands true, embedding in his throat. I don't retrieve it just yet. Time is precious now.

I veer to the right, where the hidden servants' stairs rest. Meanwhile, men rouse from their beds and burst out into the hallways. I see them on each landing as I make my way back to the top level. The dark works to my advantage. I'm used to being in its caress. I doubt there's a soul alive who has better night vision than I do. While I can see the outlines of Vordan's men, they haven't a clue I'm a handful of feet away.

Not a soul even looks in my direction. No one thinks to use the servants' stairs. They might not even know they're tucked away here. These are murderers, thieves, and all other manner of foul scum. They're not used to the layout of fancy accommodations such as these. And since

Vordan kept the staff on hand, his men would never have had occasion to use this route.

I reach the third floor, where Vordan's corpse has started rotting, and peek through bedroom doors one by one.

When I find a man who wasn't roused by the shouting, I enter, tread to the bed, and slice open his neck. It's not the most creative way to end a life, but it is the most efficient with the least amount of effort. And I have many more throats to slit, so I've got to reserve my energy.

"Six down!" someone from below shouts. "Spread out and search the mansion, and you there, go rouse the captain."

I bolt back for Vordan's rooms and slip under the bed. The blood has stopped trickling. It's partially congealed on the floor at the opposite side of the bed.

The door sways open, and boot-clad feet reach Vordan's resting place. "Captain, there's an intruder." He steps back, likely because his hand has come away sticky.

I pull his feet out from under him, climb atop his wriggling body, and prepare to go for the throat.

At the last moment, I turn my hand to the side and land a punch with my knuckles still wrapped around the dagger, right where Mandsy taught me to if the intent was to render someone unconscious.

The lad can't be more than twelve. He's all height with no muscles to his limbs. He's fallen in with a bad crowd, but even I don't murder children.

Back out in the hallway, I creep through the house, quieter than a ghost. I hear doors slamming beneath me, swords coming out of their sheaths, and men murmuring to one another. I search the rest of the bedrooms on this floor, slitting three more throats, before returning to the servants' stairs and taking them down to the next level.

With just my head peering down the hallway, I watch a pirate enter into a bedroom to secure it. I follow after him, sneak up behind him, and cover his mouth with one hand while my dagger rakes across his throat. Back out in the hallway, I note that only some of Vordan's crew are holding lanterns. Should they see my silhouette, I will merely look like another pirate searching through the mansion just like everyone else.

I follow another man into another room, employing the same tactic as before. This one gets down on his knees to look under the bed and doesn't hear me as I come up behind him. Blood trickles onto my fingers from the knife as I right myself, so I take the time to wipe it and my hands off on the bedsheets before exiting again.

Two figures come toward me down the hall without their own light sources, so I flatten myself against the wall to let them pass.

I pull a second knife from my person as I follow them into another room. The first man gets a dagger thrown to the back where his heart rests beneath the skin and muscle. The second turns, but I'm already launching myself at him, slitting his throat with the second knife.

As I rise, I try to remember the last time I killed so many men in a single night. In fact, I don't think it's happened before.

I'm making new memories.

Some men continue up to the third floor, where they're about to find more dead. Others leave for the first floor. I follow the men upstairs first.

I reach the last one in line, covering his mouth as I kill him and catching him before he can land on the floor with a thud. The next one is too heavy for me to catch as he lands, so I flatten myself into one of the closed doorways as a couple of men look behind them.

"Shit!" someone says. "Find 'em."

I'm not sure if he said *Find him* or *Find them*. Should I be insulted or flattered? I launch from my hiding place when someone passes by and slam his head against the opposite wall. I hear the hammer of a pistol being cocked back, so I turn the man, letting him take the shot.

I reach for another dagger before I let the body drop and throw it at the person holding the lantern. The light sputters out as they fall.

More footsteps pound up the stairs, bringing more lanterns with them, and I drop to the ground, as though I'm just another dead body among the mess.

"Where is he?" one of the newcomers asks.

"He vanishes like smoke," someone from the first party says.

Definitely offended.

The men tread past me, and I hold perfectly still. One of my arms is looped over my head, concealing my long ponytail from discovery if anyone tries to look down.

A boot knocks into me, but I hold back a grunt as I wait for the newcomers to pass me by.

When they do, I descend upon them one at a time. Slitting throats. Bashing heads. Catching bodies. Kill. Repeat. Kill.

My hands are slippery with blood again. My front is covered with it from all the blood spatter. I dodge a swinging cutlass on my way to deliver an attack to another pirate. He blocks my first strike but doesn't expect me to deliver a second one so quickly. It pierces his heart.

I spin as the man I dodged comes charging at me with his sword raised; I leap aside but land atop one of the fallen bodies, and my ankle rolls. When I land on my good leg, I pivot in place, ducking a slash and stabbing the man in the gut. I finish him with another slice to the throat.

Then the mansion is perfectly silent.

I rise, take a look around at the carnage. A throbbing pain lances up my leg when I try to put my full weight on my ankle. It slows me down as I retrieve all my daggers and find unmarred cloth to wipe them clean on. I scrub at my hands, though they're still red when I'm done. Dried blood has worked its way into the creases of my skin. I sheathe my rapier and daggers into their respective holsters. I pull my braided hair out of its loose ponytail and redo it.

Then I search through the mansion until I find the servants' quarters. Most have barricaded themselves in their rooms or hidden under their beds.

It takes some time, but I finally locate Miss Nyles's room.

"These are for you," I say, and I drag the two unconscious men from the kitchens inside, one at a time, ignoring the shooting pain in my ankle. Thankfully, the servants sleep downstairs; otherwise I wouldn't have managed transporting them.

I pull out one of my daggers and hand it to Miss Nyles, hilt first.

The young woman looks between my dagger and the two unconscious brutes tied up on the floor of her bedroom. She takes the weapon offered to her.

"I suggest waiting until they're awake," I offer. "It'll be better that way."

Then I put the mansion behind me and sail home.

CHAPTER 2

THE SEA BREEZE IS warm against my skin as the ship lowers anchor just off the tropical shores of Queen's Keep, an island gifted to the pirate queen by her siren mother. Initially, Alosa had wanted to name the island Alosa Island.

"I'm the queen. Why not name it after me?" she asked.

"Makes you sound just a tad conceited," Niridia, her first mate, answered.

"Whatever. If a man named an island after himself, no one would bat an eyelash."

"You're not a man."

"No, I'm far better."

"Which means you're too good to name an island after yourself."

Alosa glared at her.

"Why not something more subtle?" Mandsy, Alosa's best healer, offered. "Like Queen's Keep?"

Alosa grimaced as though she tasted something sour in her mouth before turning to me. "What do you think?"

"Name it Queen's Keep."

"Ugh. Fine."

I'm rowed to shore in a dinghy by a blessedly silent party. When I step foot on the beach, a gun fires somewhere in the distance.

It's not necessarily a sign of danger. Someone could be at the firing range. Still, my instincts beg me to check it out, so I make my way toward where the sound originated. Palm trees line the sandy shores, but a well-worn path leads to the island's center, where Alosa is still in the process of having her stronghold constructed. Builders are hard at work, hammering and sawing. I pass them by and hear another shot fired, this one followed by a whimper, and I pick up my pace.

When I arrive at the firing range, a peculiar sight greets me. There's a man tied to a dummy some twenty paces off from where Alosa and Riden stand. A crowd has gathered, and I push through it to get myself a better view.

The queen cocks back the hammer of her pistol, takes aim, and fires. A bit of straw just above the man's right shoulder explodes, raining down upon him. He shrinks away from it.

"That was the closest yet," Alosa taunts, turning to Riden.

The smile he gives her makes her own grow, and I refrain from frowning. I liked Alosa better before she had a consort. Now she's all dove eyes and too much laughter, and I have to put up with Riden at all hours of the day.

The pirate tasked with reloading their weapons hands him his pistol. Riden doesn't take his eyes off Alosa as he extends his arm and fires.

The hat upon the restrained man's head blows off, and the crowd applauds.

"Are you ready to talk yet?" Alosa calls out to him. "Or are you going to let me win this wager first?"

The captive rolls his lips under his teeth to keep his mouth firmly closed, and Alosa is thrilled. She accepts another pistol, puts her back to the target, and rests the gun atop her shoulder.

"Wait!" the man calls out. "All right, all right. It was Draxen. Draxen sent me to kidnap his brother and—"

Alosa fires, and the crowd gasps as the shot skims the fabric of the man's collar, not even an inch from his neck. He faints from the ordeal, and Alosa doesn't bother to turn around to see if she missed or not. She's simply that good of a shot.

"Show-off," Riden says to her.

"Don't be a bad sport just because you lost. Now," Alosa says, turning to the crowd, "who's next?"

No, not to the crowd. To the line of men and women bound with rope at the forefront, being guarded by the crowd.

Alosa approaches them, blowing the smoke from her gun as she does so. "You all came in on the ship bearing the newest recruits. This man was among you, and he was caught in Riden's rooms." Alosa gestures with her thumb over her shoulder to the one serving as her target. "Draxen's far too obsessed with overkill to send only one man to do his dirty work, so who wants to offer themselves up willingly? Now's the time. I'm in a good mood after winning that wager."

Not a soul says a word, and I know exactly what's to come next.

The queen starts singing.

To hear Alosa sing is unlike anything I've ever experienced. It has no effect on me because I'm female, but it's still achingly beautiful. There are no discernible words in the melody, as far as I can tell, but the first man with his wrists and ankles bound says, "No."

The second says, "No."

The third, "Yes."

Riden steps forward and separates the man from everyone else.

On and on Alosa goes, singing down the line, rooting out the spies from her midst with just a few sung notes. Men under her spell have to tell the truth. They have to do exactly as she says. They are completely powerless to her will. And though it makes her terrifying, I have never once seen her abuse this power for her own purposes. Alosa keeps herself and those who serve her safe. Nothing more. Nothing less.

She is a queen I am proud to serve.

I catch a brief movement at the end of the line. A moment later, one of the pirates runs free, having cut his bonds with something he managed to keep hidden. Alosa could easily stop him with her voice. Instead, she gives Riden one look.

He takes after the escapee while she finishes her work, skipping the two females in the lineup. She'll probably save them for me to question later. I have ways of getting information out of people without uttering a single word.

Another pirate tries to beat Riden to the running traitor. Instead, he's disarmed and gives a weapon to the man fleeing.

That had better be a recent recruit. How green do you have to be to lose your weapon to someone without one?

Riden's faster. The queen's consort can run and fight, which is part of the reason he's so insufferable. The man is cocky. He has lots to be proud of.

I have far more respect for those who know their skills and keep them to themselves.

Eventually, the running man has no choice but to turn and fight or be struck down by Riden from behind. They face off, steel against steel, while Alosa finishes her lineup.

That's when she notices me hiding in the crowd.

"Sorinda, you're back!"

"Just now. Heard the shots and came to investigate."

Alosa puts her arm around me as she leads me away from the others. Her women are already carrying off the traitors and the two women for questioning. The others are being released. We walk past where Riden is still engaged in battle.

"First time we've had a breach on the island. And who's behind it? Not the land king. No, Ladell is far too stupid for that. It's whiny, useless, blasted Draxen. The perpetual thorn in my side. Riden, stop toying with him. You're not even breaking a sweat."

"He broke free of his bonds. Least I could do was let him feel like he had a fighting chance."

"Just put him with the others. Will you oversee the prisoners while I decide what to do with them?"

In a quick move, Riden kicks the man's feet out from under him, steps on the hand holding his weapon, and puts his cutlass to his throat.

"Will do, love."

Alosa fights a grin as she leans forward and whispers something into Riden's ear. He nods once, never taking his eyes off the threat below him. Then Alosa Kalligan, Queen of Pirates, leads me into her office—one of the few rooms actually completed in the stronghold.

"How did it go?" she asks me, and I know immediately what we're talking about.

"He's dead."

"Did he know it was me who sent you?"

"He knew."

"Good. No complications?"

I shrug. "Nothing I couldn't handle."

Thankfully, my limp is gone, and the few scrapes I acquired have healed well enough in the month it's taken me to travel to the keep from the Seventeen Isles.

Alosa gestures to the chair on the opposite side of her desk, inviting me to sit.

"How are you doing?" she asks.

This is one of the things I love about Alosa. She genuinely cares about everyone in her crew and likes to ensure their well-being, whether physical or emotional.

"I'm fine," I answer. I always am. Just fine. Never better. Never worse.

Holding on. Staying steady as long as I can keep busy.

She says nothing in return, likely hoping I'll offer just a morsel of information more.

"I'm sleeping better," I say because it will make her happy. It's not really a lie. I slept much longer each night while my body was healing.

"That's good."

"And you?" I ask, desperately trying to get the attention off me.

She purses her lips. "Busy."

"Are you saying that running a piratical empire is taxing?"

At that, she smiles. Her eyes are mostly green after all the siren song she used today, and she wears a magenta corset that looks stunning with her red hair.

"There are so many things that need my attention. The fortifications we're erecting here, for one. Then there's the constant monitoring of the money coming in and out of the keep. Teniri is happier than ever, counting and recounting the gold. I'm building new relationships with my father's old clients, so all who wish to cross the sea pay me my dues. Don't even get me started on the enemies I have to monitor to ensure no one gets any stupid ideas."

"Is being queen not as wonderful as you thought it'd be?" I ask.

Her smile grows wider. "It's even more wonderful than I could have imagined. I'm only complaining about the bad things. It's the trade-off for the wealth, respect, notoriety, and fun I get to have."

"Speaking of fun, do you have a new assignment for me?" I ask. "Perhaps some prisoners to question?"

"You just got back!"

"I like to stay busy, and you have a lot of enemies, remember?"

"I know. I just miss you when you're gone."

My lips twitch, but I can't find the words to reciprocate her sincerity. I'm not one for sharing feelings or making lengthy statements when a few words will do the job. Besides, Alosa already knows how much I value our friendship. And Mandsy is usually around to express enough love for five people.

Alosa says, "If you're sure . . ." She pauses, as though thinking something over. "Do you know what I hate the most?"

"Men who don't do what they're told?"

"Yes, but after that?"

I shake my head once.

"Delegating."

"Delegating," I deadpan.

"I like being in charge, but I also like seeing things done myself. But now? I don't have time to do everything, so I have to delegate."

"Isn't that the purpose of having lackeys?"

"Is that how you think of yourself?"

"Hardly. Lackeys are replaceable."

"You certainly are not."

"What do you not want to delegate?" I ask, getting us back on track.

She rises, as though she can't stand sitting a second longer. Her boots clip on the floor as she begins to pace. They look new, not a scuff on them, but that could just be because Alosa takes excellent care of her things. "I have a situation."

"Tell me."

"You know how I like to keep eyes on the land king?"

"Of course." He's been wanting to dismantle the pirate monarchy since he took his throne.

"I had six girls undercover on one of his excavating vessels."

"Why? I thought you only bothered to have someone in his court?"

"This voyage was different. Ladell sent out a larger crew than usual. There was lots of fighting power aboard the ship, too. Harpoons, enough muskets and pistols to outfit an entire army, cannons that could be transported onto land. He anticipated finding something dangerous. I wanted to know what it was."

"And?"

"They've been gone over three months. I've heard no word for the last two. The ship seems to have vanished into thin air."

"You need someone to find it."

"I do." She looks at me pointedly.

At first, I assume she's joking. Alosa is prone to sarcasm (something I've picked up from her). I'm not who you send to save people. I'm the complete opposite of that—an assassin among pirates. But

Alosa keeps staring at me, and I realize she genuinely means to ask me to do this.

"Why me? Why not send Niridia?"

"Niridia is already on a mission for me."

I raise a brow.

Alosa growls one word. "Draxen."

Alosa loves Riden Allemos more than anything else in the world. Unfortunately, he has the most despicable human being for a brother.

"That was fast," I say. She'd only just gotten the man tied to the firing dummy to admit who sent him.

"I dispatched her before this little temper tantrum of Draxen's today. I've always known he contests my rule and wishes to set himself up as the king of pirates."

"Boy doesn't know when to quit."

"Indeed not."

"Why not send me after Draxen and Niridia after the missing girls?"

Alosa sighs wistfully. "I'm not allowed to kill Draxen. For some unfathomable reason, Riden still has a fondness for him. Since I care about Riden, I'm forced to allow that scum of a man to walk the world. Hence, I sent Niridia."

"Mandsy?" I ask.

"Is with Niridia. I thought he might be a two-woman job."

"Wise," I say.

"Thank you."

Silence fills the room.

"Sorinda, you're the only other person I can trust with something this important. I know it's outside your usual duties, but would you please consider it? For me?"

I cannot believe she even has to ask. I would do anything for Alosa. She found me when I was at my darkest. She gave me a purpose. Gave me a family again. There is nothing I wouldn't do for her.

"I'll do it."

She must hear me clearly, but she doesn't relax yet. In fact, she looks even more on edge now.

"What is it?" I ask.

"You will be sailing into uncharted waters."

"I gathered that. I'm not afraid."

"I know you're not. But for that kind of voyage, you'll need a seasoned helmsman. . . ."

She lets her words trail off, allowing me to come to my own conclusions.

And, oh, do I. I know exactly who she means.

My blood heats, the desire to kill seems to prod at my very skin, and I can't help the frown that takes over my face.

"I know, I know," Alosa says, holding her hands up defensively. "I really do know how much you hate him, but he's the best I've got. I can't give those girls anything less than that. If there's any hope of finding them at all, Kearan will manage it."

"He stares at me."

"You're lovely," she says, as though it's meant to be some sort of compliment.

"He tries to speak to me."

"You're a fine conversationalist."

"He *wants* me, Alosa."

She taps her foot on the ground twice, but she doesn't back down from my stare. "Yeah, probably."

"*Definitely*," I stress. "He cleaned himself up. He stopped drinking. He started exercising. He *changed*, Alosa."

"Those are good things," she points out.

"Not if he thinks those changes entitle him to *me*. I'm not some sort of reward for good behavior."

At that, Alosa straightens. "Has he laid a finger on you?"

"No."

"Has he made any suggestive or lewd comments?"

"No."

"Do you have any reason to believe you're in any sort of danger from him?"

I pause, giving the words serious thought. "No."

She cocks her head to one side. "Then what's the problem?"

I finally drop my carefully composed features. I never can seem to manage my stoicism long around her. "I'm not like you, Alosa. I'm not used to men looking at me and wanting me. I like to hide. I like to be unseen. I don't want people thinking about me at all. But Kearan? He sees me. He always seems to find where I'm hiding."

Knocking comes at the door, but Alosa doesn't move to open it. "It's been over a year since he quit drinking on our trip to the Isla de Canta. Now that he's been sober so long, he's really come into his own."

I just stare at her.

She shrugs. "He's actually funny and smart and trustworthy. Besides, he likely doesn't even think about you anymore. Out of sight, out of mind and all that."

I don't even blink.

She sighs. "Have you ever considered that maybe it's time for you to stop hiding?"

The knock comes again, and Alosa leaves me to ponder that while she answers the door.

Stop hiding? Ludicrous. I'm an assassin. Hiding is what I do. It's how I stay good at my job. I have to keep sharp if I'm to remain useful to Alosa.

She admits none other than Kearan into the room.

My walls go back up immediately.

When he sees me, he freezes, before a smile graces his lips. "You're back."

"Obviously," I say.

He gives me a once-over, but there's nothing heated in the gesture. It's almost like he's . . . looking for injuries. Either way, I look pointedly at Alosa. *See?*

"Kearan," she says, succeeding in taking his gaze off me.

"You sent for me?" he asks, and I realize that must have been what Alosa whispered to Riden.

"I have a job for you. I'm assembling a crew led by Captain Sorinda Veshtas to find a missing ship, and I'd like you to be the sailing master for the voyage."

There's a pause in which I feel Kearan's gaze shift to me briefly before resettling on Alosa. I don't let a single muscle on my face twitch.

"If Captain Veshtas is amenable, I am happy to serve," Kearan says.

Of course he's *happy to.* I want to scowl, but I remain strong.

Alosa turns to me. "Are you *amenable*, Captain?"

I blink at her, let the silence fill the room until it grows to uncomfortable depths. Finally, I turn to Kearan. Stars, but he's a big man. Wide enough for two men, tall enough to tower over everyone. His white skin bears a light tan from all the time in the sun, but he's not handsome by any stretch of the word. Though he's finally trimmed his hair and beard, his nose is large and has been broken too many times. His eyes are too far apart on his face.

It's one of the few things I *do* like about him: the fact that he's not handsome. He looks *real*, like a man hardened by life on the sea, though I would never admit that to anyone. Not even Alosa.

He wears a black coat that's now just a size too big for him with his weight loss. Muscle has replaced most of the fat, and what fat is left looks good on him. Again, it makes him look *real*. The coat has dozens of pockets sewn onto it, which used to hold all his flasks of rum.

Those are now floating around in the ocean somewhere, thanks to me.

He's not much older than me. Before I left to take care of Vordan, Enwen put together a surprise party to celebrate Kearan's twentieth birthday (which he hated). I had my eighteenth birthday just last week overseas, which was nice. There was no one aboard the ship who knew me well enough to make a fuss.

Kearan doesn't look away from my stare, which is impressive. There are few men who dare to hold my gaze. I can respect that, even knowing what I do about him.

"If you can follow orders, I have no problem with you joining the crew." If I can pretend like he doesn't get to me, then eventually he'll grow bored and move on. It works on bullies, so why not enthusiastic men?

Kearan nods once. He asks, "What direction are we headed?"

"Northeast of the Seventeen Isles," Alosa says. She reaches into one of the long drawers of her desk and withdraws a map. She unrolls it and points to the new markings that must indicate the missing ship's course before it disappeared. "The *Wanderer* was meant to look for land in uncharted waters. Last I heard, she was here." Alosa points to where the trail ends.

Kearan's back goes ramrod straight.

"What is it?" Alosa asks him.

"I've sailed that way before."

Alosa points to the chair I vacated at Kearan's entrance. "Tell me everything."

I take position in a corner of the room. Near the door, I'll be able to hear if anyone tries to listen in, and I like to be the closest to the escape route. Habit of my youth.

"They called it a panaceum," Kearan begins. "That's what we were hired to search for. Didn't matter if we found it or not; our employer promised us a fortune to sail that way and dig up what we could."

"Your employer, who were they?" Alosa asks.

"Some rich heir who dreamed of fame. Said he came from a line of explorers, but he intended to be the one to actually find the panaceum."

"Which is?"

"Utter rubbish if you ask me. The git said it was a mystical object that could heal any injury or sickness, no matter how fatal. It's supposed to grant whoever possesses it immortality and immunity from death. Meaning you can't kill 'em with a blade or anything."

"I get the idea," Alosa says.

"So we sailed northeast to search for this thing. Didn't find anything but trouble. As the weather grew colder the farther we went, the sea started bubbling randomly. People would disappear from the ship in the middle of the night. Just vanish without a trace. All their belongings still aboard. Lifeboats still attached to the ship. It was strange."

"What ended up happening?"

"Crew turned against our financial benefactor after the eighth person went missing. We flipped the ship around and didn't look back."

Alosa rubs at her forehead. "This all would have been helpful to know before I let half a dozen girls join the ranks of the land king's vessel."

"Had I known, I would have spoken up."

"I know. It's no one's fault, but it doesn't change the fact that those girls are missing." Alosa looks to me.

"I said I'd look for them, and I meant it. I'm not afraid of Kearan's ghost stories."

"They're not stories. This really happened," Kearan insists.

"How drunk were you during this voyage?" My tone doesn't change, but the words do their job.

He turns to me, his eyes hardening. "This was before I took to the bottle."

Hmm. I assumed he came out of the womb with a bottle in his hand.

Alosa says, "I don't leave anyone for dead. If there's a chance they're still alive, then I'm going to use all the resources I have to locate them. I'll want weekly updates, Captain, on the well-being of you and the crew. Anything weird starts to happen, you let me know immediately."

It's still so strange to be called *Captain*. Alosa promoted me shortly after we dethroned her father, yet I never wanted my own ship or women to command. I haven't bothered to hire a crew for my vessel, and I haven't even laid eyes on the ship Alosa gifted me.

"Who will be sailing with me?" I ask. "Wallov?"

"No. Where Wallov goes, Roslyn follows. This is no voyage for her."

I couldn't agree more. The lass isn't even eight yet.

"You'll have a few familiar faces. Radita will serve as boatswain. Philoria and Bayla as gunwomen. Mostly, there will be many new women that you have yet to meet. Don't worry. I won't be sending anyone with you that I don't trust. You'll have a good crew."

"Who's to serve as first mate?"

"Her name is Dimella. You'll like her, I promise."

We'll see about that. I don't like very many people. "When do we sail?"

"As soon as the ship can be made ready. I've been having it stocked since I anticipated your return soon."

"So sure I would say yes?" I ask with a smile.

"Not sure. Just hopeful. Thank you, Sorinda. I mean it. I really wish I could go with you."

Realizing that Alosa needs some assurances of her own, I say, "Put it from your mind, Captain. I've got this. I will find them."

She nods. "I know you will." Then, as though remembering something, she reaches under the desk and pulls out a long, thin box. "Almost forgot. I have something for you."

I step up to it slowly, doing my best to keep as much distance as possible from Kearan with him still sitting right in front of the desk.

"Go on. Open it," Alosa encourages.

I find the latch at the front and pull on the lid.

What rests inside takes my breath away.

It's a rapier. Long and slender, sharp as death. The knuckle guard shimmers, as though some sort of crushed gems were mixed in with the molten iron. The inner guards over the base of the blade have been shaped to look like ocean waves. When I reach for the grip, my hands brush leather so soft it could be mistaken for velvet. It's impossibly light when I lift the sword. It blurs through the air when I test it out, moving as though it truly were an extension of my arm.

"You didn't think I'd forgotten your birthday, now, did you?" Alosa asks.

I can't find my voice right away. "Thank you."

"Only the best for you."

"It's your birthday?" Kearan asks.

Alosa's gaze snaps to him. "You're dismissed, Kearan. Ready yourself for the voyage."

He towers over the room when he stands. "Aye-aye."

Alosa and I watch his back until he shuts the door behind himself.

She says, "Now, if I might be so bold as to offer you a bit of advice before you go to meet your crew?"

"Of course," I say, still admiring my new weapon.

"I have no doubt that you will make a good captain, Sorinda, but try to remember that the crew will be looking to you always. Don't be so quiet with them. Don't hide all the time. Your presence will reassure them when times are hard. Your words of encouragement will embolden them. Remember how important it is for you to be seen and heard."

I shift my gaze to Alosa. "I'm going to make a terrible captain."

Alosa shakes her head. "We can do impossible things when others depend on us. You will make mistakes. There's no getting around that. But you forgive yourself and do better next time. I'm certain that when it matters most, you will rise to the occasion."

"You never made mistakes as a captain."

Alosa laughs. "Sailing in my father's fleet wasn't a mistake? Or how about the time I put my entire crew in danger by rescuing my mother? Or what about when Lotiya died because I insisted we stop on an unknown island for a new mast? Or what about when I got Deros killed because I didn't answer my father's questions quickly enough?"

I say nothing in response.

"Guilt is healthy when it makes us do better, but don't let it consume you."

CHAPTER 3

MY NEW RAPIER FEELS incredible against my side, the knuckle guard shimmering in the sunlight as I walk. I adjust my belt slightly so the sun doesn't catch it. Last thing I need is my enemies to see me coming.

A boy who must still be in his younger teen years rows me out to my ship. He doesn't say a word the whole trip, which I love. I tip him generously when we arrive, and he returns to shore, waiting to row out the next person. Eventually, I know Alosa means to have docks extending out from the island so ships can anchor closer. But for now, we do what we must.

When Alosa gifted me the brigantine and asked what I wanted to call her, I told her *Vengeance* more as a joke than anything else, referring to a conversation from a while back.

"The three of you make quite a set," Alosa said while Mandsy, Niridia, and I all sat around a campfire on Queen's Keep, resting after a hard day's work helping with construction and organizing our men and women.

"Because we're pretty?" Mandsy asked.

"Nah," Niridia said. "It's because we're her favorite people."

I said nothing.

"You're both correct," Alosa said, joining us around the fire. She grabbed a stick and poked at the flames, which were just as bright as her hair. More seriously, she added, "You're my inner circle, you know that, right? You're what I need to keep everything we've built. This pirate empire will continue to succeed only because I have you three to rely on."

"Aww, thanks, Captain," Mandsy said.

"You're going to make me blush," Niridia said.

True to form, I said nothing.

"I mean it," Alosa said. "Now, don't ever let anything bad happen to you."

Niridia gestured to her arm, which was still in a sling. "I could argue that this was your fault."

Alosa winced, and I wanted to smack Niridia for the comment.

"It's a joke, Alosa," Niridia amended. "The pirate king is gone. We can put everything he did behind us."

But Niridia was still suffering from the two gunshot wounds she'd received during our race against the king to reach the siren treasure. Her injuries were hard to forget when her bandages were in plain sight, for all to see.

Alosa stared at the flames. "We're going to make this empire better than he ever could."

"Because you're in charge," Mandsy said. "And you're better than he was."

"No, it'll be because it's built on the backs of hardworking, good women. Pirates who hold honor and strength above all else."

"And gold," Niridia whispered.

Alosa shook her head. "With you three setting an example for the rest, I know everything will work out. You are the best parts of me."

"I don't ever remember hearing you be so sappy, Captain," Mandsy said.

"I mean it. You are the best parts of me. Mandsy, you are my mercy."

As a healer and pirate, Mandsy deals help and death efficiently. *Mercy* is the perfect word for her.

"Niridia," Alosa continued, "you are my justice."

Niridia is more fair and levelheaded than anyone else I know. I thought Alosa's words an apt description. Then she turned her gaze on me.

"And you, Sorinda. You are my vengeance."

A hush fell over our group.

"Never forget this," Alosa said. "Never forget how precious you three are to me."

As I stare at the side of the brigantine while climbing the rope ladder, I realize that Alosa took my suggestion for ship name to heart. In bold black letters, someone has painted *Vengeance* on the side of my ship. I suppose I'm stuck with it now, not that it's a bad name.

I set one foot on the deck, take a look around at all the unfamiliar faces loading food, supplies, and personal effects, and feel a jolt of uneasiness.

I know how to sail. I know the jobs of every sailor on a ship. I know what needs to happen for things to run smoothly and efficiently. I've just never been the one in charge before. Alosa said I'd earned it, but it wasn't exactly something I ever wanted: captaining my own ship. Yet I've accepted this responsibility, and I intend to see it through to the very end.

Then I will resume duties as assassin and never captain a crew again.

In the meantime . . .

I start for the girl barking out orders to the pirates shuffling about.

"Get those barrels stored below quickly. In the back of the hold, please. We won't need them right away. And, you there! You're not on vacation. You can have one trunk of personal effects and one alone."

"Dimella?" I ask when I reach her.

"You must be Captain Sorinda. Nice to meet you."

She's a tiny thing at barely five feet, but her voice is so loud, you'd think she was twice that height. With strawberry-blond curls pulled into a band at the nape of her neck and deep brown eyes, she looks positively youthful.

"Before you can ask, I'm twenty-one years old. I can assure you I'm more than capable of serving as your second on this voyage, Captain."

"I wasn't going to ask."

"That'd be a first for me. Everyone takes one look at me and assumes I'm sixteen. Not my fault my da was a wee man. Oi, you there!"

She points to a man wearing an enormous hat. I have to do a double take once I recognize him.

"Enwen?" I ask.

"Miss Sorinda!" he says excitedly. "Wait, that's not right anymore. Captain! I was excited to hear you were in charge of this voyage!"

Warily, I ask, "Why?"

"Because Kearan is also aboard. Didn't you know?"

I don't know what he means by that, but I'm already certain I don't like it.

"What's with the hat?" Dimella asks him.

Yes, indeed. Enwen wears the biggest sailor's hat I've ever seen. You could catch gallons of rainwater with it, and the plume looks as though it came from something much larger than an ostrich.

"It's my newest good-luck charm," Enwen exclaims. "When people are distracted by this hat, they're not watching my hands." He wiggles his fingers.

"There'll be no thieving on my vessel," I warn him.

"I wouldn't dream of it, Captain! This is for if we happen to stop anywhere along the way. I never know when I might need my lucky hat."

"Toss it over or store it below," Dimella says. "I can't see half the ship when you're in front of me, and that has nothing to do with my size."

"Aye-aye, Miss Dimella."

Enwen pulls the hat from his head and clutches it to his chest. He's a tall man even without it, with midnight-black hair, small eyes, defined cheekbones, and impossibly long lashes. Enwen's body type borders on scrawny. Probably a good thing. With all the superstitions he carries around with him, the man can appear massive.

I start to follow him belowdecks to get settled before remembering I don't sleep with the rest of the crew. No, this is my ship. My quarters are at the stern. The captain's quarters. The door is unlocked, so I let myself in.

It's more space than any single person on a ship has a right to own, though I'm sure Alosa would think it too small. Brigantines are thin and easy to maneuver, valued for their speed. The captain's quarters are much smaller than they might be on other vessels.

I empty out my bag, putting four sets of identical clothing in cubbies of the closet. Cotton shirts and pants in varying shades of gray and black. My spare boots I place on the floor, tucking my coin purse within the toe of the left boot for safekeeping.

I notice that Alosa has already placed other sets of clothing in here for me. Fur-lined pants and boots. Long-sleeved shirts, wool scarves and hats, a coat thick enough for me to get lost in.

There's no telling how far north we'll have to go, but the farther we sail, the colder the weather will get. As usual, Alosa has thought of everything.

I haven't any items in the way of personal belongings save all the weapons I carry on me. I learned at a young age not to give value to such things. They can be ripped away faster than you can blink.

I store my second rapier, brass knuckles, knives, and other sharp instruments throughout the room, placing them in drawers, nooks behind navigating instruments, and wherever else I can make them fit. That done, I turn to the bed.

I can't remember the last time I slept in an actual bed. Usually, it's a hammock belowdecks for the likes of me, and I've certainly never slept in a bed big enough to fit two people.

Atop the woolen blankets, I find the key to my room, a fine-looking jacket, and a note. I pocket the key before picking up the parchment.

You're a captain now, so you need to look the part. Happy belated birthday! See you when I get back.

With love,
Mandsy

I flip the paper over, finding another scrawl of writing in a different penmanship.

You should know I had to stop her from picking out something in yellow. Since you hate attention and birthdays, I won't bother to wish you a happy one. You should also note that I refrained from giving you a gift. Who's your favorite?
It's me!

—Niridia

I'm smiling despite myself. The captain's coat is made out of a midnight-black brocade, though I note that Mandsy couldn't help but pick out something with a dash of color. A deep scarlet paints the wide cuffs at the wrists, as well as the collar at the neck. Gold buttons drift down the sides, each one so polished I can see my reflection.

It must have been terribly expensive.

I try it on.

Fits like a glove.

I find the mirror near the closet and appraise myself.

I look . . . like a captain. Like a girl who's meant to be seen and give out orders. The jacket hangs down to my knees, just above where the leather of my tall boots ends. The rest of my clothes are worn and faded, not matching at all with the fancy new coat.

Mandsy would probably say that I need to break it in. She'd point out it will get dirty and worn with usage. I've never been one to care what people think of me, but maybe that's because I'm not used to them looking my way at all, not when I'm so careful to hide myself in the shadows.

I look above the coat, at the features of my face. I like to keep my hair in small braids, which I then pull back into a ponytail. I prefer it kept out of my eyes. Makes it easier to kill things. I have pointed features, strong cheekbones, and an angled brow. My nose is wide, and my brown eyes have a circle of black at the outer edge of the irises.

Even I can admit the coat looks incredible against my dark brown skin.

It would be rude not to wear it. The voice of reason in my head sounds strangely like Alosa's.

But Mandsy's not here to know whether or not I wear it.

You're the captain, Sorinda. You need to look the part. You need to command the respect of all aboard this vessel. Just wear the damn jacket.

Before I can lose my resolve, I make for the door. When I open it, I leap backward.

A large body stands on the other side, fist upturned to knock. Kearan.

His other hand is behind his back, clutching something.

"Captain," he says, surprised by my sudden appearance. "Didn't mean to scare you."

"You don't scare me."

He blinks once at that, then asks, "Can I come in?"

"No."

"I have something for you."

"I don't like gifts."

The silence is painful, but I refuse to let it show on my face. I say not a word more, nor do I move from my position. I will not back down.

Kearan brings his other hand around, and I see the rim of a tricorne pinched between his fingers. "I just thought, as the captain, you need a hat. Besides, you won't be able to hide in the shadows like you usually do. Maybe the hat will give you some semblance of privacy. A way to hide your face when you wish. I would have given you something sooner if I'd known it was your birthday."

I absolutely loathe the thoughtful gesture. What is this? Another attempt to win me over?

"I didn't get you a present on your birthday," I say.

"I don't care."

"You're in my way."

He steps backward. "Sorry, Captain."

I haven't the slightest idea what to do. That hat is still being offered to me, and some of the crew have to be watching. The way is now sort of clear, but how will it look if I brush past him without doing anything else?

In a split decision, I take the hat, toss it onto the bed behind me, then shut and lock the door before leaving Kearan standing next to it.

There.

Now I need to find Dimella so she can save me from any further interactions with this reprehensible man.

Instead, she finds me.

"Captain, all crew and supplies are accounted for. *Vengeance* is ready to set sail."

That means it's time to give my first order as captain. I swallow my discomfort. "Then let's be off," I tell her.

"Aye-aye. Kearan, to the helm with you!" she shouts to the man still standing behind me. "Weigh anchor! Riggers, to your posts!" I climb the companionway to join her atop the aftercastle. From here, I can see a single figure on the beach, strands of red hair brushing over her shoulders. Alosa waves.

I wave back as the ship starts to turn, heading for open ocean.

Here we go.

We're sailing north to the Seventeen Isles. From there, we'll take the same path the land king's lost vessel, the *Wanderer*, did. Hopefully, we'll catch some trace of her—and Alosa's missing crew.

With the ship on its proper course and the sails set to rights, the crew is free to relax. Some go below for naps before they're expected to take night shifts this evening. Others lean their forearms on the railing to watch the sun splay over the ocean. Girls chitter in the rigging, preferring to be up high. The crew is mostly women, I've noted. In fact, I've only counted five men, including Kearan and Enwen.

Alosa prefers it that way. Simply put, women make the best pirates. They think with their heads instead of their privates. They feel they have more to prove, so they work harder. They're more honorable and trustworthy. There are, of course, the exceptions. Wallov and Deros, stars grant him rest, were fine pirates when they were on Alosa's crew. And I've known women who double-crossed their own crews.

Still, numbers are numbers.

One of the men went below. Two others stand above the bowsprit, chatting with each other.

Dimella catches sight of them, too, and we both take their measure.

"What are we starin' at?" Enwen joins us up top, placing himself between Dimella and the helm, where Kearan is stationed.

"The men," Dimella answers for me, nodding at the fore. "They're rather big."

"Lerick and Rorun?" Enwen squints in their direction. "They're not as big as Kearan, I suppose, but I've never really thought about it before."

"That's because you're a man," Dimella says. "You don't have to worry about who's bigger than you."

"I don't follow."

"She means," I say, "that you don't have to think about the fact that half the population is capable of overpowering you. We women are always wary of big men."

Kearan shifts slightly.

"Truly, Captain?" Enwen asks. "I didn't know women worried about such things."

"Because you are not in as much danger of certain violences as we are," Dimella says.

Enwen swallows, takes a look between Dimella and the two men at the bow, then steps between her and them.

Dimella rolls her eyes. "Unnecessary, Enwen. I carry around pointy objects for just such reasons."

"Sorry, Miss Dimella, you're just so small, and if there's anything I can—"

"Don't call me small!" Dimella snaps. "I'm merely in a better position to stab a man where it'll do the most damage."

Enwen crosses his legs almost involuntarily.

"Best stop talking, Enwen," Kearan puts in. "You'll only make it worse."

"Sorry, Miss Dimella," Enwen says before slamming his lips closed.

My first mate rolls her eyes before turning to me. "I'm going below unless you have need of me, Captain?"

My skin crawls. I am not used to ordering people about. It feels so terribly wrong. Alosa should be here to do this. Not me. But she has entrusted this to me. Better get used to it now. These decisions are trifling. The harder ones will come in time, I'm sure.

"Take a well-earned rest," I say. "There'll be plenty to do later."

"Aye-aye."

When she leaves, the other two men fall silent for once. I stay where I am, only because it is a good place for the crew to spot me right now, overseeing our heading, and it gives me a good vantage from which to start memorizing new faces, though I have to repress cringes when eyes meet mine. Normally, people don't know it when I'm observing.

I tug at the sleeve of my new coat, pulling it past my wrist, even though it hardly needs adjusting.

Kearan speaks up. "They seem like nice lads."

At first, I assume he's talking to Enwen, but then his eyes settle on me.

"Lerick and Rorun," he explains. "I've had occasion to speak with them at the keep. They seem polite. Don't speak ill of any of the women around them."

"Do you think Alosa would permit them to sail with us if they did?"

"Some men behave one way when they're around other men. Then pretend to be decent sorts when around women. They're not that kind. They're the same no matter whose company they're in."

"I don't care. I'm always going to be wary of men and keep my guard up around them. Especially the large ones."

His eyes narrow at me, and I narrow mine right back.

Before Kearan can respond, Enwen puts in, "Are you making new friends?"

"What?"

"Are you trying to replace me?" Enwen's voice rises in pitch.

"What are you on about?"

"Let's get something straight, Kearan Erroth. I'm your best friend. You can't replace me with someone else. I will not allow it."

Kearan takes one hand off the helm to point at the other pirate. "How many times do I have to tell you? We are not friends."

"Yes. We. Are."

"Just because someone is nice to you doesn't make them your friend."

"Sorry, I can't hear you over the sound of our strong friendship."

Kearan closes his eyes. "What the hell does that even mean?"

"I'll see you below for that game of cards later." Enwen makes his retreat.

"What game? I haven't agreed to any game."

Enwen disappears without answering, and all returns to blessed silence.

For about two seconds.

"What?" Kearan asks.

Since there's no one else around, I have to assume he's talking to me.

"I didn't say anything."

"You didn't have to. I can hear your thoughts from here."

I say nothing to his stupid words.

"You're thinking about how weird Enwen is, right? He's mad. I can't believe Alosa—"

"I was thinking," I say, if only to shut him up, "that you treat your friends poorly."

"How many times do I have to point out that Enwen is not my friend?"

I don't know why I'm still talking to him. I hardly care what Kearan does with himself or who he interacts with. Maybe I'll blame every uncharacteristic thing I do during this voyage on Alosa. She's the one who told me to speak up. Put the crew at ease. Except what I'm about to say should *un*settle Kearan, something that seems to bring me a small measure of joy.

"You forget," I say, "I was ordered to supervise you aboard the *Avalee*. Enwen was the only person who cared about you when you were too slobbering drunk to be aware of anything. He was the only one who saw your potential. Even Alosa only took you on because her navigator died, and she didn't have time to replace her with someone adept when we were fleeing from the pirate king."

"*Was* the only person who cared about me?" Kearan asks. "And now? Who else cares about me now?"

"Only Alosa."

Kearan looks disappointed, as though he hoped I'd say someone else. He recovers quickly, though. "She tried to kill me once."

"You manhandled her."

"Under Draxen's orders."

"She's killed men for far less."

"Or sent you to do it for her."

I say nothing. We both know it's true.

"You be nice to Enwen," I threaten, because this is the kind of language I understand best.

"You like him?" Kearan asks carefully.

"He is part of my crew, which means he has my protection."

"Do I have your protection?"

"Unfortunately."

"Can you protect me from Enwen's prattling?"

Our eyes catch, Kearan looking as though he's fighting a smile. Meanwhile, I'm fighting the urge to dismember him.

"Let's get something straight. If you make one wrong move on this ship, I will kill you."

He lets the smile show in full force. "I'd really like to see you try."

"You won't see me coming," I assure him.

My appearance on the deck has lasted long enough. I disappear back into my quarters, toss the stupid tricorne on the other side of the room, slide out of the coat, and breathe.

CHAPTER 4

THE NEXT MORNING, I'M introduced to the first benefit of being captain: private breakfast in the morning. One of the kitchen girls brings me a tray of fluffy biscuits and sweet porridge. I eat every morsel in blissful silence. Then I don my captain's coat, but before I exit the room, I catch sight of the tricorne Kearan foolishly gifted me. It landed upside down on the opposite side of the room. All alone on the floor.

I glare at it before leaving.

The first thing I notice is Dimella standing at the port side of the main deck. She appears to be staring off to sea, so I assume she's waiting for me. However, when I approach, I spot the bird perched on the railing.

"Good morning, Captain," Dimella says without turning.

Her back is to me, so I can't simply nod my greeting. I say, "Morning." Then, because I ought to make some attempt at conversation with my first mate, I ask, "How was our first night?"

"Smooth. The queen chose an excellent crew. I think it'll be a fine voyage."

"Until we run into trouble."

"Yes, indeed."

"Does the crew know where we're going and why?"

"Aye. Everyone aboard volunteered for this mission, though I wouldn't be surprised if most are here in an attempt to impress the queen. Either way, they're prepared."

I eye the yellow-and-black bird before us. There's a small scroll tied to its leg. We're only on day two of our journey, and Alosa's already sent a missive?

Dimella says, "I've been watching over the bird to ensure no one but you opened the queen's note."

"Thank you."

I untie the scroll from the yano bird's leg. It sits patiently, not even fidgeting at the attention. I unroll the parchment and read:

Sorinda,
We're a sailor short at the keep. Wallov's frantic. We think Roslyn might have stowed away on your ship. Would you search Vengeance and send word as quickly as possible?

—Alosa

I hand the parchment to Dimella so she can read it, too.

"I don't think there's anyone aboard who isn't supposed to be," she says after glancing it over. "I took roll and acquainted myself with each person on the ship."

"She won't be among the crew. She'll be hiding, likely in the hold."

"Impossible. I oversaw the storage."

"Don't take it personally, Dimella. Roslyn may be seven, but she's craftier than a snake. She's on here somewhere, and we need to find her."

"Shall I task the crew with it?"

"Don't bother. I'll find her. Please carry on as normal."

I feel Kearan's eyes on me as I make for the hatch belowdecks, but I don't spare the helmsman a look. Sailors rise from their bunks and stand to attention when I walk through the sleeping quarters, murmuring greetings of *Captain*.

"Carry on," I say, supremely uncomfortable with all the attention as I pass dozens of hammocks and eventually end up in the galley.

A few girls are scrubbing at the dishes from breakfast, but one a bit older than the rest steps forward. She's olive-skinned with shimmery straight brown hair. A sheen of sweat is gathered at her forehead, and she has a broom in hand.

"Captain," she says. "I'm Jadine, head cook. Was there something the matter with your breakfast?"

"Not at all. I enjoyed it very much. I'm here because I've just received word we might have a stowaway on the ship. Have you noticed any food missing?"

"Aye. I gave my cleaning crew a stern talking-to this morning for it. I thought they might have helped themselves."

"It wasn't them."

I pass through a second hatch to reach the cargo hold and brig. The ship isn't quite big enough to have a standard-sized third level. I have to crouch while walking and light a lantern to see by because there aren't any portholes this low on the ship.

Since we aren't housing any prisoners in the brig, there's no one stationed down here, which would make it very easy for someone to come and go without being seen.

I stand before the crates, barrels, and other tied-down compartments with my arms crossed. "Come out, Roslyn," I say.

I'm met with silence.

"Alosa sent word that you've gone missing. Your father is beside himself. Let's not make them worry any longer."

Still nothing.

"You can come out on your own and sleep in a bunk. If you make me search through this hold for you, I will put you in the brig."

"You wouldn't!" comes a tiny voice.

"You know me well enough to know I don't make idle threats."

"Hmph."

By the scanty light, I watch the top of one of the barrels pop off. Since the barrel is stored on its side, it's easy for her to wiggle out and return the lid. I also note she's whittled breathing holes into the barrel.

"Sorinda, I—" she starts as soon as she's righted herself.

"Hush. We'll talk in my quarters. I'm going to write Alosa back first so no one need worry any longer."

I turn my back on her and return up top. Dimella is feeding and watering the bird. I pass them by and scratch out a hasty note from within my quarters.

Found her. What would you like done now?

—Sorinda

I attach it to the bird. Without further prompting, it takes off in flight, returning to Queen's Keep. Yano birds are highly valued on the seas. They're excellent navigators, capable of finding ships on the water, and they can travel great distances without tiring. They also don't utter a note of sound, which makes them excellent for sending secret messages.

"Did you find her?" Dimella asks when the bird is out of sight.

Roslyn makes her appearance on the main deck before I need to answer. She's shuffling her feet, glaring at the ground as she walks, and fiddling with a knife in her fingers. Her blond locks are filthy from just one night in the hold.

I point to the door to my rooms, and Roslyn doesn't look at anyone as she lets herself inside.

"Anything I can help with?" Dimella asks.

"I've got this."

Roslyn is an unusual child. She's a seven-year-old pirate who's grown up around pirates. She knows how to think, act, and—unfortunately—talk like one. Really, it's like talking to a tiny adult sometimes.

"What were you thinking?" I ask when I get the door shut.

She's standing in front of my bed, arms crossed defiantly over her chest. "I had no choice but to sneak aboard the ship, Sorinda!"

Oh, but I want to reprimand her, to tell her how stupid and unsafe that was. She likely has no idea where we're going or what we're doing. This was beyond foolish.

Instead, I have a feeling this will go much smoother if I let her say everything she wants to first.

"Explain," I say.

"Ever since I was shot, Papa won't let me do anything! I'm not allowed to sail with crews; I can't walk the keep by myself. Sometimes, I think he'd like to oversee me taking a piss!"

"Language," I say.

"Sorry, but he won't leave me alone. The only thing he does is continue my knife lessons. That's it. What's the point of practicing if I'm never allowed to do anything? How am I supposed to be useful to Alosa if Papa forbids it? I *had* to sneak aboard. It was the only way to stop me from dying of boredom."

I open my mouth to speak, but she continues. "I don't need you to tell me he loves me. I don't need you to tell me that he almost lost me, so he's scared of something else bad happening to me. I already know all this. What I need are ideas for how I can have my life back. I'm bored out of my mind, Sorinda. I need this. Please don't send me back to the keep!"

I close my eyes briefly, remembering that moment when Tylon shot her. The bullet grazed her head, but it managed to hit in such a way that blood oozed all over Alosa's brig. We thought the shot killed her instantly at the time. I was ready to wring Tylon's neck myself, but Wallov beat me to it.

Losing anyone is awful, but a child? Roslyn's my friend and crewmate just as much as anyone else, yet it would be so much worse if anything happened to her.

It sounds like Wallov is coddling her for the sake of his sanity.

"This journey is very dangerous," I say. "We're intentionally headed for trouble. This was the wrong vessel to sneak aboard, Roslyn. You're seven. You—"

"I'm basically eight!"

She's over six months away from eight, but I'm not about to argue the point.

"I sent word to Alosa that I found you. Your fate is in her hands now."

Roslyn groans. "Alosa's just as bad as Papa. She takes his word as law instead of making use of me as one of her crew! I'm a pirate, Sorinda. I need to be a pirate!"

Any earlier anger or irritation I might have had toward Roslyn for sneaking aboard my ship vanishes. Because I can see exactly where she's coming from. She's being forced to be idle, and that would drive anyone insane. I understand why she did it, and though I don't agree with her decision, she's going to get enough of a punishment from Alosa and Wallov without me adding to it.

My voice is neutral as ever as I say, "No one gets free passage on my vessel. If you expect food in your belly and a bunk at night, then you had best be prepared to work for it. To the crow's nest with you."

Roslyn's whole face changes. The anger drains away, and pure gratitude replaces it. She launches at me, wraps her little arms around my waist, and says, "Thank you, Sorinda!"

"That's *Captain* to you, and this is temporary. Just until I receive word from Alosa about what she wants done with you."

"Understood, Captain." She skips from the room, singing a sea shanty as she goes.

This is already proving to be a long voyage, and it's only day two.

CHAPTER 5

ALOSA'S REPLY ARRIVES THE next morning.

Sneaky little thing. I should have known she'd try something like this. I'd hoped I was finding enough things for her to do around the keep, but she misses the sea. Still, Roslyn disobeyed her orders, so dump her arse in a rowboat at Darmont as you sail by. I'll have someone waiting on the docks for her, ready to bring her home.

In the meantime, I need to have a talk with Wallov. He needs to loosen the reins on Roslyn. We'll figure something out. Hope you find a use for her over the next month.

—Alosa

I inform Roslyn of what's to become of her when we reach the Seventeen Isles. She pouts but nods once. I suspect she's going to make the most of her month of freedom.

As the days crawl by, I make a point of getting more familiar with the bodies aboard *Vengeance*. There are twenty-nine of us in total: twenty-three women, five men, and one not-basically-eight-year-old stowaway. I've never met over half the crew, so I set about changing that. I make rounds every day, asking for names and doing my utmost to memorize them. I make a point of knowing everyone's duties and where everyone sleeps. I learn the day-shift and night-shift rotations, learn what happens when, and familiarize myself with the other inner workings aboard the ship.

I don't want to be surprised by anything.

I catch up with old friends, which include two of the gunwomen, Philoria and Bayla. They're regularly talking firearms, cannons, and other things that require any sort of explosion. They introduce me to Visylla.

"If you need anything blown up, I've got you covered, Captain" are the first words she says to me. "There's enough black powder on the ship to light up a city. Don't worry, it's all in the hold." She lowers her voice and hides her mouth behind her hand as she adds, "Don't let anyone light a candle near the storage."

"Is this an extreme use of exaggeration?" I ask, because I don't know her.

"No," Philoria and Bayla say at the same time.

"Don't worry, Captain, the queen encouraged me to bring as much as I could fit on board," Visylla says. "It's all sanctioned."

"We don't have enough cannons to warrant that much gunpowder," I point out.

"Oh, it's not all meant for the cannons. I specialize in makeshift handheld bombs."

I just stare at her, because what could I possibly say to that? As I pass by my old friends, I say, "Don't let her blow up the ship."

"Aye-aye," they reply.

I'll have to keep a careful eye on that one.

The crew behaves during the daytime hours, everyone performing their chores like clockwork. That's when I have to be out and about for them to observe me and gain confidence in my abilities.

But then the sun sets, and I get to be myself. That's when I observe them.

I often slip out of my captain's coat and tread along the shadows of the ship, trailing wherever intuition takes me. Nothing should happen aboard *Vengeance* without my anticipating it.

Iskirra, the ship's healer, makes money on the side by offering tattoo work to anyone who wants it. I like to watch her in the evenings with her needles and ink. It's relaxing. Not to mention amusing the things the crew find important enough to permanently mark their bodies with. Taydyn, the fifth and final man aboard the ship, gets some sort of musical instrument inked onto his chest, right above his heart. Iskirra, herself, has several tattoos along her arms, one of which is a black and white rose that looks exquisite against her ebony-colored skin.

Enwen arranges card games in the galley almost every night before bed. I keep an extra-sharp eye on him, but true to his word, he doesn't steal so much as a single coin from the crew, unless you count cheating at cards, which I'm sure he doesn't. He's very careful about it. Only cheats on low-paying hands so no one gets too suspicious or angry. He's so quick with his fingers, switching out cards beneath the table, that no one else notices. He distracts the other players with tales of ghosts and kraken and other superstitious nonsense. I'd previously thought Enwen didn't like gambling, but I think he does it because Kearan is often to be found at the card table.

Rorun is bedding one of the kitchen girls. I learned quickly not to go into the hold when I see the two of them ducking out of sight. Jadine, the cook, smokes a pipe in the evenings. She has her own stash of spices in the pantry that are just for her. Cyara, Unesta, and Ryndra—three of my able-bodied sailors—offer to tell fortunes for the crew, and Enwen spends far too much of his sneakily won coin to hear nonsense about the great deeds he will perform in his lifetime.

Tonight I crouch behind some crates in the galley after the lads are done playing cards, waiting to see who will venture here this evening.

A figure I don't expect enters.

I know how to recognize people by their shapes and the padding of their feet. It's a survival skill I developed at an early age.

Which is why I know with certainty that Kearan arrives in the galley alone.

My mind races with possibilities. Is he here to get into the rum where no one can see? Was the sobriety all a ruse? Or is he here to eat more than his share of the food? Or . . . what else? I didn't peg him as one to poison the crew or anything else, but—

He doesn't go for the locked pantry in the back. No, he sits on one of the benches nailed to the floor, rests his elbows on his lap, and leans forward.

After a few beats of immobility, he turns his head right in my direction. I don't move, certain he can't possibly see me in the darkness.

"Thought you might like some company," he says.

When I say nothing in response, entertaining the notion that he's added sleepwalking to sleep talking, he asks, "Captain?"

My heart beats a rapid rhythm, though I am not afraid. Merely irritated.

How did he see me?

"When have I ever given the impression that I want your company?" I ask.

He turns his gaze down to his lap. "Don't you ever get bored all alone in the dark?"

"No."

"You like your thinking time?"

"No."

Definitely not that. I loathe reminiscing about myself or my past. My entire family was murdered before my eyes, and I have spent over a decade trying to forget those memories.

"Then what?" he asks.

"None of your business. How did you know I was in here?"

"I didn't see you go into your quarters for the night."

"You're watching me?"

"Just observant, Captain."

Liar. "That still doesn't explain how you knew I was in *here*."

He shrugs. "I saw you."

"You couldn't have."

"Don't worry," he says. "The rest of the crew haven't a clue that you spy on them. I only found you now because I was looking for you."

"Why?"

He shrugs as though he thinks the question trivial.

It is anything but. I want to snap at him for making a habit of watching me, but I don't want to give him the satisfaction. Doing anything other than responding to him with my usual tone would only please him.

So I remain silent. It's what I'm best at.

Except, instead of relishing in the quiet as I usually do, there's a buzzing in my head. Something grating and irritating. It takes me far too long to realize the silence is making me uncomfortable.

You can't be afraid of the dark when you're the monster lurking in the shadows.

You can't be uncomfortable if no one knows you're there.

Yet he knows.

He's here.

And he's waiting as though he has all the time in the world.

Though the silence makes my skin itch, I refuse to be the one to break it. Then he would think I want to talk to him, and I can't allow that.

"My first time on a ship," he says, "I was just a boy. I was so nervous and unsure of what to say or do around all the men. I would hide. Listen to what everyone around me said and did. It was a comfort to learn that way. To observe without being seen."

"That's not what I'm doing."

"I know. I'm just making conversation."

Damn him. Now the record needs to be set straight. "People are patterns. They do the same things. Make the same choices. When you learn the patterns, you learn to anticipate what they'll do. It's how I can be prepared for potential threats. I observe so I can protect."

"What are my patterns?" he asks.

"Drinking, snoring, drinking, eating, drinking, yelling at Enwen."

"Those are my old patterns. I don't drink anymore. What are my new ones?"

I open my mouth but close it immediately. Because I realize I don't know the answer to that. I watched him for so long for Alosa. I had no interest once it was no longer my job. I knew his patterns. I knew exactly what to expect from him.

That's why I can't stand him.

But now he's different, and I don't know him at all. I really don't want to, either. But I need to as captain of this ship.

Shit.

I've gone too long without answering, so he says, "You're doing a great job as captain, you know. It's no wonder Alosa holds you in such high regard."

Ugh, he's complimenting me. "Yet I can't fathom why she's allowed you to remain among us."

"I'm a seasoned helmsman, and I don't cause trouble."

"Not for Alosa."

Kearan sits up, places his elbows on the table behind him, and leans backward. "Has there been a complaint made about me on this ship?"

"Not formally." After all, who would I make a complaint to? I'm the captain.

"Sorinda—" he starts.

"Captain," I correct.

"Captain," he amends, "I'm truly sorry if I've done anything to offend. I would like there to be peace between us so we can effectively carry out this mission."

"There is to be *nothing* between us."

Shit again.

My voice came out too harsh. He'll know I'm incensed, that he has an effect on me.

Kearan scoffs. "You think an awful lot of yourself. Sorinda, I *want* *nothing* between us."

The force of my glare is probably lost somewhat in the near darkness, but I'm sure he can guess my expression and my thoughts.

"Captain," I remind him through gritted teeth.

"*Captain*, stop flattering yourself."

"I— You—" I break off abruptly. I'm certain I've never stuttered before in my life, and I can't imagine why I'm starting now. When I can collect myself, I begin again. "You told Alosa you would only join her crew if I was the one in charge of watching you during your probationary period."

"I was a drunk. I said and did stupid things. I thought Enwen was good company, for stars' sake. My judgment was altered."

"Are you saying I'm only appealing to you when you're drunk?"

A silence so thick I could cut it with my rapier fills the galley. Why did I suggest something so stupid?

"I'm saying I'm stone-cold sober now. I'm different."

"Why?" I ask to change the subject.

"Why am I different when I'm sober?"

"Why are you sober now?"

Kearan says nothing for so long that I wonder if maybe he's fallen asleep. Then, "That's your fault."

"My fault?"

"You dumped my flasks of rum overboard."

"I'm to believe you were helpless to procure more?"

"No, it was a gesture that showed me you cared whether or not I was sober. You cared about me. So I did my best to quit and clean myself up."

"Care?" I ask. "I don't care about you. I did it because you stank, your teeth were yellow from the indulgence, and I knew it would piss you off. It was amusing to me, a way to give myself a reprieve from your stench."

"Well, it worked, so why are you so angry?"

I take a breath to calm my voice. "I'm not angry."

"Neither am I."

"Good."

Why does it infuriate me so when he tries to get in the last word?

"Kearan."

"Yes?"

"Don't be familiar with me again. It's *captain* to you or nothing at all."

I leave lest he try to get the better of me again.

But he still manages, "Aye-aye, Captain," before I'm out of earshot.

IN THE MORNING, IT is not a kitchen girl but Roslyn who delivers my breakfast.

"What are you up to?"

"Why do I have to be up to something? Can't I just want to do something nice for my captain?" she asks.

She sets the tray down on my desk and steps back. I keep my eyes on her as I crack one of the hard-boiled eggs. Beside them are strips of bacon and a mango cut into squares. Roslyn says not a word until I'm halfway through my meal.

"You know, Captain," she says a little too innocently. "I've just thought of something. Perhaps we should make the most of our time together."

I don't respond. Instead, I place my full attention on the food before me.

She is undeterred. "I once asked Alosa who had the highest death count in the keep. I thought it might be her, but did you know it's actually you?"

I take a long pull from my glass of water.

"So I'm thinking, who better to learn from than you? Alosa has explained to me many times that I can't grow up to be a siren like her. Ugh. If I have to hear the words *You have to be born a siren* one more time . . ." She trails off. "Anyway, all this is to say I've decided I'm an aspiring assassin instead."

I nearly choke on my water.

Did she really just say the words *aspiring assassin*?

"How many people have you killed?" she asks. "No, wait. First tell me how old you were the first time you killed someone. Then tell me how many."

I cough before turning to her. Someone has run a brush through her yellow hair and pulled it back out of her face. She's clean and bright eyed. Her dagger is sheathed at her waist.

"You think you ought to be rewarded for poor behavior?" I ask.

"Sorinda, I'm doing *you* a favor. You'll have fewer people to kill if you teach me. We can share the work!"

"Your father would murder me."

"That's the best part! He'll never know because he's not here. And he could never murder you because you're a professional murderer."

"Roslyn."

"Yes, Captain?"

"Leave my room. Now."

"But—"

"Go."

"Fine." She stomps her feet as loudly as possible and slams the door behind her.

If dealing with Roslyn is the worst of the trouble I have to handle on the way to the Seventeen Isles, I'll take that punishment happily.

Such a futile wish.

When I step out onto the main deck, there's not a breeze to stir my hair.

"Bring out the sweeps!" Dimella shouts to the crew. She yells out the names of the first sailors to take turns at the oars.

No wind is bad for morale. Rowing isn't a task anyone enjoys, and I see many downcast faces. Enwen runs up top with a pair of gloves on.

He sees me and says, "It's bad luck to be missing the wind so early in a voyage, Captain."

"Don't you dare let superstitious rumors spread on this ship, Enwen."

"Not a rumor if it's true."

"Less talking from you and more rowing."

He harrumphs as he helps the others remove the boards hiding a little inlet on the main deck. Below are benches and openings in the ship for the sweeps.

They take their positions, spread out over eight oars, four on each side.

"Heave!" Dimella calls in time, signaling the crew when to stroke. "Heave!"

Many grunt with each pull of the heavy oars, and I note that all the rowers are staring at me or Dimella. Where else do they have to look except right in front of them?

Dimella has a purpose, calling out the tempo of the rowing, but I am useless. There's nothing I can do save stand over everyone and watch, yet there's nothing worse than being the one laboring while someone near you isn't.

I would hate me if I were down there, watching myself just standing around.

I should have asked to be put in the first rotation, but it's too late for that now. I can't switch with someone; it'll be seen as a sign of favoritism, surely.

I rack my brain for ways to help the situation. I can't talk to Dimella, as she's keeping time for the crew. Kearan's gaze is boring into me from the aftercastle, but I refuse to turn and acknowledge him. Maybe I should hide in my cabin? But the rowers will see me enter, think I'm being lazy. Or that I've gone back to bed. Sleeping while they're working.

The internal struggle is making me irritable.

What would Alosa do? The *Ava-lee* doesn't have sweeps. We all suffered together when there was no wind.

This is enough to give me a headache. I never had to worry about such things when part of Alosa's crew. I was free to hide where I wished, do what I wished when I was off duty. But as the captain, I'm always on duty. I'm always expected to keep up appearances for the crew.

A figure comes up top, carrying a lute in one hand.

It's Taydyn. He's one of my able-bodied sailors, and he keeps to himself most of the time. But today he takes a seat among the rowers, pulls the lute into his lap, and starts to play. The introduction is upbeat as he strums, and his fingers move with the ease of a man who's played the instrument a long time. It makes me miss Haeli. She was a rigger on the *Ava-lee* who joined the stars during our adventures trying to secure the siren treasure. She, too, was gifted with playing.

Soon, Taydyn begins to sing in a rich voice:

> *When the wind is dead and the seas are dull,*
> *'Tis my song what keeps me goin'*
> *When the drink's dried up and the food's all gone,*
> *'Tis my song what keeps me goin'*

The music turns slower, more morose before the next verse starts.

> *When the captain's dead and the crew's all bone,*
> *'Tis my song what keeps me goin'*
> *When my lute's gone flat and I'm all alone,*
> *'Tis my voice what keeps me goin'*

He stops strumming his lute, his voice the only sound to be heard as he sings the last verse.

> *When the dark arrives and is out for me,*
> *'Tis my song what rests at sea*

It's no shanty I've heard before, and I think it a little dark, but those rowing seem to appreciate it. Taydyn plays it again, and this time, some of the rowers join in. When everyone has the words memorized, he moves on to another song and another, keeping the rowers company.

More importantly, Taydyn has taken the attention off me, which I desperately needed. I can think more calmly now. I make a mental note to thank the man later for sharing his talents and keeping the rowers in good spirits.

I turn to look up at the aftercastle, where the helmsman is tapping his foot to the music. I sigh as I force my muscles to relax from the tension of being put on display. Last night, I let Kearan get under my skin. I wasn't prepared for him to show up during my silent snooping around the ship, and I'm still unsettled from the encounter. Which I *hate*. I need to do something about it.

Then a thought occurs to me.

What better way to put Kearan back in his place than to show him he has no effect on me? To remind him I'm the one in charge?

Besides, if Kearan does anything I don't like, I can always stick him with a knife.

The man in question widens his eyes in surprise when he sees me draw near. And as I step beside him, his words from last night come to me.

Captain, stop flattering yourself.

I cannot remember the last time in my life I felt embarrassed, yet Kearan managed it with just a few words. I should have listened to Alosa when she said he'd changed. Then I wouldn't be in this ridiculous situation.

Even as these thoughts flit through my mind, I keep my face as smooth as sea glass.

"The crew doesn't need me hovering over them," I say to the man by way of explanation. "This is the most useful place for me to be until it is my turn to row."

"You're the captain," he says. "You won't take a turn rowing."

"Yes, I will."

"You don't have to feel guilty. Your job is the hardest one on the ship."

"Don't try to sympathize with me, Kearan."

Vengeance sweeps across the sea, the motion more lurching than when the power of the wind propelled us onward, but progress is better than no progress.

Kearan says, "What's got you in such a bad mood?"

"I'm not in a bad mood."

"Was it something I said last night?"

"No."

He cranes his neck fully in my direction, but I stare straight ahead. "You aren't embarrassed, are you?"

Despite myself, I blink slowly, still saying nothing.

"I didn't mean to upset you, So—Captain. Like I said, I only want things to be easy between us so we can do this mission."

"Stop talking, and things will be just fine between us." Somehow I manage to keep my tone even, but I feel my cheeks heating. Luckily, my complexion is too dark for even Kearan to notice.

He stares down at the helm, and I take the chance to let my eyes shift to him. He's not wearing his usual coat today. Without the breeze, the weather has grown rather warm. Kearan's rolled his shirtsleeves up past his elbows, and I see a series of tattoos along the length of his right arm.

I had no idea he had those.

I trace the designs with my eyes, following the shape of a skull, an ocean wave, some sort of flower, a replica of his cutlass, a helm. Random geometric lines connect everything, mere scraps of his light skin visible between designs.

"Been working on it since I was fourteen," he says, and I nearly take a step back from the shock of his voice. I'd forgotten those shapes were attached to a living, breathing, horrible human being.

"I don't care," I say.

"Sure. That's why you were staring."

"I was observing, not staring."

"Are you embarrassed again?"

I press my lips into a tight line, unable to think of a response that would help the situation.

"It's okay to ask questions, you know," he says. "You don't have to learn everything about people by spying on them."

"People can lie when they can speak."

His brow shoots up. "Damn. What happened to make you so dark?"

The question has my eyes drifting closed, a black so potent it could swallow me whole filling my vision. I hear the sounds of splashing water, of screaming.

Hide, Sora, hide!

I force the memories to the corners of my mind, where they belong. Yet I see red when I open my eyes again.

"I love being on the sea," Kearan says, his eyes fixed on the ocean before him once more. "I love it so much, I wanted to mark my adventures on my skin." He points to his arm. "I got the helm after the first time I was allowed to steer a ship. I realized I loved it and didn't want to do anything else." His finger moves to the sword. "When the captain gifted me my cutlass." The skull. "The first time I killed a man."

On and on he goes, detailing out his adventures, until he runs out of tattoos. When he starts to push up his sleeve higher, I stop him.

"I've heard enough," I say.

"You sure? Seemed like you went somewhere else for a moment. You need more grounding?"

In all the time I've spent with Kearan, it hasn't really been his pursuit of me that's angered me the most. It's the way he sees me better than everyone else—even when he was drunk. I try so hard to hide those parts of me, but somehow, he sees them.

It's beyond infuriating. If he weren't a member of Alosa's crew, he'd already be dead.

"If you love the sea," I say, "then why did you try to forget it by overindulging?"

His face falls, and he rubs idly at a spot on his arm. As he does so, his sleeve rides up, showing what I'm certain is the corner of a heart.

He doesn't answer.

And just like I did before, he seems to drift somewhere else.

The ship slips off course ever so slightly, and I rack my brain for anything to say. I want to call his name. To yell at him. But I know exactly what loud surprises do to a person when their mind is in a dark place.

"Would you like a proper look at the new rapier Alosa gave me?" I ask. I draw my sword and hold it up to the light. The sun catches on the glittering gems, making the guard almost blinding.

"I've always favored the rapier, because of its speed," I continue. "Also, it's what my father carried as a nobleman. I like that it reminds me of him."

Kearan's eyes shift back into focus, and he slides his gaze to the weapon.

"Were you so eager to replace your old weapon?" he asks.

"It was starting to feel . . . heavy."

"Because of all the blood it spilled?"

"Yes."

"Do you like it? Killing, that is."

"Don't we all enjoy the things we're good at?"

"Often. But not always. I'm good at rowing. Doesn't mean I love doing it. But I'll take my turn like everyone else."

I look down at the rowers below. Enwen's face has turned red, but he keeps on like the rest of them. They must be nearing the end of their shift.

"I love killing," I say. It's the only thing I love. Sharing that moment with Samvin Carroter over and over again. The taste of revenge on my tongue. The sight of his face when he knew it was me ending it.

Kearan says, "I love hunting. Does that count?"

"Count?"

"As killing."

What an absurd question. "Animals."

"Well, yes."

My eyes narrow. "Are you trying to find a common interest with me?"

He smirks. "Captain, you're doing it again. Stop flattering yourself."

CHAPTER 6

WHEN I ORDER DIMELLA to add me to the next rotation of rowers, she doesn't question the order. She never questions my orders, which is why I like her.

I sit at the backmost bench so I can see all the rowers ahead of me. I don't like the exposure of sitting in the middle of the ship, but there's nothing for it. I want this. I need this. Enwen offers me his gloves, and I take them, despite them being far too big. I shrug out of my captain's coat and lay it under my bench.

What I hadn't taken under consideration was the clear line of sight this position gives me to Kearan up at the helm. So I stare at the back of Bayla, as she sits in front of me.

"Heave," Dimella bellows, and I push the oar through the water, moving the ship forward. "Heave. Heave. Heave."

Taydyn is giving his voice and fingers a rest, so there is nothing to distract the crew from the tedium of rowing. Nothing but talking.

"When do you think *Vengeance* will see her first fight?" Philoria asks.

"Hopefully soon," Bayla answers. "Those cannons are looking a little too clean."

Philoria takes a big draw of air through her nose. "I miss the smell of gunpowder."

"I can see the soot in your hair," I say. "You've been getting into the powder with Visylla, haven't you?"

"Guilty." She sings the word.

"It's not the same as when we get to light it, though, Captain," Bayla says. "We need a proper sea battle."

"All in good time," I say. "You two are going to get your fight. It's inevitable where we're going." I would tell them not to be so eager, but that would be hypocritical. I'm itching for a fight myself.

"I certainly don't mind having less work," Iskirra says from where she's working at her own oar.

"Liar," Bayla says. "You miss having wounds to patch up. Admit it."

"Heave."

I'm out of practice at the oars. It doesn't take long at all before my muscles start to ache, but I will do my part like everyone else. Ignoring pain is almost second nature to me.

"Heave."

After spotting movement out of the corner of my eye, I watch Roslyn scurry down the line from the crow's nest, faster than should be possible for anyone. That girl's part monkey.

She crosses to us on bare feet and sits, letting her ankles dangle in the area where the rowers labor.

"Captain," Roslyn says. "I've been thinking."

"You're getting dropped off at Darmont, and that's the end of it," I say.

"But what if you can't find me on the ship? Or what if I climbed back aboard after you dropped me into a rowboat? Alosa can't very well blame you if—"

"I'll not make myself look incompetent or complicit in your schemes, Roslyn."

"I don't know what *complicit* means, but no one would ever think you incompetent."

"Exactly. The answer is no."

"But, Sorinda—"

"No."

"I could help row! I could serve food in the kitchens. I'll take night watches. Whatever you want. Please, I'll do any task on the ship if you please, please don't drop me off."

"If you bring this up again, you're bound for the brig. You understand?"

She huffs. "What about assassin lessons? Have you given more thought to—"

"The answer is still no."

She stands. "You're not my favorite anymore."

"Favorite what?" Though I hardly care for the opinions of an enraged child.

"Pirate," she says simply, and for some reason, the word stings just a bit. She stomps away again, this time joining Kearan at the helm, of all places. She sits on the railing before him and says something that makes him laugh. When his eyes dart to me, I can guess she's complaining about my rulings.

Let them talk about me. See if I care. I have no wish to keep Kearan's gaze, so I return mine to Bayla's back.

After a half hour, my arms, stomach, and legs all burn. Muscles I forgot I had throb from the workout.

I keep rowing.

Alosa's missing girls could be hurt somewhere, so we'll not slow down or delay in reaching them. If they're alive, we'll find them. If there's any chance that anyone can be saved, I will always fight.

I couldn't save my sisters, but I will save Alosa's crew.

THE WIND FINALLY PICKS back up three days later, though it blows in the least favorable direction, so we have to tack the ship, making the voyage even longer.

I make the days count in the only way I know how. I shrug out of my captain's coat and readjust my knife sheaths. What shall I observe tonight? I could hide myself in the sleeping quarters and see who rises earlier than they should. That's always a fun one. Or I could position myself high on one of the masts and watch the main deck below me. I can't hear interactions from up there, but it's always interesting to see if anyone rendezvous with someone they don't usually talk to.

I fold my coat and place it in its cubby. Then I turn.

That tricorne is still on the floor, the smallest layer of dust coating it.

The door to my rooms closes without a sound, because I keep the hinges well oiled for just such activities. Kearan is no longer at the helm. His shift ended a few hours ago. Let's find out what he does when his time is his own. He insisted I don't know his new habits. I should set about changing that.

He's not in the bunk area, where Iskirra is halfway through inking a compass onto one of the girl's upper thighs. He's not in the galley with the men playing cards. Nor is he anywhere on the top deck. That leaves the lowest level, which isn't off-limits, but there's very little reason for anyone to want to be down there, unless they're trying to hide something.

The hatch barely makes a sound as I open it, and I lower my head into the opening, looking at the area upside down. There's a small light toward the fore of the ship, so I drop down, my toes connecting with the hull before I land into a crouch. Behind me is all the storage for the journey. Ahead are the cells for those who misbehave. And after that—

I hear crying.

But it's definitely not coming from a man.

I creep closer, keeping my body low to the floor and hugging the edges of the rounded walls, using the beams of the hull to hide behind as I inch closer and closer.

When my ears catch up with my instincts for silence and nearness, I realize the crying can only belong to one person.

Only Roslyn can manage to sound like that, and her little whimpers break my heart.

"I came down here to be alone," she says.

For a heartbeat, I make the mistake of thinking she's talking to me.

"I know," a deep voice answers. Kearan's. "I also like to be alone when I cry."

She makes a sound like a snort. "You don't cry."

"Don't I?" he asks.

"No. Grown-ups don't cry."

"Oh, yes, we do."

"What do you have to cry about? Sorinda actually wants you here."

At that, Kearan laughs. "No, she doesn't. I'm here because Alosa wants me here."

"Then at least somebody wants you here. Nobody wants me." A little sob makes her shoulders shake.

"That's not true, and you know it. You know why you're not allowed to be here."

"If you're trying to make me feel better, you're bad at it. Go away."

There's a beat of silence, and then Kearan says, "I miss my mother. It's okay if you miss your father, even if you want to be here."

Roslyn cries harder, but this time, she wraps her arms around Kearan, and he pulls her to his side, completely enveloping her in his arms.

"How did you know?" she asks.

"I was once a little boy away from home."

She sniffles. "I miss him, but I also want to be here. How come I have to feel both things at the same time?"

"That's just life. You can feel joy and pain at the same time, just like you can want to be here and be somewhere else at the same time. But it's okay. You get to have your little adventure on the sea, and then we'll get you headed back to your papa once we reach the Seventeen Isles."

She rubs at her eyes. "That's just it. I don't want to leave. I wish Papa could be here with me on this adventure. I've never been sailing without him before. But he's different now. He doesn't know how to enjoy being with me on the open ocean anymore. And nobody understands that. Everyone thinks I almost lost my life when I was shot, but the truth is, I *did* lose it. No more pirating. No more adventures. No more sailing. I say I'm bored and angry, and that's true. But even more true is the fact that I'm sad. I miss my life and my old papa."

Most of Roslyn's tears fade into Kearan's clothing from where he still holds her.

"It's okay to be sad," he says. "And you don't need to hide being sad ever. If it's okay, I'd like to stay here while you be sad. You can squeeze me as tightly as you want and get my shirt as wet as you want. I won't go anywhere."

She nods against his chest as more tears fall, and I find myself backing away.

This is what I find Kearan doing when he's not on duty? Comforting a child?

Damn him.

Damn him to the stars and back.

FIRST THING THE NEXT morning, I rouse Roslyn from her bunk before the day crew even rises to prepare for their shifts.

Her sleepy eyes widen when she sees me hovering over her bunk. "What is it? We can't have reached the Seventeen Isles yet!"

"Shh. No. Grab your dagger and meet me on deck."

The weather is a bit chillier than it was yesterday. We're slowly making the transition from the tropics to more temperate climates the farther north we go. The cooler air feels nice in my lungs, and I take a deep breath.

Roslyn's changed her clothes and slid on her knife holster by the time she reaches me. She looks thoroughly confused when she notes that it's just the two of us at the fore of the ship.

"Don't be seen or heard," I say.

Her face turns downcast as she says, "For the rest of the trip, you mean?"

"It's the first rule of being an assassin."

It takes her a moment, but her eyes widen, and her smile comes out in full force. "Don't be seen or heard," she repeats.

"Take out your knife and walk around the deck. Learn which floor-boards creak. Follow the pirates on board without them knowing you're there. Learn to place yourself in shadows and little nooks."

"Why do I need to have my dagger out while I do it?"

"Because assassins must often be sneaking about while balancing their weapons, but for stars' sake, do not stab anyone."

"I won't," she promises.

"When you're ready, we'll move on to the second rule."

"How will I know when I'm ready?"

"Bring me a secret. Something you observe or overhear. Not something trivial. Something good. Then I'll know you're ready."

She gets to work that very instant. She tests her little feet out on every square inch of the ship. From my usual position on the aftercastle, I watch her following her crewmates around. More often than not, they catch her and ask what on earth she's doing.

But she is undeterred. If she's not up in that crow's nest keeping lookout, she's snaking her way through the ship, desperate to catch a juicy secret to bring me. I hadn't realized just how busy it would keep her. I thought for sure she'd grow bored by the task, but she's more determined than I've ever seen her.

"Something weird is happening with the little one," Dimella informs me one day. "I caught her riffling through the ship's log. It's not exactly a thrilling read."

"She's hunting for secrets," I say.

"In the ship's log?"

"Do you not have a personal journal that you write in at night?" I ask my first mate.

"I do," she says, her voice showing her surprise at my noticing.

"And was your journal where you'd left it after you spotted her at the ship's log?"

"No, I thought I'd maybe forgotten where I— That little sneak!"

I fight a smile as Dimella goes to punish the little one as she sees fit. Later that day, I find Roslyn swabbing the deck instead of enjoying her time off.

"Captain," she says. "Couldn't you tell Dimella the nature of our lessons to get me out of this?"

"Oh, no. If you get caught as an assassin, the consequences are far worse than extra chores. This is how you learn not to get caught. Be more careful next time."

She grumbles, "Dimella doesn't have any juicy secrets anyway. That journal is as dull as the ship's log."

"Keep looking."

She does so, and the crew is so busy trying to keep her out of their things that they're far too distracted to notice me observing them, even in broad daylight.

Kearan's new patterns prove to be . . . unexpected.

For one, he's on the move more than I would have thought. He takes his exercise routine very seriously, and he's often running up and down the stairs belowdecks or hauling items out of the cargo hold and then repacking them. He'll do push-ups and sit-ups next to his bunk or some weird movement where he jumps into the air over and over again.

He works himself up into a sweat, then cleans himself off. He likes to take naps every once in a while, and he still talks in his sleep. Rarely are the words understandable. But sometimes he'll say a name. "Enwen." "Alosa." And once. Just once. I hear him say my name.

"Sorinda."

Must be having a nightmare.

If he's not exercising, he'll be playing cards with the lads or chatting with Roslyn. He seems to spend more time with her than anyone else. For some reason, my mind can't wrap itself around the fact that he's good at talking to children. In fact, he's good at talking to everyone.

He jokes with the lads, makes polite conversation with the lasses. I even witnessed him make Dimella laugh, though I was too far away to hear what he said. The only person he isn't nice to is Enwen. But only sometimes.

They're perfectly fine until Enwen makes some comment to specifically address their friendship. Then Kearan gets all defensive.

Yet Enwen continues to bring it up, and Kearan continues to contest the label.

"Kearan, could you please pass me the water jug?" Enwen asks during the midday meal.

Kearan does so, and Enwen says, "Thank you. You're a good friend."

Kearan picks up his tray and switches tables.

I eye Enwen. "Why do you do that? Goad him so?"

"One of these days, I'll get him to admit it, Captain."

"What's his deal?" Dimella asks from where she sits next to me.

"With me? "Enwen asks. "I'm not sure. But in general? There's definitely something he's hiding. A trauma, most likely. And the only way to deal with trauma is to address it. Over and over again until it doesn't hurt you anymore."

"How would you know about trauma?"

My question exactly.

"Everyone assumes I've led such a happy life because I'm such a happy bloke. Do you think I'm a good thief because I had all this free time on my hands? No, I had a keeper on the streets, and if I didn't bring him enough valuables to satisfy his greed, I didn't get a proper place to sleep or food in my belly. Nor did I get to keep my skin free of his beatings. My friends who weren't as good at thieving didn't make it."

"I hope you killed the bastard," Dimella says.

"As soon as I was big enough to take him on."

"Good."

"Point is, I don't let my humble beginnings get to me. Neither should Kearan."

"Not all traumas are created equal," I say.

"Of course not, but that doesn't mean anyone should have to continue to be hurt by them."

I finish my drink before also switching tables.

CHAPTER 7

IT TAKES US FIVE weeks to reach the Seventeen Isles, and when I catch sight of Darmont, my mood picks up considerably. After this, things are going to get dangerous. After this, I might get to do some killing.

We sail within a quarter league of land before dropping anchor. Then the little lass is lowered in a rowboat.

Roslyn looks up at me with worry. "What if my rowboat capsizes before I make it to shore?"

"Then you'll have to swim it," I say. "Good thing your papa taught you how."

"What if some unfavorable folk grab me once I make it to shore?" She's overdoing her tone immensely. She'll have to work on her acting if she expects anyone to believe her.

"Alosa's contact is already on the dock waiting for you. She has her spyglass on you now. I can see her from here."

Roslyn growls. "Sorinda, I need this! I'm so close to getting you a juicy secret. Please, you can't—"

An explosion sounds in the distance, and I turn my gaze toward the shore, where several buildings are now going up in flames.

"Spyglass!" I shout, and Dimella places one in my hands immediately.

The dock is pandemonium: people running to carry water toward the fire, others simply trying to get out of range of the danger. I see the land king's soldiers fighting against a group of heavily armed men. I don't recognize them, and last I heard, the land king wasn't dealing with any sort of rebellion.

Catching movement on a nearby rooftop, I center the spyglass there. Women crouch on the tops of buildings, observing the damage and watching the fight take place below. I recognize one figure.

Niridia.

Those men fighting against the land king's must be Draxen's. Alosa said she'd sent Niridia and Mandsy after him. Their travels must have taken them here. But did they cause the explosion, or did Draxen?

"What is it?" Dimella asks.

"Fire and chaos," I answer. "The docks aren't safe for Roslyn."

"Do we wait? Do we engage? See if we can help?"

This feels like the first big and important decision I have to make as captain. Alosa gave me orders. Find her missing vessel. Drop Roslyn off at Darmont on the way.

I can't do them both. We haven't time to communicate with Alosa and explain the situation. Her contact can't safely get to Roslyn. In fact, I can't even see the pirate any longer. She must have gone to help.

"Pull her back up," I say.

The lads haul the rowboat back onto the ship.

"We keep going," I say, returning the spyglass to Dimella. "The queen's forces are already on the island seeing to the situation. No one is free to take her." I turn my gaze to Roslyn, who clambers out of the rowboat as though the boards might burn her. "Your fate now lies with us,"

I tell her. "You better hope you last the voyage or your father and Alosa will both have my head."

I OFTEN HAVE TROUBLE sleeping. Nightmares plague my dreams most nights, and I'm easily woken by the quiet creaking of the ship or even a change in temperature or lighting. I always have a weapon on me or beside me.

Tonight it's worry that keeps me awake.

What if I made the wrong decision? What if Mandsy and Niridia needed help? What if I've doomed Roslyn to death?

I try to reassure myself that I made the best decision with what information I had. I've already written to Alosa to explain the situation. All I can do is wait for her response, but it hardly matters.

The decision has been made. There's no turning back now.

The bed is too soft as I roll over, trying to find a comfortable position. I hear the doorknob to my room rattle, and I go to the door before asking who it is.

"Roslyn."

I let her in, and she throws herself into my arms.

"I'm sorry, Sorinda. I didn't mean to be so difficult. Do you think my bad actions caused this?"

"Caused what?"

"The fire? The explosion? Enwen says that bad things follow bad intentions, and I—"

"Don't listen to anything Enwen says, you hear me? You made a poor decision, but you didn't cause that fire or explosion. It was a squabble between Draxen and the land king. Nothing more. It was poor timing."

"Do you think Papa will die of worry before I can return to him? Do you think we could send a bird?"

I point to the bed behind me. "Climb in."

She does so, and I tuck her in. "Everything will be all right. You get some sleep. I'll let you know what Alosa says when I hear back from her. For now, I'm going to keep watch. Make sure no one followed us from the island."

"Isn't that my job?" she asks as she rubs her eyes, hiding tears she doesn't want me to see.

"You're relieved of your duties for the evening. Now sleep."

ANOTHER LETTER COMES two weeks later:

Damn Draxen. Damn him to hell. Apparently he went after one of the land king's banks. Naturally, Ladell is going to think it was me until Mandsy and Niridia can prove otherwise. Riden is torn between wanting to help the girls and worrying his presence will only make things worse. But don't you worry about that.

You did the right thing. Those missing girls are top priority. Roslyn has no choice but to go with you now. I trust you'll keep her safe. Now I've got to tell Wallov. Let's hope he doesn't have a heart attack.

—Alosa

We're into uncharted waters now, viewing an ocean that few have traveled before. Enwen clutches a string of pearls within his fist at all times. I've known him long enough to recall he thinks it wards off evil. Kearan has grown more alert, his eyes not only checking the sea in front of us as we sail but also the south and west, as though he anticipates something coming upon us without the lookouts noticing.

A rock extends out of the water to our right, and a colony of seals have climbed upon it, sleeping in the early morning. Dimella lets Roslyn borrow her spyglass so she can watch them better. We dare not get too close in case other such rocks are near the surface.

Many romanticize a life on the sea, but few consider the realities of being stuck on a ship for months at a time. Nowhere to go. Very little to do outside of chores. All social interactions limited to the people on the ship. There's no privacy for anyone save the captain and sometimes the first officer.

Many take to gambling, playing instruments, reading, and making idle chitchat.

What I hadn't anticipated was a demolitions demonstration.

True to her word, Visylla has been making handheld bombs in her free time. I've often spied her in the evenings collecting empty bottles of rum, coconut husks, and anything else she can find. She'll fill them with black powder, hollow out corks to give them a neck if necessary, and use twine or other bits of discarded materials to make a fuse.

Today she pulls out her collection and gives the crew a lesson in handling the bombs.

"The trick is to time the fuse carefully," she explains. She pulls out three small bombs, each the size of an orange, from the pile. She lights the first with flint and steel before using the lit fuse to ignite the last two.

And then she starts juggling them.

Juggling them.

"If you throw too soon, the husk or bottle will break before the powder can ignite, which of course creates a smaller explosion or no explosion at all. Throw too late and you risk injuring yourself. Observe."

She alters her hold on the bombs, grasping one in her right hand while juggling the other two in her left. She throws the stationary bomb right onto the deck of the ship. The outer husk breaks, and powder skitters across the floor. The fuse was separated from the powder, so the fire went out before igniting.

The second bomb, she tosses out to sea, throwing it high up in the air. Just before it makes contact with the water, the bomb explodes in a flash of color.

And the third she simply holds in her hands.

I push off from the railing I'm leaning against, but before I can do more than that, Visylla pulls the fuse from the bomb, so it peters out harmlessly.

"Wait too long, and you best stop the explosion from happening at all," she says. "Just like that. Now, who would like to give it a try? We'll practice by throwing out at the ocean. Time your throw so the bomb ignites just before it hits the water."

Roslyn hops off the crate she'd been sitting on, and I grab her by the shoulder. "Not you."

IN THE DEAD OF night, a slight scraping at my door wakes me. I throw it open, already anticipating who's on the other side.

"Practicing my lockpicking," Roslyn explains as she rises from her crouched position.

"Practice on doors I'm not sleeping behind. And who's teaching you lockpicking?"

"Enwen."

I rub at my eyes. "Is there another reason you're here?"

"Oh, yes! I have a secret for you."

"Let's hear it."

"Not so fast. I have to work up to it."

"I'm going back to bed."

"No, wait!" She reaches for my arm and tugs me around with her little strength. "Fine. I overheard many things while snooping around, but I wasn't sure at first what would count as *juicy*. Cyara has a daughter who she sends money to. Iskirra fancies some soldier in the land king's ranks. She writes him letters in the evenings. Taydyn stole his lute from some merchant trader who had unreasonable prices. I learned these and more, but nothing felt right. Until tonight!"

I close my eyes. I told her to get to the point, and she still went on a roundabout way to get there. "And?" I demand.

"Dimella is with child."

That wakes me up all the way. "No, she's not."

Roslyn grins. "Yes, she is. I saw the medicine she takes in her room."

"That's for seasickness."

"It's for morning sickness. She also doesn't drink with the rest of the crew, and she rubs her belly when she thinks no one is looking."

Obviously, I noticed those things. I just didn't come to the same conclusion that Roslyn did. I have not been around any pregnant women. I don't know what to look for. I thought maybe she liked to stay sharp like me and didn't bother with drink. And that she really liked food.

But now that Roslyn's pointed it out, it seems embarrassingly obvious.

"So what's lesson number two?" she asks.

"Don't wake your instructor in the middle of the night."

She doesn't look amused.

"What are you going to do with this secret you've learned?" I ask instead of answering.

"What would an assassin do with it?" she fires back.

"Dimella is not your target, nor is the information useful to you in any way. So what do you think?"

She pauses to think about it. "Dimella is my friend. If she wanted anyone to know about her condition, she'd tell them. It's not my place to do anything with the information."

She looks up cautiously, as though scared she's given the wrong answer.

I nod once. "Lesson number two is always go for the throat. It serves two purposes: killing and silencing your opponents in one go. Problem is *you* can't reach the throat easily unless your target is sleeping. Tomorrow, I'll show you the best places to put your dagger to immobilize your targets."

"Immobilize?" she asks.

"Stop them in their tracks."

"Oh. Why didn't you just say that? Papa's already been teaching me how to use a knife."

Aye, but Wallov is likely teaching her tactics to give her time to run away for help, not how to deliver the more difficult wounds that people won't recover from.

"It's good to learn new tactics from new people."

She shrugs. "You're probably better at it anyway. Can we start now?"

"Good night," I say as I hold the door open for her.

"Night, Captain."

THE DAYS CONTINUE TO pass slowly, yet there's no sign of the *Wanderer* yet. We haven't seen any land save the few rocks jutting out of the ocean. There haven't been any signs of ship debris or anything else to suggest someone passed this way, but we continue to follow Alosa's map.

The temperature grows ever colder, making exploring the water by swimming impossible. We don our winter wear soon enough, Dimella loaning Roslyn an extra set.

"Don't you tell anyone you got these from me," she says to the little girl.

"They almost fit," Roslyn says. "Even the boots."

Dimella glares at her and walks away.

"What did I say?" Roslyn asks.

The winds grow harsher, moving the brigantine along faster. Floating bits of ice appear on the sea, growing larger and larger with each passing day. It's like we've sailed into a whole new world. I've never seen anything like it. The waters are so dark, we can't see anything below the surface.

One morning, a knock comes to my quarters. Expecting one of the kitchen girls with my breakfast, I call out, "Come in."

But it's Dimella.

"I've just done morning roll call, Captain. There's a sailor missing."

I stand after tying off my warmer pair of boots. "Who?"

"Cyara."

One of the fortune tellers.

"I want to talk to whoever saw her last," I say. "And to Unesta and Bayla. They have the closest bunks to hers."

"I'll be back," Dimella says.

"Be discreet."

"That's the plan."

As I shrug on my coat, I tack on, "Also, bring me Kearan."

She nods as she leaves.

As much as I loathe talking to the man, he's seen this before. It would be foolish not to include him in the happenings when he might prove knowledgeable about what's going on.

Kearan arrives first. I imagine he was on duty at the helm, closest to my room. I let him in and shut the door. It's freezing outside, the little stove in the room the only reason I'm able to sleep comfortably at night. I dread to think what would happen should we run out of wood and coal.

I forget how big he is until he's filling up most of the room. His eyes land on the tricorne he gifted me. Still on the floor where I left it. There's no time to give that a second thought.

"A girl's gone missing," I explain.

"Who? When?"

"Cyara. We're going to find out more soon."

We wait in stark silence until Dimella returns towing three girls with her, the two I asked for and Roslyn.

"You first, little one," Dimella says.

"Dimella says you want to know about Cyara? I saw her late last night. She was up in the rigging chatting with me. We didn't talk about anything important. She went to bed before I did. Didn't see her again before I turned in. Am I in trouble, Captain?"

"No," I say. I turn to the other two girls. "Did you see her at all last night?"

Unesta shakes her head in the negative. Bayla says, "I think I woke briefly in the night. Saw her get up to use the privy. She has a small bladder. I fell back asleep. Didn't see her again."

"No one else saw anything?" I ask.

"I've asked around, Captain," Dimella says. "No one saw anything suspicious."

"Turn the ship inside out. I want every nook and cranny searched. If she's on board, find her."

"Aye-aye. Do you want me to tell the crew anything?"

"Tell them we've a sailor missing."

The girls leave, but Kearan doesn't move. He says, "It's just like what happened last time I came this way. Disappeared without a trace."

"No one just disappears. If there's a body on board, we'll find it."

"You won't find anything."

"You think she fell overboard?"

"Trained pirates don't fall overboard without a trace. Something is at work here."

"We'll double patrols."

"That's what we did."

"No one will go anywhere on the ship without a partner."

"Tried that, too. People started disappearing two at a time."

"Do you have anything helpful to say?"

Kearan bites his lip and scratches at his beard, giving the question serious thought. "They always went missing at night. Light every lantern on the ship. Have most of the crew active at night rather than during the day. Have people watching over those who are sleeping."

"We risk going through our oil and candles too quickly," I say.

Kearan shrugs. "Better than going through our crew too quickly."

Indeed. "We'll see it done. Thank you," I tack on belatedly. Awkwardly.

"You're welcome," he says.

Then he just stands there.

"You can go now," I say.

"Right."

The hold is emptied and refilled; every box, barrel, crate, and nook searched. Jadine riffles through her kitchen with her helpers.

We come up empty. Not so much as a drop of blood is to be found. She's not anywhere on the ship.

I see Kearan's advice carried out. The day and night crew swap shifts. We light every candle and lantern we can find at night, setting them along the railings, tying them up in the rigging. There's not a speck of darkness to be found above deck. I write to Alosa, appraising her of the situation, but I don't turn back. We've a job to do. We can save more than we've lost at this point.

The next evening, Enwen is whistling loudly while he checks the lines on the ship. When Kearan barks at him to keep it down, Enwen completely ignores him.

Kearan doesn't like that. I can tell by the way he tightens his grip on the helm, but he follows Enwen's example and ignores him right back. Dimella, however, is not content to let Enwen carry on. She marches up to him and says something I can't quite hear. When he stares at her blankly, I can tell something is wrong, and I start to head for the pair.

Dimella reaches out for Enwen's coat, pulls him down to her level, then grips him by the ear.

"Ow," he says loudly.

She starts parading him in my direction by the ear, and he's helpless to do anything but follow. I meet her in the middle of the ship.

"He's got something in his ears," Dimella explains.

I inspect for myself. Is that . . . wax?

I'm about to gesture for Enwen to remove it, but Dimella has no qualms about doing it for him.

"Ow!" he says again.

"What the hell are you doing?" my first mate asks.

"My duties," he responds.

She holds the glob of yellow-white wax up to his eyes to make her meaning clearer.

"Cyara has gone missing without a trace," Enwen says. "Only thing I know that can do that is a siren."

"Sirens sing *men* to their deaths. Cyara is a woman," I say.

"We're in new waters, aren't we? Why can't there be menfolk sirens out this way?"

"Then why would you have need to fear?"

Enwen pulls himself out of Dimella's grip and stands up straight. "I wouldn't presume to assume the preferences of menfolk sirens. Besides, what if there's both out this way?"

"Alosa has a deal with the siren queen, *her mother*," I emphasize. "Her ships and crews are safe. You have nothing to fear from sirens."

"Something took Cyara, and I'll not be next."

"You will keep your ears uncovered so you can hear orders," I tell him. "If you don't, the brig is finally going to receive its first visitor."

His eyes light up. "That's a great idea. Nothing can sing me overboard if I'm locked up. Let's do that."

"Dimella," I say, "kindly go take the helm for a few minutes and send Kearan over."

"Aye, Captain." She gives Enwen a disappointed look as she passes him by.

When I check our surroundings, I note that most of the crew has halted their chores and is looking on. "You may eavesdrop, but you do have to keep working," I say to them in my stoic way.

They immediately jump into action, still casting looks this way whenever they get the chance.

When Kearan arrives, his face is blank.

"Helmsman," I say, raising my voice, "when you passed this way on a previous voyage, did you ever hear singing coming from the sea?"

"No, Captain." He answers loud enough for the rest of the crew to hear, too.

"Did you ever see folk swimming in the water?"

"No."

"Did you see or hear anything at all that would suggest sirens, male or otherwise, were behind your sailors missing?"

"Not a single thing, Captain."

"There," I say, turning back to Enwen.

"But—he could be wrong," Enwen says.

I want to snap at him. I want to throw him in a cell below and be done with it. But I can't have the crew worried into stupid mistakes. I try to think of what Alosa would do.

Despite how ridiculous the words are, I say, "Are you saying you don't trust the word of your best friend?"

Kearan tenses beside me, but he says nothing.

Enwen gets defensive. "Of course I trust his word! I'd trust Kearan with my life."

"Then follow your orders, and don't chalk this up to sirens again. I need everyone fully alert if we're to get through this. Lives depend on us. Are you dependable, Enwen?"

"I'd like to think so, Captain."

"Then fight your mental impulses and be the hero we need everyone to be right now."

"Aye-aye."

"Back to work," I say, and the words are for everyone, including Kearan.

The two of us return to the aftercastle, and Kearan takes the helm back from Dimella, who can barely see over the pegs.

"That was crafty," Kearan says as he looks out at the dark sea in front of us. "But did you have to encourage him by using me?"

It is with great effort that I don't let any expression show on my face. "If I didn't want everyone on the ship falling into panic? Yes, yes, I did. I don't put your feelings before the safety of the whole crew."

"I wasn't suggesting you should."

"Then what were you suggesting?" I ask, though I really don't care.

"You enjoy irritating me."

I don't answer, because I know it will irritate him further.

CHAPTER 8

A FEW MORE DAYS go by without change.

And then the water starts churning.

Bubbles float to the surface. The water turns gray. I'd think it a whale feeding, except there are no whales to be found, and the tumultuous water follows the ship, rather than staying in one place. The state of the water doesn't affect our pace. The wind carries us true as ever, but that water is concerning everyone on the ship.

"It's a bad omen," Enwen says.

"It's air in the water," I shoot back. "Even you should know what makes bubbles."

I stand on the deck among the new night crew, our ship lit up like a tavern at night. Kearan's at the helm. Enwen's seated on the ground with his back to the exterior wall to my rooms.

"Maybe the sea is warning us to turn around," Enwen says. "Air doesn't follow ships, Captain. There's no explaining that."

He's got me there.

"Until Alosa orders us back, we stay our course. We're taking precautions, Enwen. No one else has gone missing. And need I remind you that you volunteered for this mission?"

"Of course I did. You think I'd miss out on witnessing this?" He does some weird motion with his hand, gesturing over his shoulder at Kearan and then to me.

I'm so glad he finds our arguments entertaining.

When I say nothing, not taking his bait, he continues. "You know, your epic romance?"

My whole being freezes up, but I shift my head toward him in an owllike way.

"Don't look at me like that, Captain. You know something is happening there. But don't think about it. Just let it naturally evolve."

"I am not romancing anyone, Enwen."

"Well, not on purpose."

"Not on accident, either."

"You can't help it. Everything you say, everything you do—it just draws you nearer to him. There's no stopping it."

"I can stop anything with a well-aimed knife. Including your mouth, Enwen."

"I'm shutting up now, Captain."

Kearan steers us around larger and larger chunks of ice the farther we go. At one point, he threads two large icebergs, sailing between them with practiced ease.

And the churning water beneath the ship calms.

Until we reach the other side of the strait. Then the bubbles resume once more.

I climb the aftercastle, positioning myself next to Kearan.

"It's a beastie of some sort," I tell him.

"Aye," he agrees.

"Too big to fit through that strait we sailed."

"It had to go around, which means it's sticking close to the water's surface. Something that has to breathe regularly?"

"We've seen nothing crest the waves."

"Perhaps it only does so at night, far out of our lanterns' reach."

"That means it's enormous."

"Yet it can sneak off with a single sailor in the night?"

I keep my voice pitched low as someone walks by in front of us. "Why wouldn't it wreck the ship? Take us all out at once? It clearly knows there's food aboard."

"Maybe it has a small stomach. Wants to make its meals last."

"Then how long before it's hungry again?"

Kearan's face grows solemn, for it's a question neither of us knows the answer to. "Do we dare attempt to attack first?"

"We have cannons and a single ballista, and we don't know what would happen if we make it angry."

"So we wait?"

"We wait."

I NORMALLY KEEP NIGHT hours as it is, but I can tell some of the crew have a hard time adjusting. Dimella occasionally has to wake up sailors who slump against the companionway or other hard surfaces of the ship. Too many are less alert, their internal monitors relaxing in the bitter evening air. Night is for sleeping. It's hard to convince the body otherwise.

I can sympathize, but if I'm to keep everyone alive, I need the crew to try harder.

The reason I kept my theories about the beastie between myself and Kearan is because I thought that would keep everyone calm and levelheaded for the fight ahead, but it would seem they need a little more fear in them to stay alert.

That means I need to . . . make a speech.

As I survey the sluggish night crew from atop the aftercastle, I swallow back my distaste and push through my discomfort. "Listen up, you lot!" My sudden shout startles many, and Enwen nearly falls over from where he's leaning against the railing. "There is some sort of sea creature following us. It's already fed on one of our own. Look alive or you might be next."

That does the trick.

Philoria, Bayla, and Visylla keep the cannons loaded at all times in the evenings. They're cleaned and unloaded by the scanty day crew, then readied again at night. I have a sailor stationed at the ballista at all times, scouring the water in front of us.

Many hold their pistols in their hands for comfort. Some even get into the muskets from belowdecks. Visylla brings up her collection of hand bombs, and I welcome it. Better to be overprepared than under.

I have a brave crew full of good people. Only the best would volunteer for this mission in the first place. They prove their mettle in their commitment to stay course. Only Enwen's superstitions get the better of him from time to time.

And then it happens finally.

A change.

The water stops churning, despite the fact there are no obstacles around.

"Lerick's gone!" Rorun shouts, and my eyes find him across the ship. "He was standing right behind me a second ago."

"There's something in the water!" This from little Roslyn up top. "I can't make it out."

When the water begins churning again, I realize what it must mean. It's feeding. It releases air while eating, and the churning water is from its efforts to keep apace with us. But we can't let this go on. Not when it just snatched another of the crew without a soul noticing.

"Weapons out!" I shout. "Gunwomen to your posts. Backs to the deck, everyone. Eyes on the water. Stay vigilant."

Dimella takes up the call, repeating it belowdecks and waking the rest of the crew. I run to the ballista at the other end of the ship. It's already loaded, harpoon slung in place. My muscles strain as I turn the weapon, angling it straight down into the water. The trajectory isn't perfect, but if this beastie's as big as I think it is, the harpoon will hit.

"Ready yourselves!" I shout.

I fire.

A larger rush of bubbles flies to the water's surface. Something like a clicking sound erupts from the midnight depths below.

"Reload," I order.

Visylla uses two hands to put another harpoon in place. She helps me at the crank to pull back the spring. I change angles, this time aiming for the other side of the bowsprit. I shoot.

This time the noise is unmistakable: a keening moan akin to a whale yet sharper. The sea is frothing madly beneath us, and something finally makes an appearance above the surface of the water.

It's a tentacle of some sort, but not like that of an octopus. It's smooth, not puckered with suction cups. It looks like a thick whip, except at the very end, which doesn't come to a point. No, it's large and rounded. And when the tentacle finishes rising out of the water, my eyes widen.

An unblinking eyeball stares at us all.

Enwen shrieks, but I've already got my pistol out. I take aim, sighting that bulbous eye at the end, and pull the trigger.

Blood and flesh rip apart. Another moan sounds below the ship, and I hear the splashing of water as the wounded tentacle retreats.

Not for long.

More of those whiplike appendages breach the surface. They surround the ship, each with a large, grapefruit-sized eye on the end. One of them still holds Lerick's body, the tentacle wrapped around his neck. It releases him onto the deck of the ship with a horrible crunch. We stare at our fallen crewman, who is missing the lower half of his body.

There's a moment of silence where I wait for Alosa's orders; then I remember Alosa's not here. This is my ship. And the crew looks to me.

"Open fire!" I yell, and gunshots erupt into the night. More eyes explode, bits raining down into the sea. But a lot of the shots miss, skimming the arms of the beastie or flying wide.

The boat shakes, the creature moving us from beneath the waves. I don't hear the cracking of wood, so I hope that means we're all right. I see Radita take off belowdecks to check. Then those whiplike arms lurch forward.

"Swords!" I shout, but it's too late to be a warning.

Tentacles wrap around the crew, trying to drag them into the sea. One catches Visylla around the neck, and I hack downward with my rapier. Rapiers are usually for stabbing, but I keep the edges of mine nice and sharp. The beastie must not have bones in its limbs, because my sword goes straight through, severing the tentacle. Visylla shrieks as she unwraps the eyeball-tipped limb from her person.

Looking toward the stern, I see sailors being pulled toward the edges of the ship, nails scraping along the deck, trying to find purchase. Kearan drops the helm and lets his cutlass slide free, rushing for the nearest caught sailor. I'm doing the same from this end.

I manage swings with my sword as I run, freeing sailors left and right. I stomp on tentacles, stunning them for a time, allowing other members of the crew to step in. Soon the deck is covered with sticky black blood. Explosions sound from behind me, and I know it means Visylla has begun making use of her bombs.

When I reach the mainmast, Kearan is already there, covered in black streaks of beastie blood, a path of destruction behind him. We've met in the middle, each of us panting and filthy. There's a moment of quiet where we both survey each other. And then, without even communicating, we turn back-to-back, preparing for the next wave.

It is utterly bizarre how attuned to him I feel in this moment, but I don't question it. A fight is happening, and instinct drives us both.

Someone screams as they're pulled into the sea, and I don't see who it is in time. The deck is a mess, pirates running for cover, reloading weapons, tripping over severed limbs.

"Reload the ballista," I call to Visylla as I slice at a slimy limb that tries to grab me by the neck. I'm faster than it is, and I sever the tentacle right below the eyeball. It bounces twice before rolling across the deck.

Once Visylla has another harpoon ready for me, I resume my position at the ballista. More arms sprout from the water, unblinking eyeballs trained on individual members of the crew. We crank back the mechanism as shots blast through the air and shouts fill my ears. I take aim and fire again.

The creature grunts, but its limbs don't falter. We're not doing enough damage.

When an idea comes to me, I have the absurd thought to tell it to Alosa, only to once again remember that I call the shots now.

"Philoria!" I shout.

"Captain?" she says from somewhere within the bedlam.

I finally catch sight of her and race across the deck, slicing at more limbs as I go. She's stationed against the outside wall to my quarters as she reloads her pistol. I cover her while she takes the time to add powder to her weapon.

"I need the cannons pointed into the sea. Can it be done?" I ask.

"Without shooting through our own ship?" She thinks for a moment. "Well . . . sort of."

"Do it."

"Aye-aye. I need five people to pull it off."

"Take them. The rest of the crew will cover you."

She pushes off from the wall, shouting as she approaches the first cannon on the main deck. "Bayla, Visylla, Kearan, Enwen, Taydyn—to me!"

I find Dimella from where she's slicing through beastie appendages right and left. "We need to give the gunners cover!"

"Aye-aye. To the cannons everyone! Backs to the gunners. Protect them with your lives."

Philoria disappears belowdecks and returns with ropes slung over her shoulders. She uses them to tie the first cannon to the mainmast with a few feet of slack.

She calls out to her helpers, "Shove the cannon over the water!"

"The railing's in the way," Taydyn calls back.

"Then you'd best push really hard! On my count."

On three, the men shove with all their weight, smashing the cannon right through the railing until it hovers over the water, the ropes attached to the mast keeping it from tipping into the sea. The girls angle the first cannon straight down, before moving to the next one to repeat the process. Philoria tosses separate lines to Bayla and Visylla so they can tie off more cannons to the masts.

Another scream and another crewman disappears over the deck. This time I catch sight of Rorun before he goes into the water, arms flailing.

Dammit.

"Dimella, lower the anchor!" I shout. "We need to buy us some time."

She widens her eyes, and I can see her desire to question the order, but she hasn't failed me yet. She nods once, then races for the capstan.

"Brace yourselves!" I shout to the crew.

The ship jolts when the anchor is lowered, the weight slowing us down considerably. Because there's no one at the helm, we start to spin. But a satisfying wail erupts from below. We hit it. Pierced it likely. Those eyeball limbs disappear back into the water, probably to attempt to dislodge the anchor from wherever it struck the beastie.

"Philoria, quick!" I shout.

Only four of the cannons are ready. Half. We're going to need them all if this is going to work.

"Reload!" I say to the rest of the crew, most of whom are already preparing their pistols for the next round.

"The water's churning again, Sorinda!" This little shout comes from way up in the crow's nest.

Roslyn. Still doing her job, despite everything. Stars, but how could I forget about her?

"Roslyn, go shut yourself in my quarters! Now!"

I anticipate an argument, but none comes. Instead, I hear the slap of feet landing on the deck. Roslyn starts for my quarters, but a wayward tentacle comes out of nowhere. It grabs her by her left arm, pulls her straight up in the air, and I watch in horror as it drags her toward the edge of the ship. I'm running for her, but I know I can't get there in time. My pistol isn't loaded yet.

The light of a lantern glints on the knife Roslyn pulls from her waist. She jabs it into the eye attached to the arm that has her. She pulls it free and stabs again and again with increasing rapidity. Eventually, the tentacle releases her, and she hits the railing, teetering off the ship.

I barely manage to catch her arm before she falls into the water.

I hoist her back onto the ship and shove her into my quarters before anything else can happen. "Under the bed," I tell her before closing the door. "Philoria!"

"Two more to go."

The ship lurches again, a sure sign that the beastie has dislodged the anchor. The ship sails a little quicker, the water too deep for the anchor to hold us in place.

"Visylla, fire the ballista again!"

"Aye-aye."

She does so, but the creature doesn't even make a sound this time. I don't know if the harpoon missed or if we're doing about as much damage as a toothpick would to a person. Probably the latter.

"Ready for another wave!" I shout.

Kearan suddenly looks up from the cannon he's maneuvering and races back for the aftercastle. I line my sight up with the bowsprit, realizing we're on a collision course with an especially large block of ice. The ship jerks as our course is corrected, and Philoria and the boys stumble. I replace Kearan's post, helping to position the cannon.

One left.

"They're back!" Dimella calls out. "Fire!"

More shots. More screams. More glinting steel. The ballista fires again. I hear a splash, and I pray it's one of the beastie's limbs falling back into the sea and not another lost sailor.

The anchor catches on something under the water before tearing free, and the ship spins. Kearan struggles to right it. Radita appears above deck. "We're taking on water! I need bailers while I make repairs."

Dimella orders a few of the crew below, while the rest guard our gunners. I hear more screams and shouts, but I have my attention on the cannon. This has to work. This has to be the right call.

The last cannon finally breaks through the railing and hovers over the water.

"Light it up!" I scream.

Philoria and Bayla light their linstocks before touching them to the fuses on each cannon one by one.

"Brace!" Philoria shouts.

Each cannon goes off, one right after the other. The force of the blasts sends the cannons bolting upward before slamming back onto the ship. One cannon breaks free of its lines and falls into the sea. One splinters the deck of the ship and falls through to the next level. The others hold.

The water stops churning. One final cry sounds from below the depths. Then all those many limbs fall lifelessly to the sea.

CHAPTER 9

"GET THE ANCHOR UP!" I call out. "Put up the sails. Stop this ship now."

Dimella runs the length of the ship, calling whatever remains of the crew to their duties. I run below to take stock of the hull. Radita is in the hold with a few sailors. They're boarding up a few holes, while others carry buckets of water to the portholes.

"How bad is it?" I call down to her. She's in water up to her calves.

"Not bad so long as I have the time to patch these up. I have to start over every time the ship lurches!"

"We're stopping," I tell her. "I think we killed it."

"What is it?"

"I've no idea."

I leave her to it, return back above deck, and assess the ship and crew.

It's bad. The ship is a mess. Debris is scattered along the deck. Blood and severed limbs cover almost every inch of space. The railing is almost nonexistent where the cannons tore through. Part of the deck is missing from the cannon that went through it from the recoil. I know some of the crew are below, but we look like so few above deck.

"Dimella," I say. "Roll call now."

"Aye-aye."

"Iskirra!" I shout, but I spot her a moment later. She's already making rounds. I watch her put someone's shoulder back into its socket, likely torn out while the beastie tried to haul her overboard. Many of those waiting to see her aren't bleeding. Just holding their limbs still. Broken bones and more sprains.

The ship finally slows as we get the sails up. Kearan turns us, angling the ship back the way we came. We retrace our path slowly, and I know exactly what he's looking for.

The beastie has risen to the water's surface now that it's dead, and we all get a good look at it.

The body is bigger than the ship. It's fleshy, bell shaped, and almost transparent with the tentacles streaming out of the underside. It glows faintly in the moonlight with some sort of natural bioluminescence. Inside the body, I can see the outline of something humanoid. I don't know who it is yet.

Lerick's body is still on the deck. It could be Rorun, but it looks too small to be him. He's likely lost at sea or clasped within one of the tentacles underwater. Dead either way. That water is cold enough to freeze a person to death long before they could drown.

"Captain," Dimella says. "We're missing three. The two lads who were pulled over and Unesta, who must have fallen during the fight."

Unesta. That's who's inside the beastie.

Three more fallen. That's four in total on this trip. We're down to twenty-five now.

I say, "We stay put until we can make the repairs Radita needs.

All the crew is to turn to her for direction, save those who are injured. Order rest for them."

"Aye-aye."

Then I go to my quarters to see to Roslyn.

She's huddled under the bed. Right where I told her to go.

"It's okay," I say. "It's dead. Are you hurt?"

She cradles her left arm as she wiggles out from under my bed. "Just bruised, Captain. Nothing bad."

"You're quick with that knife."

"Because someone's been making me practice every day." She rubs at her sore arm. "Captain?"

"Yes?"

"Is it wrong that I don't feel scared?"

"What do you mean?"

"I mean, I ought to be terrified that a giant monster tried to eat me. That it almost pulled me off the ship. But I'm not."

"What do you feel?"

"Alive. Sorinda, my heart is racing, and my hands are shaking, and I can't remember the last time I felt this good." She adds quickly, "I'm sorry I snuck aboard your ship and didn't tell Papa. I feel bad, but I can't regret the decision when I finally feel useful and like I'm right where I'm supposed to be."

She's a proper thrill seeker. Just like Alosa. Just like me when I'm about to kill.

I say, "It's good to be scared from time to time, even if you aren't right now. Terror is what keeps us alive. It stops us from being reckless."

"But you're not scared of anything. I want to be like you."

"I was scared when I saw that tentacle hauling you away. I was terrified."

She thinks about that for a moment. "I suppose I get scared for other people, too."

"That's what makes you a good crew member. Excellent job today. I'm proud of you for listening to me when I told you to go into my quarters."

"Thanks, Captain, but . . ."

"What?"

"I can't help but notice that the creature didn't attack me until I followed your orders, so sometimes isn't it a good thing that I disobey?"

I have to turn my laughter into an exasperated sigh. "Adults have to make tough decisions. Sometimes they're wrong decisions, but we still have far more life experience than you, so you should listen."

"All right." She looks sadly down at the ground.

"Go make yourself useful. There's lots of cleaning to be done."

"Aye-aye."

She leaves, and I write up a hasty report to Alosa before attaching it to the leg of a yano bird. As I move to exit the room, I find Kearan standing on the other side of my door.

"Kearan—" I start, prepared to tell him how I am in no mood for his antics today, but one look at his face has me slamming my mouth closed.

His eyes are red and swollen. He holds his body too still.

He looks . . . distraught. No, more than that. He looks broken.

What happened to the focus and ruthlessness he showed in battle just moments before?

"Captain, I need a moment alone, and I wondered if perhaps . . ."

I step aside to let him into the room, then exit and close the door, thoroughly thrown off-balance by his change in demeanor.

Did I miss something? Or did he just find out who we lost during the battle? I know he said he liked Rorun and Lerick, which is plenty enough for grief. But he looked thoroughly wrecked.

I should have asked what was wrong. Now I have to stew about it as I get to work. As I deal with what *I'm* feeling. He looks how I feel. Until recently, I could believe that somehow Cyara got off the ship and was alive and well somewhere. It was an unlikely scenario but possible. Now the reality is before me.

Four dead on my watch. Four I failed to protect.

And Roslyn was all too close to joining them.

I was the wrong person for this job. This proves it. Alosa will surely call us back now, surely reprimand me for this. But I'm not allowed to lose myself to panic and distress. I have to keep it together for the crew. I need to stay busy.

I send the bird off and get to work on the ship, cleaning tentacles from the deck. Dimella works beside me silently, using a broom to scrape blood and guts overboard. We've buckets of salt water to use to aid with cleaning. Meanwhile, Radita has finished making repairs below, and she now instructs the crew on fixing the upper.

But then I see her teeth chattering. She's still in her sodden boots.

"Radita, you and those who repaired below are to warm up before you do anything else. Get fires going. I'll not lose anyone to frostbite."

"Aye—aye—" She descends through the trapdoor with her bailers.

Stars, I wasn't thinking. How can I expect her to do anything after being exposed to that icy water? Why didn't she say anything?

I massage my temples.

Four dead.

Almost everyone else injured or hurting.

How did I let this happen?

There had to be something I could have done better.

"Do we know what it is?" Enwen asks, interrupting my thoughts. He's sorting through pieces of broken ship for anything that can be salvaged.

"Who cares what it's called?" Dimella asks. "You just thank the stars we don't have them back home."

"Them? You think there could be more out there?"

"No," she says quickly. "Something that big in these waters? Its hunting ground would need to be massive. If there're more of them, they're far away, where they can find other food."

"I'm going to have nightmares for weeks," Enwen says. "I'm staring right at the creature, and I still can't believe it existed."

"I can't wrap my mind around how smart it was," Dimella offers. "Attacking only at night. Going for one sailor at a time when no one was looking."

"Not as smart as the captain, though," Philoria says from where she's putting a cannon back to rights. "We killed it good and proper. Too bad it's too large to bring a trophy home. No one will ever believe what we saw."

"The queen will believe us," Dimella says.

"Yeah, but everyone else will think we embellished its size."

"It doesn't matter," I say. "Four people are dead. That's what matters. You honored them by killing what killed them."

Philoria looks guiltily at the cannon as she keeps cleaning. "Sorry, Captain."

"You did well today."

"As did you," Dimella says to me. "I thought for sure the anchor would be the death of us, but it bought us time. Quick thinking, Captain."

I can't say anything in response. Four people are dead. I shouldn't be praised for anything.

AFTER HOURS SPENT HELPING with cleanup, I make my rounds. I check in with each individual aboard the ship, asking how they fare and if there's anything they need. Everyone puts on a tough face for me, pretending as though they are unaffected. I can't really blame them since I'm doing the same thing.

For many of them, this is their first true mission under the pirate queen. They don't want to let her down. Everyone is ready to give their all.

I praise them for their bravery and skill. I try to say the things I think Alosa would say. I can only hope I'm not making anything worse. I know that people skills are not one of my strengths.

For the millionth time, I wonder why Alosa thought I could do this.

When the ship is in a less hazardous state, we clean ourselves up, heating water at the kitchen stove and wiping ourselves down as best we can. Jadine said she could have her kitchen girls pour me a bath in my quarters, but I opted out. Those girls have done enough work for the day. Everyone has. I wipe myself down with soapy rags like everyone else.

When I enter my rooms early the next morning, I'm startled to find that Kearan never left. He's standing right where I saw him last, staring at nothing in particular in the corner. Dried tearstains cover his cheeks before disappearing into his short beard. His face is red, like when he used to drink, though I know he hasn't touched a drop since he quit.

I realize now that I've checked on the well-being of every member of the crew except one person.

"Sorry, Captain," Kearan says when I enter.

He moves to leave.

"Wait."

He halts in place but doesn't turn around.

I find my courage. "How are you?"

"You don't have to do this with me."

"I asked you a question, sailor."

He turns. "I feel like shit, Captain. There's nothing I want more than a drink or five. Don't suppose you could have Jadine lock up the rum tonight for me?"

"You have more self-control than that."

"Right now I don't think I do."

I don't want to be stuck in this tiny room with him, but I can't pinpoint why, and that frustrates me more than anything else. He's different, I remind myself. Things don't have to be weird around him.

"What's wrong?" I ask. "Do you mourn the fallen?"

"Of course I do, but these wounds are deeper than that."

"Tell me."

He looks up. "Is that an order?"

I gentle my tone. "Tell me, if you want to. I'd like to understand."

"Why?"

"Because I'm your captain, and I care about your well-being."

"You're exhausted and ready to drop."

"Not anymore." I realize the words are true as soon as they're out. My body might be ready to never move again, but my mind is alert. Ready to fix another problem.

"Captain—" Kearan starts.

"Are you scared to tell me?"

"No."

"Then what is it?"

"I don't think you actually want to hear my petty traumas."

"Yet I'm telling you I do. You going to call me a liar?"

"No, ma'am."

"Then out with it."

He heaves himself into the chair in front of my desk. It looks too small for him, but he doesn't complain. He's probably used to everything being too small for him.

"You were there when I told Alosa I had sailed this way before," he starts.

"I remember."

"I wasn't alone. There was a girl."

"Parina," I say.

Kearan looks up, startled to hear her name from my lips.

"You talk in your sleep," I say by way of explanation. When I was ordered to watch Kearan aboard the *Ava-lee*, I saw him do and heard him say all kinds of things. But one name he always repeated. At least, he did before he quit drinking. I've never heard him say her name since then.

"I thought she was the love of my life," he says. "How fanciful we can be when we're seventeen."

I don't point out that I was seventeen just over a month ago, but he seems to realize his error immediately.

"I meant no disrespect. We all age differently, and I was . . . different then."

"None taken."

"Good. Like I said, I thought she was the love of my life, but she . . . started taking on with a different lad on the ship. I caught her at it, and I ended things. That was hard, but not so hard as when she died."

"She died on your last voyage out this way?"

"Went missing. Disappeared off the ship. Now I know what took her. What . . . ate her."

He sighs heavily, fighting another bout of tears, I expect, and I try to think of something comforting to say.

"It would have been quick," I reassure him. "It seems the creature snapped necks before it took its victims. That way they couldn't scream. She didn't feel a thing. Wouldn't have even been scared before the light was snuffed out."

"That is . . . surprisingly comforting to know. Thank you."

I relax at the words, relieved I didn't make his suffering worse. I dare to say more. "You shouldn't care for a woman who discarded you. You should let her go."

He laughs once without any mirth. "Should have known you'd say something like that, but you see, I can't let it go, because I'm the reason she was on that ship. I convinced her to go with me."

"You can be as persuasive as you like, but a person is still going to make their own choice in the end. Unless I'm to believe the girl had no say in the matter? Was she some docile thing who did whatever you wanted?"

"No."

"Then stop fretting. You were young. You couldn't have known. And she made her choice before she died. It wasn't you."

"I was trying to get her back."

"Do you think you would have succeeded? Or that even if you had, her attentions wouldn't have strayed yet again?"

After a long pause, he says, "No."

"Then don't mourn her. She didn't die because of you. She wasn't on that ship because of you. If she truly cared for you, she wouldn't have chosen another man over you. So she wasn't on that ship *for you*. She was there for herself. She chose someone else for herself. What happened afterward was an accident."

Kearan swallows. "Those words are about as soothing as a blunt knife."

"And just like a blunt knife, they still get the job done."

He rolls his eyes, and some of his normal coloring returns.

"You really turned to drink because a woman died? And one who treated you like rubbish, at that."

His gaze narrows. "That's not why I started drinking."

"Then why?"

He doesn't answer right away. "I did lose Parina. That hit me hard. I came back from the voyage without pay. Then I found out my mother had passed. Some ridiculous cough that wouldn't go away." He looks up. "I had nothing. No money. No one left who cared for me. Nothing but a house with a fine stock of ale, courtesy of my good-for-nothing father, who'd quit the world a few years previously.

"So I started drinking to cover up the pain. I took on with Riden's father's crew when I grew too hungry for the drink to be enough."

Confusion settles within me. "And then you stopped because of me?"

He grins. "I may have exaggerated that a bit. It wasn't just you. It was Alosa's crew, where I could see myself part of something bigger again. Not a family, exactly, but something like it. It was Enwen, who stuck with me all that time, even though I never deserved it. I still don't deserve it, yet he keeps trailing me around like a lost puppy. He goes around insisting I call him my best friend, as if we're a couple of little girls. Grown men don't go around calling each other their besties." He catches himself digressing and pulls himself back on track. "And then there was you, who gave me an excuse to stop in that moment because my easy access to rum was gone."

"Drink is not an answer to pain," I say, because I don't know what else I can say to help. I'm entirely out of my element. Kearan just gave me his entire life story, full of pain and loss. I'm unused to being entrusted with such vulnerabilities. I add, "We can't change the fates of those who are gone. We can't unmake decisions—our own or others. All we can do is keep living, ourselves, and if you hate yourself, then live for others."

He looks at me with the most peculiar expression. Disbelief? Confusion, perhaps?

"That sounded far too self-reflective to be advice you just thought of," he says.

"I did just think of it," I lie.

"Do you hate yourself?"

"I didn't say that. You're reading too much into—"

But I can tell it's too late. Kearan has deduced far too much about me. When I was trying to focus on him, no less.

"You think your life isn't worth living, so you live for others?" he asks. "Is that what drives you? All this time I've been trying to figure you out, and—"

"Kearan, we were talking about you. Don't change the subject."

"Is that why you serve Alosa? Because you'd rather let someone else make choices for you? You think you're not capable of directing your own life?"

I round on him. "This from the man who let drink control him for three years?"

"And you turned to killing. What was so bad that you became an assassin? What did Alosa save you from?"

Everything is cold and dark. I hear splashing and gasping, a shriek that cuts off into gurgling. The screaming of my sisters.

A body floating in bathwater. My mother's sightless eyes staring at the ceiling.

I blink the thoughts away, refocusing on the man sitting in my room. How did we even get here?

"Alosa saved me from nothing. I saved myself. And then I got my revenge for what I couldn't save. Alosa just gave me a purpose again."

"Again? What was your purpose before?"

"It's none—"

"Of my business. I get it. I'll just pour out my deepest hurts and insecurities to you, but you stay bottled up. I hear that's super healthy."

He stomps out the door without looking back.

WE HONOR THE FALLEN by lighting lanterns the next night. Though we've been doing this for days to prevent the beastie from sneaking off with anyone, this time it's different. The lanterns are for the dead, not the living. Souls lost at sea are able to follow the lantern light to the water's surface. From there they can see the stars and be guided home. Each star is someone who has passed on, living a bright new life in the heavens.

When I was little, I would search the sky for hours, trying to guess which bright dots of light belonged to my family. So many nights I longed to join them, and many times I thought of speeding the process along.

Then I met Alosa. She reminded me that the stars have a plan for each of us. I shouldn't cut my time short. My family will still be waiting for me no matter how much time I spend on the seas. There is still much good I can do before I reunite with them.

Now there are four new stars up in the sky. I can't distinguish them, for the stars in the heavens are as numerous as the sands on the beach.

But I can't help but wonder if there's anything I could have done to prevent them from joining the night sky so soon.

IT TAKES A FEW days to put the ship to rights, but we thankfully had everything we needed on board to fix things. Radita is truly the best at what she does. She has the ship perfectly functional once more. *Vengeance* certainly shows signs of wear, but if anything, it makes her look more hardened. Like she's seen tough waters and survived. I like her better for it.

We set sail again, our ship following the *Wanderer*'s path, though we've long since passed the point where Alosa last heard from them.

Since the water beastie didn't attack the ship until we attacked it, I have every reason to believe they kept on sailing. *Wanderer* had a far larger crew. I don't think a few missing sailors would have deterred the land king's men.

When Alosa's response to my report arrives, I feel relieved as I open the scroll. I want her advice. I don't want to be in control for a moment. I just need to know what she would have me do next.

It was bigger than the ship, you say? And you still managed to take it out? I've said it before, and I'll say it again. There's no one better at killing than you. I know you're downplaying your role in defeating the creature. Good work, and I'm proud. I am also saddened by the losses. We will honor them tonight after dinner. I know you'll have already done so on the ship.

And don't worry. I won't say a word to Wallov about what happened during the attack. He need never know Roslyn almost went over. We had enough of a scare during that nasty storm. You remember? The one where Riden got himself tossed overboard. He can be such an idiot at times.

The next call is yours to make. I respect your choice as captain and trust you to make the right decision for your crew. You know the situation better than I, so proceed as you see fit. Stay the course and find those missing girls or turn around and come back.

Just know that I have every confidence in you. The land king's ship was captained by one of the land king's men. He doesn't have you or this crew I've handpicked. You can all do incredible things. Better yet, no one was ordered to go on this voyage. You're all there by choice. If anyone can pull this off, it's you and this crew.

But again, the choice is yours. Remember, as captain, you can change your mind at any time. You can stay course, and then if things get worse, turn around.

I trust you.

—Alosa

Alosa's faith in me is emboldening, but I wish she would order me to do as she sees fit. Instead, she's leaving the choice up to me. What if I make the wrong one? Alosa didn't lie when she said I would make mistakes. I've made at least four, and they have names: Cyara, Unesta, Rorun, Lerick. But Alosa's lost sailors, too, and she's kept going.

I know I have to do the same.

We can save more than we've lost, but even if we lost half the crew, we still need to fight for those who need our help. It's what we do. We give our lives for our fellow crewmembers. It's what being a pirate under Queen Alosa means.

I hate this responsibility, but I also can't leave those girls to whatever fate befell them.

We keep going.

CHAPTER 10

WE SWITCH BACK TO a daytime schedule, with most of the crew alert when the sun is out.

Not that the sun makes much of a difference these days. The air is so cold I can see my breath in front of me. I keep the hood of my warm jacket over my ears and regularly have to cover my nose with my hands. Any burnable debris from the fight was stored belowdecks to dry out. We've plenty to burn to keep everyone warm below. But taking shifts on the deck is hard.

The floating ice gets bigger and bigger, until we have icebergs bigger than the ship. They slow us down considerably, as we have to alter course to avoid hitting anything.

"I didn't know it could get this cold," Kearan says with his hands firmly on the helm. He has thick gloves encasing his fingers. I can't imagine how cold the wood must be to the touch. I'm surprised the ocean isn't frozen solid yet.

"Talking is hard," Enwen says in response. "Whoever thought talking would be hard? It's as if I don't want to risk that little breath of heat leaving my body."

"And yet you're still speaking."

"I do it for you, Kearan."

"Lucky me. How do you feel, Captain?" Kearan asks.

"Cold." The question is stupid, so I give a stupid answer.

"That all? You know you can tell us if there's anything else."

Enwen blows heat into his glove-covered hands. "Yeah, Captain. Kearan's a good listener. He can go hours without saying a single word."

Dimella is a little ball of furs beside us, but she perks up at those words. "That's because he's probably fallen asleep, Enwen."

Enwen looks at me out of the corner of his eye while shushing Dimella.

"Don't you shush me."

"Sorry, Miss Dimella, but I'm trying to encourage a conversation here, and you're ruining it."

"I don't follow."

Enwen mouths the words *epic romance* to Dimella, but she doesn't catch them. I immediately look at Kearan and relax when I realize he's not paying a wink of attention to Enwen.

"Miss Dimella, why don't you come show me the starboard side of the ship?" Enwen asks.

"What?"

"I think we should leave the aftercastle and go on a stroll."

"Why?"

"You're useless," Enwen says to her before storming off.

"Excuse me? Sailor, you get back here."

She takes off after him to give him a tongue-lashing, but it doesn't matter. Enwen's plan worked, and I'm now left alone at the helm with Kearan.

"I've been saying it for years," Kearan says. "Enwen is mad."

"You're not much better. *How are you feeling, Captain?*"

"It's your first time captaining a ship. You've lost four sailors. You should talk to somebody about it."

"I did. I wrote Alosa and told her all about it."

"And what did Alosa say?"

"None of your business."

Kearan grunts. "Did she tell you not to blame yourself? Or did she assume you're unaffected because that's how you always act?"

I say nothing.

"So she did assume you were fine. Then let me tell you not to blame yourself. It's not your fault. Don't focus on the four souls you lost. Think of the twenty-five you saved."

"Why don't you keep your thoughts on yourself? Better yet, keep them *to* yourself."

"You look out for everyone on the ship. Someone needs to look out for you."

"I don't need looking out for. I'm a damned pirate assassin, Kearan. The only looking out you need to do is for the knife at your throat when you finally piss me off enough."

He grins. *Grins.* And says nothing more.

This is why you can't let them know they get to you. They smile at your expense. My hand goes for my closest knife.

"I care," Kearan says. "I want to know how you're doing. I want to know how I can help. We've been through some things together. Storms and broken masts and fights against the pirate king. That doesn't leave anyone unaffected. I just want you to know that you're incredible, and I want you to be okay."

My clenched fingers release the knife as sense finally slams back into me.

"Stop trying to flatter me!"

"I'm not."

"You are."

"Just because I'm telling the truth doesn't mean I have an angle. I'm not trying to get anything from you."

Except he is.

Because men always are.

"Then stop talking. Because your words are purposeless."

I see his mind turn as he tries to work an argument around that one, but a call interrupts us.

"Land ho!"

When I join Roslyn up in the crow's nest, I think all she's spotted is another iceberg at first. It's much larger than the others, for sure. I can't even see the edges on the sea, but as we draw closer, I begin to spot other things.

Green. There's vegetation, and with vegetation comes life.

The little lass has eyes sharper than a hawk's.

I put the spyglass to my eye, making out the shapes of trees and mountains and snow-covered terrain, but there's not anything terribly exciting to see on land.

The water surrounding it, however, is another matter.

Dead ahead, I see a bowsprit jutting into the air. To its right, a hull rests at an angle, the structure tottering with the incoming tide. A sail billows atop a broken mast, an unfamiliar flag streaming in the wind. Shattered planks float on the waves, and downy white birds sit atop some of them. A coil of rope has become entwined with seaweed, the brown mass floating alongside a frozen body facedown in the water. Who knows how long he's been dead? The cold keeps everything perfectly preserved.

The island is completely surrounded by ship wreckage. I can't look in any direction without seeing it.

We've surely found where Alosa's women went missing.

But right now I'm more concerned with what caused all of this.

I climb down the mast, where Dimella and the rest of the crew wait patiently.

"It's a ship graveyard out there," I say, forgetting to be tactful until after the words are out of my mouth.

Enwen clutches his beads to his chest, and my gun master climbs the mast without another word.

"Is the *Wanderer* among the wreckage?" Dimella asks.

"We're too far to tell."

"We're going closer?" Enwen asks with alarm.

Kearan puts a hand on his shoulder to steady him. "Find your mettle, man."

"We're going to circle the island without getting too close," I say. "We need proof that the *Wanderer* docked here before we go ashore."

"A lot of ships permanently docked here, Captain," Dimella says. "What do you think got 'em?"

"Cannons," Philoria says when she returns to the deck. "Definitely cannon debris. I'd stake my life on it. Nothing else tears apart masts like that."

"No more beasties, then?" Enwen asks.

"Not this time."

"Someone doesn't want anyone going ashore," I deduce.

"For what purpose?" Dimella asks. "Not like it's a prime vacation spot or anything."

"There must be something valuable here," Kearan says. "Gold or other precious metals."

"Gold, you say?" Enwen perks up.

"Take us closer, Kearan," I say. "I want a better look at that debris."

He does so, but it's not easy. For hours, he maneuvers us around blocks of ice and ship debris. But we eventually find what we're looking for.

I see the letters *Wan* painted on the side of one of the wrecked ships. The rest of the letters disappear into the water. Alosa's missing vessel is here. Just from what I can see in either direction, there is enough wreckage for at least nine full ships. And the destruction continues as far as the eye can see. Surely there's even more surrounding the whole island.

"Dimella, I want to go ashore alone," I say to my first mate. "Have the crew lower a rowboat for me."

Dimella narrows her eyes. "Captain, I know you mean to put no one in danger but yourself, but if anything should happen to you, then you'll leave the crew without their leadership. It isn't wise for you to go anywhere alone. Please consider taking a scouting party with you if you intend to go exploring. Alosa has chosen some fine girls for this voyage."

"I'll go with you," Kearan offers immediately.

"And me," Enwen says.

We all stare at him.

"Kearan mentioned gold. Perhaps I could keep an eye out for it while we're out and about." He shrugs.

I think it over, weighing all my options, and ask myself for the hundredth time what Alosa would do.

"I'll take half the crew ashore," I decide. "Should anything happen to us, you'll still have enough sailors to make the trip back home."

"I'll guard the ship with my life," Dimella says.

"Don't be ridiculous," I say. "A ship is only a thing. You protect the rest of the crew."

She grins. "Well, I'd at least try to save the ship. The crew was a given, Captain. Who will you take ashore?"

"These two," I say, gesturing to the men beside me. "Taydyn, Philoria, Bayla, and Visylla." I list a handful more names.

"What about me?" The small voice comes from somewhere nearby, yet it isn't until Roslyn's head pokes over the companionway that I realize she was spying.

Sneaky little thing, indeed.

"You're the ship's lookout," I say. "You need to be on the ship to keep a lookout. That's the most important job right now."

She scrunches up her face, as though trying to decide if I'm being sincere or just tricking her into staying. The answer is both, but she seems placated for now.

"I'll have the boats lowered," Dimella says, and she sees to it.

I make a stop at my quarters, grabbing as many weapons as will fit into my clothing. Knives in both boots. Knives inside my coat. Knives at my waist. I lose count somewhere after twelve. I take extra pistols, slinging them through a holster over one shoulder. Normally I prefer quiet weapons, but if we're ambushed, stealth will cease to matter.

I grab my old rapier and bring it out on deck with me. When I spot Roslyn at the port side staring off at the island, I approach her.

She turns, and her eyes go straight to what I'm carrying. I hold it out to her.

She takes the rapier and unsheathes it, holding it up to the sky.

"We'll work on form and stance later, but for now, you should have a weapon with a longer reach in case anything bad happens."

"You're giving me your old sword?"

I nod. "You'll have to ask Dimella if she has a spare belt for you. You'll likely have to cinch it high so the sheath doesn't drag."

I can't tell if she hears me or not. She's swinging the rapier in unpracticed arcs, lunging at invisible foes.

"I'll take it away if you injure yourself or anyone in the crew with it," I say.

She turns a glower on me. "I would *never*. I haven't done so with my dagger, and I'm not about to with my new sword. Thank you, Sorinda!"

She tries to run at me with the sword. Then remembers to turn the blade downward before grabbing me in a hug.

"Keep a sharp lookout," I tell her.

"I always do."

She's staring at the weapon when I turn from her, approaching the party that's gathered near the lowered rowboats.

Enwen squints out at the land. "I don't see any sort of settlement. No one could survive in this temperature long without shelter."

"Someone sank all these ships," Kearan responds. "Maybe they're hiding in the woods."

"What if what lives out here isn't human?"

"We'll soon find out."

Enwen tucks his beads into his coat.

I don't say a word as I climb down into the nearest rowboat. Those chosen to go ashore follow quickly. We fit snugly into three boats and start the trip for shore.

Kearan rows in my boat, and I watch the land grow closer from over the top of his head. I get an eerie feeling as we drift farther from *Vengeance* and the rest of the crew, but I can't quite place it. I'm not afraid. I don't think anything is going to jump out at us the second we reach shore. Besides, we'll be able to take cover in the trees shortly after docking.

Yet I feel as though I'm forgetting something. Or as if my subconscious is recognizing some danger that my brain can't quite place. But it has nothing to do with the land we're approaching.

I turn in my seat to look over my shoulder. *Vengeance* is anchored far enough out that she'll have plenty of warning if an attack comes from the shore. Then I look to my right and left, taking special notice of the shapes jutting out of the water. Now that we're close to shore, I can see them all the more clearly. From the ocean, the land appears to curve with hills of snow and cliffs of ice. But from this angle, I can see that the solid block of ice to our left is *hollow*. The water within only had the appearance of solid ice. It's actually an enormous water cave. Some trick of the light?

Whatever the case, I feel my heart sink toward the icy depths beneath me as I peer into that dark crevice. My eyes focus on the darkness, trying to make out any movement within.

And then I see it: a line of shadow more potent than the others. The shape of a bowsprit.

"Turn the boats around!" I shout. "Now!"

The order is followed immediately, despite Kearan facing the ship and having no reason to listen.

"What is it?" Enwen asks from the next boat over.

"Row faster," I order.

And then we hear shouting. Roslyn yells something from atop the crow's nest. Dimella barks out orders in return. Bodies scramble atop the deck of *Vengeance*.

I return my eyes to the left, and sure enough, a ship unlike any I've ever seen emerges from the ice.

The hull is pale white, the sails dark gray. Many of them are ripped and tattered, streaming uselessly in the sparse breeze. It doesn't matter, because the mainsail is enormous and intact, and the sweeps carry it plenty fast. It approaches the bow of *Vengeance*, out of our cannon sights, which are only located at the starboard and port sides.

It is easily twice the size of our own ship, with two extra decks, and a massive forecastle.

A galleon big enough to do some serious damage.

The bows of the two ships face each other. One anchored, the other closing in fast.

As we try to race the new vessel to the ship, I force my tense shoulders to relax. The enemy ship will need time to get within range. Then they'll need to turn and line up their cannons just so. They have more control with those sweeps, but we might have chance to reach *Vengeance* in time.

And then I hear a cannon fire. Confusion settles within me until I see smoke billowing just below the bowsprit of the enemy ship.

Fore cannons.

Shit.

The first shot misses, but the second lodges into the hull of *Vengeance*. I hear the anchor of my ship slowly cranking, as Dimella must be trying to get the crew to weigh fast enough to turn the ship so we can face it with our own cannons.

"Come on, come on, come on!" Philoria shouts beside me. Her

fingers twitch, and I'm sure she's just aching to get behind a cannon and return fire.

We've still a ways to go.

"Scoot to the left," I order Kearan. He moves over, allowing me to take the right oar and help him row. He was doing just fine on his own, but I need to do something before I go mad with anticipation.

I hear more cannon fire. Water splashes as missed shots connect with the sea. Wood shatters as another cannon hits its target. I'm at my limit, rowing as fast as I possibly can, and it's still not enough.

Stupid. So stupid. I should have seen the enemy's hiding spot sooner.

Another blast of cannon fire has my heart pumping at impossible speeds. It's followed by an earsplitting crash and the creak of wood. I look over my shoulder, already knowing what I'll see.

They hit the foremast, and it falls to one side, ropes snapping, and sails tearing.

Some sound escapes me. A throaty shriek of frustration.

And then we're finally there.

I fly up the rope ladder, land on the deck, and survey the crew. Four girls are at the capstan, trying to get the anchor raised. Meanwhile, Dimella is at the helm, cranking it for the turn that will finally get our cannons in range. Radita is nowhere in sight, likely already below seeing to the damage.

Girls race to prepare the cannons. The anchor finally comes free of the water. The enemy ship is almost lined up with our cannons.

I try to make out figures on the enemy ship, but all I see are heavy coats and gear, just like we wear, though in different colors and styles. And whoever wears them is definitely human, not that I really took Enwen's fears into consideration.

"Return fire!" I shout.

Philoria sets the first cannon off, and it just barely skims the ship, as it's not quite lined up with the cannon's sight. Visylla's shot goes wide, but Bayla's strikes true. She takes out one of the enemy's cannons at the fore, striking right through the gunport and destroying both the weapon and whoever was manning it.

There's a small cheer on our side as we see the enemy scrabble out of the way and take longer to reload their weapons for the next bout.

But when it comes, it comes hard. Their cannons go off in rapid succession. There are still at least three at the fore, and *Vengeance* jolts from the hits she takes.

There's a breathless, silent moment as both sides refill their cannons before firing once more. The ship finally comes within musket distance, though just barely. Shots ring out on our side, and crossbow bolts and gunshots answer from the enemy.

Another cannon hits us low, and the sound of rushing water is all I can hear for a moment.

Until another shattering *boom* sounds, and a cannonball streaks to us, skimming too high to hit the ship, dodging the mast.

It hits Bayla square in the chest and carries her off the ship.

She's dead before she even hits the water.

I stare at the spot where she disappeared in stunned silence.

Radita is shrieking at me from below, and I barely make out her words.

I don't want to believe what is happening. I want to go back in time, retrace my steps in such a way as to save the four—five now—we've lost on this journey.

I would have attacked the beastie the first time we saw bubbles in the water. I would never have left the ship to explore the shore until I was certain the crew I was leaving behind was safe.

But it's too late for any of that, and regret will not save the souls who remain within my care. The truth strikes my heart like a physical blow.

We're not going to win this fight.

Perhaps if we'd had the whole crew on deck. If we hadn't anchored. If we'd had our weapons ready.

But it didn't happen that way, and I know we've already lost.

"Dimella!" I shout. "Get the rest of the rowboats lowered. Now! Jadine!" I find the head cook somewhere in the bedlam, loading a musket for another shot.

"Captain?"

"Get as much food as you possibly can loaded into the boats."

"We're abandoning ship?"

"Preparing for the worst. Now go!"

Philoria gets her cannon reloaded and takes another shot. It strikes true, but the behemoth doesn't slow.

I go belowdecks and call for Radita.

"Forget about patching the holes," I tell her. "Have your workers haul up what supplies they can from the hold before it's all below water. Anything we might need to survive on land."

"Aye-aye."

I return up top. Girls are firing muskets at the approaching ship, but the enemy's volley is three times as large as ours, and my crew constantly has to duck out of sight to avoid being shot themselves.

The enemy vessel puts another hole in us. All three of our shots make contact with the ship now, but we can't spread out the holes to do the most damage with just the fore pointed at us.

"Philoria," I bark out. "Slow that ship down."

She wipes unshed tears from her eyes as she lines up her next shot. "Aye-aye."

The next few blasts aim higher, and one finally clips a mast, slowing the approaching vessel.

"Keep firing!" I order, and then I help the girls below. We bring up food, cooking supplies, tents, blankets, tarps, and anything else that might be necessary to survive on land. Meanwhile, the ship shatters and splinters around us. When I'm back up top, I can see our yano bird in the distance, fleeing the destruction. Someone had the sense to let it free. It'll return to Alosa without a note.

"Everyone into the boats! Now!" My crew scrambles to the side of the ship, everyone squeezing onto the rowboats. Some girls even sit on each other's laps to make room. Roslyn lands on the deck after climbing down the mainmast.

"There's some movement on land, Captain," she says, "but they're too far away for me to make out anything."

"Do you think you can steer us away from them once we reach shore?"

She nods.

"Good work. Get in."

Philoria gets off one final shot, and *Vengeance* lists to one side, the water finally overcoming her.

"Let's go!" I shout to her.

She races for the boats, the last of the crew, and nigh jumps into the waiting boat below. Only then do I sit myself and order the rowers to take us ashore.

More and more cannons fire upon *Vengeance* as we flee. When the enemy ship is close enough to take notice of the little rowboats in the water, it turns, lining those fore cannons up with us.

But the shots go wide. We're too small of targets, and the fore cannons don't have as much range of motion. Our boats hit the frozen shore, and we pull them onto land. Everyone grabs something to carry from the supplies we managed to bring with us, and we run.

I've got one hand clasped around Roslyn's, the other around a pack of food. The terrain is rough, full of rocks and slick snow. It's far too easy to slip, and many of us go down as we hurry. Roslyn takes me down once as she falls, but we quickly right ourselves and continue. A cannon shot sends a patch of snow flying into the air and then raining down upon us.

"Blast all this snow!" Dimella says as she rights herself after a fall.

Roslyn points to the right, indicating a patch of woods. "The movement came from there. We should go another way."

I veer the crew to the left, and we run and run and run until we can't run anymore. Until the cannon fire is just a small thrumming in the distance. Until the wreckage of *Vengeance* is entirely out of sight.

Until there is no visible reminder of my failure.

Just the pain and shame I carry within my chest.

CHAPTER 11

WHEN I'VE RESTED LONG enough to catch my breath, I climb the nearest snow-covered tree. It's an evergreen with long daggerlike needles. Some sort of vermin scurries out of my path when I'm halfway up, my hands near frozen through from the cold bark. I had to remove my gloves so they wouldn't get covered in sap.

From above, I can see the galleon in the distance, circling the shore, looking for stragglers. Rowboats meander to the remains of our ship, likely looking to see what they can scavenge.

Our new friends on land are not too far off. They're just about to enter our section of woods to search for us.

I return to the ground and order everyone to keep moving.

Dimella monitors a compass regularly to keep track of where we're going and how we can return to the water if need be. We don't head in one direction but continue to make turns to confuse our pursuers. We hug the thicker trees, where the snow isn't as soft, to hide our tracks.

"Is it safe yet?" Little Roslyn asks after another hour of movement.

"Not yet," I tell her, "but don't you worry. I'm not going to let anything happen to you."

"I'm not scared."

I believe her.

It isn't until dusk is threatening the skies that we finally stop for the night. Radita was smart enough to bring waterproof canvas intended for the sails, and we lay it down below our tents and let the trees cover us from above. Dimella stations lookouts around the camp, and I order Jadine to under no circumstances build a fire. For I can see smoke far in the distance, where the enemy must be camping. We'll not let them know our location so easily.

We've only a few tents between us, so we'll have to pack the girls and lads tightly, but at least no one will be freezing at night.

We dust the snow off a few fallen logs and use them as makeshift chairs. Jadine passes out a rationed meal of hardtack and jerky to all. I eat mine quietly while the crew converses among themselves.

"Well, shit," Kearan says.

"Could have been a lot worse," Dimella says. "We made it to land without losing another soul. That's no small miracle."

"Yeah, but we walked into the same trap that all the ships before us did."

"No one could have seen that coming."

Alosa would have, I think to myself. She would have the moment she saw the sunken ships. Not when she was practically to shore and unable to save her vessel.

Enwen's off in a corner, shoveling at the snow.

"You digging a latrine?" Dimella asks him.

Enwen looks between her and the hole. ". . . Yes."

Kearan shakes his head. "He's looking for gold."

The two laugh. Laugh! How can they laugh when I've sunk our ship and stranded us on this frozen wasteland? I may keep a strong face and act capable, but I've never felt more confused and out of my depth.

I want to kill something.

Taydyn approaches our group. "I'd like to set some traps outside of camp. See if we can catch some food to add to what we salvaged from the ship. If we cook during the daytime, the fire will be less visible."

I nod. "Enwen, go help him."

Enwen hands his shovel to one of the girls before scurrying off with Taydyn through the brush.

Roslyn scoots closer to me for warmth, and I throw my arm over her.

"You haven't said much, Captain," she says. "Are you all right?"

Everyone within hearing range of her comment looks at me.

"I'm fine."

This time, it might not be true, though.

"We'll have an early start tomorrow," I say to the group. "You best all turn in."

I may be a captain without a ship, but the crew heeds my orders, piling themselves into the tents. Roslyn follows the remaining gunwomen into one, eager for the promise of warmth.

Only one person stays behind outside. One man. The one I knew would wait.

Kearan.

How's that for learning his new patterns?

He always sees through me. I may have said I'm fine, but he knows that's not true. He means to talk, hopes to get me to open up yet again. I brace myself for what he'll say to me. *It's not your fault. There's nothing you could have done. No one blames you. You're a good captain.* He'll try to make me feel better but only infuriate me instead. I begin to ready my argument.

He says, "Get over it."

I expel a small breath of surprise. "What?"

"Get over it. You messed up. Now move on. Think about your next move."

I can't say anything for a full five seconds. "You blame me?"

"Didn't say that."

"You said I messed up."

"Isn't that what you're thinking?"

"I asked what you were thinking."

"You don't care what I think. You respond better to tough love. So there it is. The advice you would give yourself if you could think past your guilt. Get over it."

He didn't tell me what I expected to hear, yet I'm somehow angrier than if he had.

Alosa said I would make mistakes. She was right. I just didn't expect to fail so miserably. Or to feel the way I do when it happened. The pain of my shortcomings is a constant pressure against my skin. Something trying to beat its way out of me. I want to be alone. I want to hunt. I want to *do* something so I don't have to think.

But none of those are options right now.

I stand from the log I'd been perched on and begin to pace. Sitting still is driving me mad, despite the hours of running we all had to do today.

"I failed them all," I say after a moment, because talking is the only thing I have left, and he's the only one who stuck around to listen.

"You saved them," he says. "We're here. We're alive. We have food. Alosa will come for us if we can survive long enough."

"Alosa isn't supposed to save us. I'm supposed to save those girls. Instead, I've gotten more of us stuck here."

Kearan picks a stick from the ground, dusts the snow off it, and begins breaking off the smaller branches. "Plans change."

"That's your advice? *Plans change.*"

"Captain, you don't want advice. You want someone to yell at and fight with so you can take your own attention off yourself."

I am so sick of him telling me exactly what I'm thinking.

I pull a knife from my waist and throw it. It lodges into the trunk Kearan's sitting on, barely an inch away from his leg.

He looks down at it, grins, and says, "Do that again."

I reach for another knife and fling it. It lands just a bit above the first.

"Throw until you miss," he challenges.

I grab a knife with my left hand, toss it to my right, then hurl it with all my strength. It strikes near Kearan's thigh. But he doesn't have to encourage me anymore. I grab and throw, grab and throw. Five knives. Ten knives. All making a neat outline surrounding where Kearan sits.

The fifteenth and final knife lands near his left calf, tearing through the thick pants he wears. When he dislodges it, a small line of red appears on the blade.

"Missed," he says, not showing an ounce of pain or shock. He throws the knife back at me, and I catch it out of the air by the blade without slicing my skin.

As he somehow knew I would.

We stare at each other. Me out of breath, him with that ridiculous grin, and something within my chest shifts ever so slightly.

"Now," Kearan says, "what's the plan, Captain?"

I wipe the knife free of blood on my own pant leg and return it to my person. "We find those girls. Get them to safety. Wait for Alosa to arrive. I keep this crew alive and well until then."

"Good. What's the first step?"

"I need to get a closer look at whoever lives here to see if they've captured Alosa's crew."

"Let's go," he says, standing and revealing the outline of himself left behind by my blades.

I LET THE GIRLS on watch know I'm going off scouting with Kearan, and then the two of us take off.

Perhaps it was a foolish thing to agree to. Nothing about Kearan is stealthy, but I'd disappoint Dimella if I tried going off on my own. I like having her good opinion. I want to maintain the mutual respect we have for each other. Besides, Kearan probably won't be able to keep up, and I'll lose him in the dark. He'll have no choice but to return back to camp. Dimella can hardly be upset then.

It's so very dark under the trees, but thin beams of moonlight break through the canopy, illuminating our way. The small scurrying of night-life sounds around us. Some sort of nocturnal bird hoots in the evening air, and the leaves and needles rustle around us, despite the lack of breeze.

The needle-strewn floor masks any sound and prints we might leave on the ground. I dart from tree to tree, searching our surroundings carefully before moving on to the next stopping point. Small plants appear here and there, and I skirt them so as not to leave a trace.

Kearan makes barely a sound behind me.

In fact, I have to look over my shoulder more than once to ensure he's keeping apace with me.

"You remember what I used to do for a living, right?" he asks. "Stealth was often required."

Still, there's so much of him. I don't know how he manages it.

"You make a lot of assumptions about me based on my size," he says. "I don't like it."

I halt in place and turn, staring at him.

"I'm a big man. Always have been. I have no problem with it. Do you?"

"Of course not."

"Good."

I turn back around, thoroughly puzzled by the exchange. I can't tell if he wanted to know what I thought about his body shape or if he was concerned it might affect how I treat him or something else entirely.

I like his shape, not that I would ever tell him that. And I would assume anyone who isn't me would make more noise than usual, but maybe I need to be more careful with my thoughts and words if they're coming out wrong.

Talking has never been my strong suit.

Still, I say over my shoulder, "I'm sorry if I've offended."

"If? You remember that you once pitched me off a ship and into the ocean, right?"

"I meant with my words."

He seems thoroughly shocked for a full second. Then he mutters, "Apology accepted."

"Good. Now, quiet; we're getting close."

It is a thing I sense, rather than see, that tells me we're nearly there. I halt in place, and Kearan does the same two steps behind me. The moon hides behind cloud cover, obstructing my vision, but I am endlessly patient, waiting the fifteen minutes for it to return. My eyes take in the surrounding landscape, checking every tree and bush twice.

I spot the man up in the canopy to our right, even before he coughs loudly into the frigid air. The glint of a pistol in the moonlight appears near some shrubbery, and there's a rustling not too far off to our left.

We skirt them all, moving slowly. Waiting, waiting, waiting. Crouching, springing forward. Crouching again. Soon, I can smell the smoke from the campfire, and my mouth waters at the scent of whatever they are roasting.

Kearan taps my back and points, having spotted yet another guard up in the trees. I nod, and we continue on, tracing a circle around the entire campsite, until I know the location of every person on watch, including the one who fell asleep leaning against another tree. He's the one we tread past to get closer.

A large boulder rests just outside the firelight, and Kearan and I press our backs against it. I look around the side, peering through some bushes to take a look at what's before us.

There are ten of them. Big, built men wrapped in furs and armed to the teeth. They carry spears and quivers of arrows. Bows resting beside where each of them sits. Swords at their waists. The hilts of knives peeking over their boots. A few sport pistols.

They don't look different from us. Their skin and hair come in the same colors. Their facial features are arranged in the same shapes. They are human just like us.

Though their language is far different.

I listen carefully as they speak to one another around that campfire. The words are nonsense to me, the vowels softer than we say them, but their laughter is the same. Our known world is so small, consisting of one inhabited country made up of seventeen islands. There are other islands spread throughout Maneria, of course. The late pirate king used some to house his keep. Alosa uses another for her stronghold. The sirens have some that they frequent. But outside of that? There was nothing. No other people.

Until now.

They're here on the most unlikely place for habitation, and twenty men are stationed at this specific location with . . . very little.

There aren't any tents or other shelters here. Nothing to suggest this is a campsite at all. In fact, aside from the food they're eating and the fire they manage, there's nothing. If this is the search party meant to find us, they are poorly equipped.

My eyes do another sweep of the area, searching for what I missed.

Kearan finds it before I do, pointing to what I originally thought was only a shadow, but is actually an opening between two boulders on the other side of the fire.

They're guarding something. An opening into the earth.

A prison, perhaps?

This is no campsite but a guard watch.

It's impossible to sneak past them all right now. Not without some sort of diversion to draw them away or at the very least get them to look in another direction. It's not something we can manage with just the two of us.

I've no choice but to turn away and come back again later.

WHEN THE LIGHT IN the tent first starts to brighten, I rise and exit. It was a fitful night's sleep. Though I've slept on the hard ground many a night, I am not used to having other people touching me. I would doze, only to wake at the first movement of another body in the tent.

I stretch in the frigid morning air and rub at the spots where my weapons dug into my skin. Like hell was I removing my knives while I slept.

Jadine soon joins me outside with her helpers, and they set to getting breakfast ready. While waiting for the rest of the crew to wake, I do sweeps around the area, checking in with each of the girls on watch, who all report seeing nothing in the night. As I do so, I rehearse in my head what I'll say to the crew this morning.

Kearan's words are never far from my mind.

Get over it.

And his accompanying grin as I threw knife after knife at him.

I shake those thoughts from my head as I return to camp. The cabin girls pass around the food, and Roslyn jumps down from the nearest tree to receive a bowl. Even on land that girl likes to be up high.

"See anything interesting?" I ask her.

"Snow," she says, deadpan.

I wait for everyone to have their morning oats before I dare to speak. It is my experience that folks are more amiable when they're not hungry.

"Yesterday was a rough one. I . . . apologize for not speaking about it last night. You all worked admirably. Short of seeing the future, there's nothing we could have done to save the ship. The moment we anchored, we were sitting ducks.

"But we're all here now. Alive with food and shelter. We're going to be okay. Our yano bird will return to the queen. She will send more ships this way, and they'll have a far easier time of it now that we've taken care of that beastie."

A few shouts of *raw!* go up at the pronouncement.

"We need only survive until they get here," I continue, "but that doesn't mean we can't still do the job we were sent to do." I explain about the underground entrance and the men guarding it. "I want to get a better look at it today during the daylight."

Dimella and I spend some time together talking strategy, but in the end, we decide it's best if Kearan and I scope it out again. As always, I'd rather go it alone, but it's not just me I'm putting in danger anymore by doing so. I have a whole crew depending on me.

Before the two of us head out, Philoria and Visylla approach me. I ache to see their saddened faces. Bayla's death hit them harder than everyone else, for they knew her best.

"Captain, we'd like permission to go down to the water tonight and light a lantern for Bayla's soul."

"Of course. We should not delay. I will accompany you."

They both nod before striding away, and Kearan and I take off.

The landscape isn't terribly different during the day, though I swear it's just as cold and difficult to see. The sun reflects off all that white snow, blinding anyone who dares to look at it. The plants we saw last night now have color to them, and these purple blossoms poke through the ground at uneven intervals. Kearan and I wear white to blend in with our surroundings. (I had to borrow clothes from some of the other girls, since I don't own anything in a light shade.)

There isn't much more to see at the campfire in the daytime.

New men have taken watch. The same number as before: ten around the fire, ten more keeping watch from the trees or surrounding foliage. They stare out at their surroundings with vigilance.

There's definitely something down there they don't want anyone to find.

Or perhaps people they don't want broken free?

At first, I thought it wishful thinking to hope for Alosa's crew to still be alive if they were captured, but if the natives have underground prisons for newcomers, then maybe we have a chance.

The crew and I find a new rhythm in the days that follow. I observe the natives, listening to them speak to one another, watching them exchange shifts guarding that entrance belowground. Dimella has a watch rotation all worked out so everyone can take turns keeping lookout. Instead of maintaining a sailing ship, we have to keep the camp stocked. We send out parties to collect firewood, go hunting, and scavenge for anything we might be able to use.

Everyone takes turns teaching Roslyn how to fight with her new rapier. She has a sparring buddy for every hour of the day to keep her occupied and out of trouble. Though she doesn't know it, her fighting partners are whoever is charged with guarding her in that moment. I'm taking no chances with her.

Enwen always lets her win.

Dimella puts her in her place.

And I make her work until her limbs drop with exhaustion.

CHAPTER 12

"DO YOU THINK ALL the natives look like that?" Kearan asks, obviously referring to the sheer size of the men on watch, as we return to camp from another night's scouting. "Or is there something dangerous in those underground tunnels?"

"We won't know until we can get a look down there."

"I don't like our odds going up against them. I think we could win, but not without many losses."

"I wasn't planning on fighting them for access to the tunnel."

"Then what were you thinking?"

"A diversion to draw them away."

"How?"

"We'll cross that bridge when we come to it."

A few days later, and I think we're ready. We've observed that small clearing surrounding the never-dying campfire long enough to know when they swap guards or restock the place with more firewood and food.

Once I know the patterns, I feel confident striking.

I approach the crew just over a week after landing upon this frozen place. We've switched camp locations every evening, always keeping on the move.

I say, "Today, I want to get inside the cavern the enemy is guarding, but I'll need help doing it."

Before I can ask for ideas, Visylla perks up. "Perhaps now would be a good time for an explosion?"

"With what?" Philoria asks. "We didn't bring much black powder. We'll need it all for the guns."

"That's not strictly true . . ." Visylla kicks a barrel, and I hear a soft *tink* within.

Dimella rounds on her. "Are you saying you brought your hand bombs instead of more food?"

"Everyone else grabbed food. We needed protection, too! Besides, you can hardly grumble when the captain needs them."

Both girls turn to me, looking for a verdict.

"Visylla, in the future, you will listen to your first officer. Dimella may discipline you as she sees fit. But today, we'll use those bombs."

KEARAN AND I SLINK between the trees like jungle cats. We've done this a dozen times now, but that doesn't make us careless. If anything, we're more cautions than ever. This has to go smoothly if we're to pull an escape off.

Flowers pad my steps through the snow. It's hard to believe that so much greenery survives in these temperatures, but I suppose almost anything can adapt. Maybe the type of flora here can only survive in a freezing environment.

As we approach the camp, it starts to snow. Little pinpricks of white make it through the canopy, brushing my head and shoulders. I hold out a hand in front of me to catch a large flake. It's been a long time since I've seen it snow. The northern islands in the Seventeen Isles sometimes have snow in the winter, but most of my time lately has been spent in the tropics.

When I come to a stop, Kearan doesn't miss a beat. I crouch behind the brush, looking through icicle-covered branches to observe the look-outs in the treetops.

I haven't seen the same men on guard duty twice yet, so their numbers are large enough to accommodate that, at least. I wonder how many live here and why our arrival was met with such hostility. Why did it have to result in Bayla's death? Why am I stuck here now trying to keep twenty-three other souls alive?

There has to be a way to make up for all of it. If I can just save Alosa's missing girls, then surely this will all be worth it. If I can still save more than I've lost.

Or maybe I don't want to admit that I've bungled everything up and I never should have accepted this mission.

I shut out the doubts crowding my mind by replaying some of my latest kills. Knives driven through hearts, knives raked across necks, knives plunged into eye sockets. Every encounter ending the same way.

Samvin Carroter dead. Again and again.

His look of shock and disbelief accompanies me as we stay crouched low in the snow.

Waiting.

And waiting.

And waiting.

The girls spent the morning cutting down dry branches, covering them with what oil we could spare, making a pile perfect for a bonfire.

I don't know how many of her hand bombs Visylla will use to ignite it and make a sufficient sound to draw away the guards, but I get an idea when the first blasts go off. Snow slides from a nearby mountain, the sound a deep rumbling that's enough to get anyone's attention.

While the men are distracted, Kearan and I creep ever closer, waiting for some of the guards to run and explore the sound. When their numbers are sufficiently thinned, we gain more ground, until I can see the opening in the rocks.

They left only two men behind aside from the lookouts, who now have their backs to us.

I don't need to signal Kearan what to do. We each get behind one of the men and simultaneously slit their throats.

Normally, I know the men I'm killing. I know their misdeeds and their characters. I know why they deserve to die. This doesn't feel quite the same. I don't really know these men. All I know is they sunk my ship and killed Bayla.

But that's reason enough for me.

Samvin Carroter dies again, and that small high carries me through the opening into the ground.

The light dims at first, only the sunshine at our backs lighting our way through a thin, rocky tunnel. But soon more light shines ahead, and I follow it into a cavern opening.

I am not easily impressed, but the sight before me takes my breath away. The ground, the ceiling, the walls—they all look as though made of light blue glass. But I know it's ice. Cicles from the ceiling hang over our heads; some have grown so long they connect with the ground at our feet, making columns of ice. The sun shines through the transparent ceiling above us, lighting up the whole place brightly. There must be feet of snow above the icy ceiling, hiding this cavern from sight, but it's not deep enough to keep out the light.

As I take my first step onto the ice, I nearly lose my footing.

"It's slick," I tell Kearan. I put one hand on the wall to my left to help me keep my balance, and we continue. Past the chamber of ice is another tunnel, this one just as slippery, and we traverse ever deeper and deeper. So far, the path hasn't forked at all, so I'm confident about the return trip.

When more light streams ahead, I hurry for it, silent as ever, and come to a stop before I step foot in the new chamber, taking it in before I expose myself.

It's much larger than the last opening, with more pillars and blocks of ice strewn about the place. Only this time, I can see shapes within the ice. When I deem the area empty, I creep closer to get a good look at one of the frozen blocks.

There's a skeleton within its depths.

Kearan scrambles on the ice behind me, and I look in time to see him reeling from the discovery of another skeleton in the ice.

"Is this a graveyard?" he asks.

"Why guard a graveyard?"

"I don't know."

I meander around the ice, counting compilations of bones as I go. When I reach the end of the room, I get to thirty-six.

"Now what?" Kearan asks.

"There's another tunnel."

He follows me through it.

The light does miraculous things to the ice, distorting the shapes hidden within. Still, I know for a fact that the first skeleton I see in the next room belongs to a child. No trick of the light can mask that. The curious thing is the skeletons are all bare. No clothing or weapons or anything else to suggest who they were. Just bones frozen forever in a timeless rest.

"It doesn't make sense that there's nothing remaining but bones," I say. "In this cold, it would take forever for the bodies to decompose."

"Unless someone carved them up. Ate them first. You remember when we met those siren-enchanted cannibals?"

I don't want the reminder. We lost Lotiya that day. I squint at another block of ice. "Look at them; they're perfect skeletons. Not a bone out of place. Standing upright. What held them in place like that while they were frozen? How were they frozen like this to begin with?"

"There's something at work here more than just the elements," Kearan says. "Do you think any of these people were from the *Wanderer*?"

"I can't say. I don't even know how to tell if a skeleton is male or female. Should have brought Mandsy with us." She knows more about the human body than anyone.

We pass through more and more rooms, or rather crypts. Each is the same. Columns and blocks holding skeletons encased in ice. Some even stand in the very walls of each cavern. We walk deeper and deeper underground, passing hundreds and hundreds of the dead.

"Enwen would lose his shit in this place," Kearan says.

I bite back a laugh, his comment so random it takes me by surprise. More surprising still is my response. I can't remember the last time I wanted to laugh at something he's said.

Just when I think it's probably time to turn back before we're caught, I catch sight of something new. A dark spot beneath the ice floor at the foot of the next tunnel. I crouch down in front of it to get a closer look. It appears to be some sort of metal plate?

I pull out a dagger to chip away at the thin layer of ice covering it. The second the tip of the blade presses down on the ice, there's the *twang* of a bowstring, and an arrow shoots just over my head. Kearan, luckily, had been standing to the side of me, out of range.

He says, "It's booby-trapped."

"Then we're getting close."

"To what?"

"Whatever it is they're hiding down here."

I tap the plate a second time, but nothing happens, which means the traps have to be reset once they're sprung. That makes things easier. I eye the tunnel ahead of us, seeing more dark spots down the path, and I start flinging daggers to activate the depression plates.

The second one sends a giant ax slicing through the frozen hallway. It cracks through a thin layer of ice in the ceiling before swinging down and across, embedding back into the ceiling once it reaches the peak of its arc. The third depression plate springs spears up from the ground.

"They're not just guarding this place. They're also maintaining these traps," I note. "Else everything would just freeze over completely and be useless. They clean and sharpen and reset these constantly. They'd have to."

"Best we see what they're hiding from us."

More daggers fly from my hands. A few more arrows spring free from different directions. A guillotine-like blade falls from the ceiling. I start to notice the holes and divots along the walls where all the traps spring from. When I strike the last plate, which deposits a net of some sort, I tread the path down the tunnel, retrieving my knives as I go.

Kearan follows but has to stop halfway down the tunnel, where some of the still-swinging weapons block too much space for him to squeeze past.

"I'll wait here," he says. "Talk me through what you find."

When I reach the end, I enter a small room. Five skeletons stand in the ice walls, as though guarding the tomb in the middle.

"There's another dead person," I say. "Only this one is inside some sort of ice coffin. And he's . . . not a skeleton."

Far from it. His skin is pristine. Smooth yet hardened, like a boy who's just become a man. His eyes are closed, each of his dark lashes visible underneath the inches of ice that separate us. His torso is bare, his legs in some sort of leather breeches. He doesn't wear any boots. The man is well built, with tanned white skin, brown hair shorn close to his scalp. His jaw looks sharp enough to cut the glass around it. His nose comes to a soft point, and his brow is on the small side.

Why is he tanned if he's in this place? Is this another prisoner who was captured? If so, why did they take the time to place him in a tomb? And *why* is he still made of flesh while everyone else is made of bones?

"What is he, then?" Kearan asks.

"Looks like he was frozen minutes ago. His skin doesn't look pale, like the dead. His cheeks have some pink to them. He looks . . . alive but in ice."

"That doesn't make any sense."

"I'm just telling you what I see."

"Is there a lid to the ice coffin?"

"You want me to open him?"

"I'm just asking if it opens. I think it's a valid question."

I reach out a hand to touch the ice coffin, testing for a seam.

"Yes. It opens."

He says nothing, and I say nothing.

After some deliberating, I announce, "I'm opening it. He looks like he's still alive. Maybe he's from the *Wanderer*."

"Be careful."

As if I'd be anything else.

It takes both arms and bracing a leg against the wall, but eventually I'm able to shove at the icy lid. It skids loudly, until it lands on the ground and cracks into a few pieces. The noise doesn't rouse the man in the tomb.

I reach for a blade and place it near his lips. It doesn't come away foggy.

"He's not breathing."

"Maybe check for a pulse?"

Right. I reach down my free hand to the side of his neck.

The second my fingers touch his skin, his eyes open, which should be a good thing. Rousing him is exactly what I was trying to do.

Except those aren't human eyes. They're a blue as iridescent as a peacock's feathers, and they're *glowing*. My body floods with cold, and instinct moves the hand holding the knife.

I stab it right into his heart.

The blade doesn't skim bone and sink into a soft organ. Instead, it makes a chinking sound as if I've struck metal.

And then the room before me disappears.

I peered into the room where my little sister slept, knowing it might be the last time I saw her sweet face. I always liked to see her when she slept, because it was the only time she wasn't in pain.

She was twelve, and the doctors were sure she wouldn't see thirteen.

Unless I did something about it.

I had a plan. The ship would leave tomorrow, and there were already whispers about what we would find when we made port.

The panaceum. The cure to any ailment. Just what Kayra needed to survive.

I was going to find it. I was going to steal it for myself. I was going to keep my family together.

And I wouldn't let anyone get in my way.

I know the memory isn't mine, but I'm transfixed by it all the same. The determination and love of the owner fills my whole being. It's akin to the warmth I remember feeling with my own family. That sensation of belonging gathers under my skin. It moves toward my chest, as though all the warmth within my veins is pulled to the very center of me, leaving my limbs numb from the lack of it.

Everything that I am, everything that I have—it's all contained where my heart is.

And then it moves upward, a gentle tugging that I barely recognize, until there's a pressure at my lips.

I wrench away so forcefully that I nearly drop my knife as it pulls free from the man's skin. My eyes shoot open to find him sitting up now, and his lips were—

They were on mine.

My free hand wipes at my mouth while the one gripping the dagger prepares for another strike. Except that the last time that happened . . .

I halt the attack and instead back up from the tomb and the being now standing free from it.

"Sorinda, what is going on in there?" Kearan sounds exasperated, as though he's been calling my name for quite some time. I hear ice crack-ing, and I think he's trying to force his way down the tunnel, but I dare not take my eyes off the threat to check.

"*Lourech nem construnun mzchen nuow.*"

The words should mean nothing to me. I know they're in a lan-guage I do not speak, but my mind offers the translation: *Thank you for freeing me.*

"Get out of my way," I say in Manerian. No, not Manerian. The world is Maneria, and it is far larger than we ever even imagined. I am of the Seventeen Isles, so I suppose I speak Islander.

The being's gaze lands on my mouth. His eyes constrict, his pupils grow-ing a darker blue, and he says, this time in my language, "You taste like hope."

"The hell?" Kearan asks, his voice echoing lightly in the cavern.

I want to repeat Kearan's question, but the being in front of me is looking me up and down in a very uncomfortable way.

"I said move," I say.

"My name is Threydan," he says instead of moving. "We're going to do amazing things together, Sorinda."

"The actual hell?" Kearan says, "Sorinda, get out of there. What are you waiting for?"

Threydan eyes the tunnel over his shoulder, and I take the chance to attempt leaping around him, but he moves with me, keeping himself between me and the exit.

"He's in my way!" I call back to Kearan.

"Then gut him!"

The man called Threydan says, "Yes, gut me."

If I was hesitant before, I'm now determined to do no such thing again. I don't feel right. It's almost like being sick, with every limb weakened from the body's fight with the disease.

Except, instead of feeling weak, I feel nothing.

Something is very wrong, and it happened after I stabbed him. What would become of me if I did it again?

I pull out another dagger, just so my free hand can have something to hold.

"You have nothing to fear from me, Sorinda," the being, Threydan, says. He tries to approach me, and I bring my daggers together in an X to ward him off. He halts. "Tell me your heart's greatest desire, and I swear to let you pass."

The hair on my arms stands on end, and I am overcome with the need to get out of this room *now*.

"I'm looking for some missing people," I say, because what else can I possibly do? I've never had a situation I couldn't get out of with something sharp.

Threydan steps away from me until his back hits the ice wall, leaving the exit clear. "I will help you find them. Then you will help me exact my revenge. I have it on good authority you excel at that."

Horror seizes me in place for a full second as I realize he must have seen one of my memories just as I saw one of his. "What did you see?" I ask, tightening my grip on my daggers.

"You were so little, yet you dealt death so beautifully."

My breathing picks up. I want to kill. I envision knives sticking through his skin. Blood dripping from a dozen cuts. His look of agony just before his eyes go blank . . .

A morsel of sense wheedles its way through my murderous thoughts.

I start to inch my way toward the exit, taking careful steps, ready to back away should Threydan prove to be a dishonorable liar.

When I reach the tunnel entrance, Threydan moves as if he means to follow, and I raise my knives higher.

"I'm not about to stay in here," he says, looking around. "It's all right, Sora."

That nickname coming from his lips almost makes me double over. I haven't heard it in over a decade. I didn't give him permission to use it.

Consequences be damned, I raise one of my knives and fling it. It lands square in his throat.

But Threydan doesn't choke.

Doesn't fall.

Doesn't die.

He pulls out the knife and examines it.

Kearan's cursing comes from behind me. And I inch back another step.

The sound of cracking ice thunders around me, and there is a rumbling above my head. Threydan and I both look at the ceiling. I register the ice above us crumbling, just as I realize I must have stepped on another pressure plate I missed the first time around.

A large shard of ice tumbles down, shattering against Threydan's head and sending him toppling to the ground. At the same time, hands grip my hips fiercely and pull me backward.

Kearan hauls me out of the tunnel. When we reach the cavern on the other side, he shoves me ahead of him and yells, "Run!"

Just this once, I obey.

I slip onto my arse three different times as I try to make my escape back through the rooms of frozen skeletons. Kearan is not so quiet as he keeps up with me, just a step behind, though he sometimes manages to keep his feet better than I do.

Because I'm still reeling from the encounter. I saw things I shouldn't have. I was distracted enough by them that he was able to *kiss* me. And I don't feel right in my skin anymore.

I can't feel the freezing temperature around me. There is nothing except my heart, which feels too hot within my chest. I would swear it has its own sentience. Pounding and turning and writhing with heat. It isn't painful exactly, but it's impossible to ignore.

And then I remember the moment my dagger pierced his heart. The way it changed me. The way it was drawing some sort of essence out of me. My stomach turns.

I shoot out through the last tunnel, finally landing aboveground. I fall to my knees in the snow and wretch and wretch and wretch. Up comes my breakfast and last night's dinner and anything else that might have been within my system.

My ponytail is pulled behind my back the moment I start to heave, Kearan holding it out of the way from behind me.

When I think I'm done, I grab a handful of snow and shove it into my mouth. I know it should feel so cold against my teeth that it burns. But there's nothing. No registering of the temperature.

Yet it still melts, and I swish it about and spit. Repeat. Repeat. Repeat.

Don't think about the fact that snow doesn't feel cold anymore. That's the least of your concerns.

"Did he . . . kiss you?" Kearan asks.

My body convulses again, but there is nothing left to upend.

"He did something to me," I say when I can speak again. "Something is very wrong."

"It's all right," Kearan says. "He's dead now. No one could have survived that cave-in."

I shake my head. "He's alive."

"How do you know?"

"I put a dagger in his heart and another in his throat. He's still walking and talking."

And then there's the bit I don't want to admit to.

The fact that I can *feel* him.

I don't know exactly where he is, but I know that he *is*. We are connected somehow. From the moment I struck his heart.

"He called you *Sora*," Kearan says.

"That was my family's nickname for me."

"How could he have known that?"

"I—"

The point of a spear juts under my chin from where I still kneel in the snow. I was so distressed that I didn't realize we were no longer alone.

And then it happens again.

"You took something that wasn't yours to take, Threydan. The siren artifact is the property of the king, and you will return it immediately."

Spears were pointed directly at me from a dozen different directions, but I only laughed at their presence.

"You can't kill me. You can't take the artifact. I am the panaceum now."

A spear embedded into my shoulder, but I couldn't feel the pain of it. There was only numbness as I pulled it from my skin. It dripped blood onto the green earth, but my skin was already healing, the blood replenishing and the wound disappearing.

Then I rushed them, determined to kill every last one of my crewmates. They chose their side.

When the memory subsides, I look up to see more weapons pointed at Kearan. It's the men returned from our distraction, finding us at their camp.

I can't find the proper fear within me right now. Not when my body and mind no longer feel like I control them. That's far more distressing.

One of the men says something in that unfamiliar language, but my eyes widen as my mind translates the words.

"You've woken him."

Why can I understand him now?

What did Threydan *do* to me?

I stand slowly, so as not to get stabbed, and stare down the man who spoke.

"What is he?" I ask, somehow speaking their language back to them.

The man's eyes widen in shock. "He's already changed her."

"What is going on?" I ask.

A different man steps forward, presses his spear against my cheek, and slices across my skin.

Kearan tries to leap to my side, but burly men restrain him. One throws a punch into the center of his stomach, toppling him. Meanwhile, my head whips back from the sting of the cut. I feel my blood drip down my face, though I can't feel the cold air against the open wound.

"She still bleeds. He hasn't performed the ritual yet."

"What ritual?" I ask.

"Sorinda, what's going on?" Kearan asks. "How are you talking with them?"

"We need to make sure he doesn't find her body," the one who spoke before continues.

"What do you want done?" another asks.

"To the deep with her."

Something hard crashes against the back of my head, and everything goes black.

CHAPTER 13

WHEN I REGAIN CONSCIOUSNESS, my eyes feel so very heavy, so I keep them closed.

And then I realize I must be dreaming.

For I feel weightless, and my body drifts as though it were floating.

At least I'm not falling, I think distantly. Or having some nightmare about the night my whole life was ripped from me.

I think it curious how muted and strange everything feels. Sounds seem too far away. Or perhaps too close? There's a whooshing that sounds nothing like wind and a pressure on my skin that has no temperature.

And finally, I register the sensation at my heart. That warmth that seems contained. Out of my reach. Yet vital somehow. My entire life force held within one spot.

And then I remember Threydan.

My eyes shoot open.

I blink several times before I can make sense of what I'm seeing. Light threading down from above. Thick shapes hovering above me. A large void spread out in front of me: darkness in every direction as far as I can see. Which admittedly isn't that far.

I try to stand, to move my fingers. Pinch myself awake.

But then I realize I'm restrained.

I look down, my head moving more sluggishly than usual. Some sort of iron weight rests on the ground, dirt flecks stirring when it shifts. My arms are bound in front of me at the wrists, and as I try to free myself, to thrash, bubbles drift upward.

Bubbles?

The realization sends my pulse hammering away at lightning-fast speeds.

I'm underwater.

I've *been* underwater for stars' know how long, and yet I've been breathing just normally. Or at least I was before I realized my predicament.

Now my lungs have increased their pace.

This is a horrible nightmare.

Except . . .

That heat within me, the numbness to temperature in my limbs. That all really happened, didn't it? Some frozen, sleeping man did something to me. The faint taste of bile still sits on my tongue.

I don't know what's real and what's not at the moment, but I know one thing. Regardless of whether or not I'm dreaming, I do not want to be down here.

I lift my head, realize the floating blocks above me are ice. I'm still in the frozen northeast. The water should freeze my limbs into immobility, yet I cannot feel it.

But my cheek still stings from where the man cut me on his spearpoint.

Right after I came out of that ice tomb with Kearan.

Kearan.

They've taken him or killed him.

And that thought, while it once would have not made a difference to me—now I feel incensed.

That is a member of *my* crew. He is no one's for the taking. Not while I'm still alive.

I need to get out of here.

My cutlass is gone, of course. So are a good majority of my knives. But surely, I had far too many on me for those men to find them all.

I slip my fingers into my boots, only to come up empty. I try for pockets in my clothing, but the water has made the fabric stiffen, and it's hard to reach inside my coat with my hands bound. I hear something move behind me, and I go very still.

Sound travels faster underwater, doesn't it? It could be something very far away, I reason.

You can't be afraid of the dark when you're the monster lurking in the shadows.

That's always been true on land. But underwater?

Believe it.

I have to.

I am the deadliest thing in this ocean. I will not let panic consume me. I have nothing to fear in death.

Except, Alosa gave me a job to do. I have not yet done it. I cannot die before I save those girls.

I try to bend my arms and legs. The ropes are too tight at my wrists. My legs have little sway from the weight of iron bound to them. Thinking to pick up the iron and take it with me, I reach for it, but it's far too heavy to budge.

I search the seabed, looking for something sharp, but there is nothing in sight save a bit of seagrass.

I have to find a knife.

Bending myself in half, I try to feel for where one single weapon could be. Those men couldn't have found them all. I own fifteen knives, damn it.

And then, at my side, I feel the pressure of steel digging into my skin. I twist my arms, trying to reach for it, fingers scratching against my clothing. Eventually, the tip of one finger presses against steel, the pommel of the dagger. I try to grasp the edge with my fingernail, but I always keep them short and can't get a grip.

A fish half my size swims in front of me, and I nearly scream from the surprise of it. With the scant light, it looks brown with no remarkable features, save its sheer size. It circles me once curiously before moving on.

I try again for the knife, twisting until my muscles burn and my fingers cramp. But finally, my fingers pinch at the hilt, and I pull it free.

Another ten minutes and I have my hands free of the ropes. In just two more, I have my feet free of the iron weight. I push for the surface, swimming fast as I kick my legs.

When my head breaches, I gasp in a hard gulp of air, despite not needing the extra burst of oxygen. My stomach sinks as I look ahead, seeing nothing but endless ocean on the horizon.

When I turn, I feel sick because there is still nothing. I'm in the middle of nowhere. With nothing. Just emptiness above and beneath me.

This is a nightmare.

Except it's not.

I know it's not. Because I am fully alert, fully aware of myself. I may be different, but I am present. No dream is this real.

Across the horizon, the sun is close to setting. I've never been afraid of the dark before, but it's never been combined with the void of an ocean beneath me. It is so very quiet except for the softly moving water breaking against my skin.

I want to scream. I want to look down, for fear of what else could be below me. I'd estimate that a good thirty feet of water waits between me and the ocean bottom.

I am not afraid.

I will not be afraid.

I am what people fear.

And then I see it. Far, far in the distance to my right. A stripe of green.

Land.

Those bastards sailed me out here, dumped my unconscious body overboard. What had they said? Something about putting me where *he* couldn't find me? Well, I'm going to find *him*. I'm going to find *them*. They're all going to pay.

For there is nothing I excel at more than vengeance.

I start to swim. One arm in front of the other, kicking my feet behind me. I push my limbs as fast as they will go, swimming as though something were chasing me.

After what feels like an hour but is surely no more than fifteen minutes, my limbs are too tired to move any farther. Too limp to even hold me up. I start to sink below the ocean's surface. And somehow, I'm still breathing as though oxygen were flowing into my lungs normally.

It feels wrong. I'm wrong. Threydan did something to me, and he needs to fix it.

I focus on nothing but breathing as I hover in the space between air and seabed, waiting for my limbs to regain their strength.

Then I swim for the surface, find land once more, and start the process all over again.

IT IS VERY, VERY late when I finally drag myself onto frozen, snow-covered ground.

I flip onto my back and stare up at the sky. Only a few stars poke between the cloud cover, but their presence is a welcome sight. Little pinpricks of light after I just spent hours hovering in the gloom of the open ocean.

I must fall asleep like that, for when I wake, my limbs feel sore and stiff from the hours of swimming. The sun is well overhead, not that it's done much good for the landscape here.

When I try to stand, I find that I cannot move. Cannot so much as sit up.

I yank on my right arm, hear some sort of crack, and then finally feel the tension release. When I look to my arm, I note that it is covered in ice.

I'm frozen to the ground.

I should be dead three times over by now. From the water, from the cold, from the night exposed to the elements.

Yet here I am. Breathing, heart pounding, muscles sore.

Numb to everything except that sting on my cheek.

My left arm comes free next, then my legs. I have to wiggle in place for a couple of minutes before my back finally breaks free from the ground. I pat at myself as I stand, ensuring all my clothing is where it should be. The dagger I used to cut myself free is frozen into my clothing. Useless at the moment.

I try to get my bearings. There are snow-covered peaks in the distance. Evergreen trees dot the expanse in front of me. Purple flowers break through the frozen ground, flourishing where they shouldn't, just like me now.

I've no idea where my camp and crew are. Dimella must be frantic with worry, but I trust her to keep everyone safe until I can find my way back to them.

I start walking.

My stomach grumbles for the want of food, but there is nothing I can do about that. My thirst is remedied by scooping up snow and letting it melt in my mouth before swallowing. I can't feel the cold of it, so it's very satisfying, if slow.

My eyes sting from all the salt water they've been exposed to. Burns and scrapes cover my fingers and wrists from tugging and clawing at the ropes as well as misplaced slices from the dagger as I sawed my way free.

My hair and skin are covered in frost. My clothing is frozen to my body. I wish I could remove the outer layers, since I don't need them, but I don't know how to get free of them without tearing my skin off.

My gait is more of a waddle than a walk with the way my limbs are stuck to my clothing. It makes my pace slower than it should be.

But I am not dead.

That is the important thing.

Even if it's impossible.

As the sun traces the sky, I make my way farther inland. Finally, when night falls, I can see pinpricks of light through the trees. It's not my crew, that's for sure. They know better. But neither is it the camp of men who guard the tomb entrance. For there must be dozens of fires spread throughout the woods to what I think is northeast.

I pick up my pace, finally having a heading.

I make noises as I move, no matter how much I try not to. The ice crunches and my clothing rustles with every step. Though my stomach kills me, I force myself to take it slow. Observe the area thoroughly as I approach. The natives on watch make themselves known to me slowly with their small movements. One scratches his nose. Another shakes himself awake. A third rubs his hands together for warmth.

For hours, I watch, until I'm certain I see all the lookouts. Only then can I plan my path into the camp.

I can smell the cooking meat on those fires, and it presses me on when my limbs feel ready to drop. My stomach encourages me when my head feels too heavy to lift.

I crawl through the trees, passing the watch one by one until I can see into the camp. Here, I pause, taking the measure of the space. Log cabins spread before me in an endless line. It is the first I've seen of any permanent residences from these people. Smoke billows out of the chimneys, and I spot covered areas housing chopped wood. Toward the center of the settlement, I see what appears to be the outside of a smithy and a tannery, though it's hard to be sure with only firelight to see by.

Not far off, two men stand guard outside of a hastily erected tent, and I wonder instantly if that is where they are holding Kearan.

There is only one way to be certain, but I'd never make it over there without being seen, or more importantly, heard. Not in my current state.

There are a series of firepits, where spits roast meats, likely food for those on watch to help them stay awake. There is one person tending to the food, stopping at each fire to turn the meat. I watch her carefully, waiting to see if she will leave a fire untended long enough for me to approach it.

She does, for after she makes her rounds, she disappears inside one of the cabins, likely to prepare more food, and I take my chance, helping myself to the mostly cooked meat. Because the heat doesn't hurt me, I don't have to wait for it to cool before I let it slide down my throat and fill my aching belly. When done, I check for anyone coming this way.

Most of the people are sleeping, and those in the camp are unconcerned about intruders when those on watch haven't raised an alarm.

They've clearly never had a run-in with someone like me before.

I hold my hands out toward the fire, and my frozen clothing crunches as I try to get myself closer. The ice melts from my sleeves at an agonizing pace, so I decide to hell with it all.

I thrust my hand into the flames, waiting for the pain of the burn to surface, but it doesn't happen. My skin doesn't catch fire, though the fabric does.

Throwing caution to the wind, I step fully into the firepit, stand atop the crackling logs, and hold back a sob.

I can't feel it. Not the cold or the heat or anything in between.

What. Did. He. Do. To. Me?

I fall to my knees, grab on to a fiery white coal with my bare hand, squeeze it within my fist, waiting for something, anything, to happen.

But the fire doesn't burn my skin. The smoke doesn't clog my lungs. The heat doesn't sting my eyes.

Instead the fire sizzles and sputters under the water melting off my skin and clothing. There is no pain. No consequence.

This isn't right.

I catch movement out of the corner of my vision, and I duck down farther into the fire. A woman approaches the tent I noticed earlier with a young boy at her side.

Kearan. I still need to save Kearan. I can't break down now.

She disappears inside the tent, and I remove myself from the fire, patting out my clothing in the few places that have caught.

Now I have a smell that follows me, surely, but at least I don't make a sound when I move anymore. I creep closer to that tent, waiting until the guards aren't looking before placing myself exactly at the back. I lower myself onto the dark ground, making myself as small as possible.

Here I pause and listen.

A woman says something in that native tongue. My mind translates the words for me, but the boy, who can't be more than ten, translates them for Kearan.

"Let's see if you are prepared to talk now that you've had a chance to calm your temper." I can only imagine the look she must be giving him. "I am Dynkinar, a Speaker for our people. This is Zarian, my translator. What are you called?"

"I'm not feeling especially chatty after you sank our ship and killed my captain. Just run me through and be done with it."

At first, I feel comforted to hear Kearan's voice, but he thinks me dead, and that, inexplicably, makes me sad.

The boy translates Kearan's words back to Dynkinar.

"There is still a chance you may live," he says after Dynkinar speaks again. "There is a chance the rest of your crew might live, but first you will answer my questions. If I like what I hear, perhaps we can talk of peace. Now, let's try this again. I am Dynkinar, a Speaker for our people. Who are you?"

I can sense Kearan's hesitation. He does not trust these people, but he also wants to keep the rest of the crew safe.

Finally, he says, "I am Kearan, sailing master of the former vessel, *Vengeance*. What is a Speaker? That like a queen?"

"No, a Speaker is one whose words hold power. One who must be listened to. There are three of us among the Drifta, but you were captured while my men were on watch, so here we are. Now, that's enough questions from you. You will answer mine now. Tell me why you have woken the King of the Undersea before I order my people to have you flayed alive."

CHAPTER 14

KING OF THE UNDERSEA?

Is that what they call Threydan?

I wish I could be the one inside that tent to answer and ask questions, but I'm stuck listening to wherever Kearan takes the conversation.

"I know nothing about an undersea king," Kearan says. "We were sent here to find a missing ship and crew. To rescue the survivors and bring them home. Instead, we lost our ship, and we're stranded in this frozen wilderness."

"Why did the first ship come?" Zarian asks on behalf of Dynkinar. It's clear that the Speaker knows about our first crew. If she hadn't dealt with them personally, someone she knows reported to her of their existence. She must know what became of them.

"To explore unknown waters. To discover more of the world."

Dynkinar humphs. "You mean to conquer. To steal. To take."

"I do not know." Kearan pauses a moment before saying, "My people are divided. The women we were sent to find were spies on the ship that traveled this way. Our queen likes to keep eyes on her enemies. When the spies did not return, she sent us to find them."

"Then why, Kearan, are you not looking for your lost crew? Why instead are you waking beings that are better left sleeping?"

"We assumed you held our friends captive. We spotted some of your men guarding what we assumed was a prison, so we searched it for the missing crew."

There is a pause so long, I wonder if I've missed Dynkinar leaving the tent.

Then Kearan barks out, "Why did you attack us, and what did you do to the crew who arrived before we did?"

A valid question.

"Our people were charged long ago with protecting the cursed tomb. We were ordered to kill anyone who came to this land, for no one must wake the King of the Undersea."

"Who charged you with this task? Who is he?"

There is a shifting in the tent, as though Dynkinar is making herself more comfortable. "A thousand years ago, our ancestors were once like your people: explorers looking to discover more of the world. A crew landed here and found a *slechian* artifact."

It takes me some time to translate *slechian*, but I find the word before Zarian translates it for Kearan.

Siren.

"They called it the panaceum, and it was not long before they realized how special it was. It granted the possessor long life, made them impervious to afflictions of the flesh. Rendered them essentially unkillable. It could heal any sickness, cure any wound.

"The travelers were excited to take the item home and share it with the world, but one among them decided he would keep it for himself instead."

Threydan.

"The King of the Undersea, though he was not known as such at the time, stole the panaceum. He found a way to make the panaceum part of himself so he could never be parted from it, and that joining corrupted the magic."

There was no explaining it, but once I fused with the panaceum, I could feel them.

The dead.

I could sense where they were buried beneath the earth and taste their ashes on the wind.

It was not long after that my crew attacked, demanding that I return the artifact, even though it was impossible to do so now. They threw their spears, and I returned their attacks with my sword, felling three of them before I grew heavy from all the metal within my body.

I tried to stand, to pull the weapons from my flesh, but they surrounded me, thwarting my efforts. For the first time, I became aware of a new horror. I was undead, but they could still restrain me for all eternity if they wished. I could be alive but trapped.

Until I tried something new.

There were dead bodies still bleeding on the ground, and I reached for them. Not with my arms, but with my mind.

They answered.

My body floods with horror as I come out of the vision.

He can raise the dead. He can command them. I *saw* it.

Dynkinar is still speaking. "... moved effortlessly underwater, which is how he earned his name. The ocean is where he would hide his undead army, when they weren't busy attacking the rest of the explorers. He hunted them down, and the survivors eventually turned to the sirens for help.

"The King of the Undersea could not be killed, so the original explorers had to restrain him, while the sirens sang him to sleep and buried him in ice. The dead were also put in ice by the sirens so he could not call them to his aid, for while he could control the undead, he could not control the elements. He'd be hard-pressed to dig each set of bones out from feet of solid ice."

I saw those bones. Perfectly captured in ice. The work of sirens. I did not know they had control over water, though Alosa said she once accidentally controlled water. She pulled it straight out of Riden's lungs after he drowned. But she has never managed to replicate it.

Dynkinar continues. "The King of the Undersea has been waiting all this time for someone to wake him. And now you have."

Her tone is full of condemnation. As if it were our plan all along to wake a being who can control the dead. As though this all couldn't have been avoided if they would stop sinking ships and just *talk* to those who arrive.

When the boy finishes translating, Kearan says, "I've told you it was an accident. Something that could have been avoided if you'd simply talked to us upon our arrival instead of attacking! My captain has paid the price for that mistake. What more do you want?"

Indeed.

"Your captain was not killed for waking the King of the Undersea. She was killed because he'd started to make her like him."

My heart skips a beat as Kearan says, "*What?*"

"She could understand my warriors. The gift of tongues was another that the King of the Undersea possessed. When she proved to have it, it was clear that he'd chosen his mate."

"*His what?*" Kearan repeats.

"The sirens warned our people long ago that this might happen. He is the panaceum now, but he can share its powers with one other. One whom he can make invincible and immortal. I'm surprised he chose someone so quickly. Your captain must have struck some sort of bargain with him."

No, that's not what happened at all.

I struck *him*, and I think that might have linked us somehow. These memories . . .

"Why would this power-hungry wretch wish to share his powers?" Kearan asks.

"He needs a woman. Someone who will be unaffected by siren song so he can exact his revenge and reign supreme over the known world."

Kearan clearly finds that notion as ludicrous as I do. "What good is one woman against an army of sirens?"

I saw what happened when Alosa rallied sirens to her cause to save us and her mother. No one human person could fight against that might.

"She wouldn't have been an ordinary woman if he'd been allowed to finish changing her. She would have been an immortal capable of commanding the dead as he does."

My fingers twitch. I *really* want to kill something.

"So you . . . spared her that fate?" Kearan asks.

"We cut the King of the Undersea's power in half by ensuring he cannot use her in such a manner. It's bad enough that we will have to find a way to capture him once again. Before there are dead for him to command."

"Well, you did. Congratulations," he deadpans. "Now where is the crew who came before us?"

Zarian translates, "Many died during the initial battle. Some who made it to land were lost to the elements, and others are still out there somewhere, surviving in the wilderness as your crew is now. Our food and supplies go missing from time to time."

They're still alive.

I hadn't dared to hope.

But they could be anywhere. They're trying to survive in this land just as we are. Hunkering down somewhere, stealing food and supplies when they can get away with it.

We have to find them.

But first I have to get Kearan out of here.

"How do you intend to deal with him?" Kearan asks suddenly.

"What?" Zarian asks.

"How do you intend to stop the King of the Undersea from slaughtering all of you to add to his army of undead?"

Dynkinar says not a word in response after Zarian translates the question for her.

"I have a suggestion," Kearan says to the Speaker. "My queen is coming. She does not leave sailors for dead. Queen Alosa has an entire fleet of ships at her disposal. I don't know how many she'll send for us, but I can't imagine it would be less than three."

Someone shifts uncomfortably within the tent.

"I assume that you only have the one galleon to fend off newcomers on this side of the island. You will lose it should you try to attack when she comes. So I propose this. Do not attack when she arrives. Let me explain the situation to her. Not only does she hold power over her people, but she is also the daughter of the siren queen. She has powers, but even if she alone is not enough, she can get the help of her people to put him back to sleep."

Kearan's words are met with silence. Then Zarian starts to translate. Dynkinar's response is clipped and abrupt, but I understand.

"You're lying."

"Clever of you to try," the boy continues translating. "I will talk with the other Speakers. You will remain here until we can determine what to do with you and your crew. I want to set you free, Kearan, but we can't have you and the others depleting our resources."

And then she leaves. Finally I hear the tent rustling. I press myself into the snow as far as I possibly can.

I wait until I see Dynkinar and the boy to ensure they're not crossing behind the tent. I don't want to be in their sights. Even now I can hear more noises in the camp. Daylight must be near.

Crying interrupts my survey of the camp.

Crying from the tent.

I wonder for a moment if the guards have entered and started beating Kearan, for he sounds terrible.

"I'm so sorry, Sorinda," he whispers. "I tried."

Is he . . . crying for me?

The sound of it hurts my heart. It is a startling pain when so much of me is devoid of any sensation.

I use my dagger to cut through the dried skins and slip inside the tent.

Kearan is thoroughly tied to a series of crossed poles. They serve to both hold up the tent and keep him prisoner. His back is to me, but

I can tell he's not in great shape from the way his body is slumped. His crying quiets, as though he's trying to get himself back under control.

On the floor far out of his reach, my rapier and remaining daggers rest. I take what's mine before rounding the pole so I'm in Kearan's line of sight. I put my finger to my lips.

Despite my clear caution to be quiet, Kearan sucks in a huge gasp. I immediately take my dagger to his bonds. They're thicker than the rope I'm used to, made with wound animal hides.

Once his hands are free, Kearan wipes at his eyes. I can see that they haven't treated him well. He's sporting a swollen eye and a bloody nose. He rubs his wrists gingerly, and I begin on freeing his legs.

The guards are mere feet from us, just on the other side of that tent flap, so it's impossible for us to speak to each other. I prefer it that way for now. Especially when he still has silent tears falling from his face. When he's completely freed, I drop onto my hands and knees to look through the cut in the tent.

More people are rousing from their cabins. The way isn't clear.

Shit.

I slip back inside and shake my head, but Kearan isn't quite all the way there yet. He's still staring at me as though I'm some sort of ghost.

There's nothing for it. We can't sneak out. We'll have to act as though we belong.

I look outside once more, then gesture for Kearan to follow me when I don't see anyone looking our way. When I rise to a standing position, I wait for Kearan to join me before moving away from the tent. He's acting far from normal, with the way he's looking at me, looking around. And I hardly blend in with the way I'm covered in soot, my clothing fire streaked.

I do the only thing I can think of and throw Kearan's arm over my shoulder, blocking most of me from view and giving him something to focus on.

Contact.

"Act natural," I whisper to him. "We have to walk out of their camp."

"How are you alive?" he fires back.

"Not now. Focus."

"I'm focused!"

"Hold," a deep voice says, and Kearan and I freeze at being discovered.

CHAPTER 15

ONLY, AS I SURVEY our surroundings, I don't see anyone talking to us. No, the order was given some thirty feet off to our right. One of the guards has his spear pointed at a newcomer who is entering the camp.

A man who isn't wearing a shirt or boots.

The hair on my arms stands on end.

It's *him*.

"I said hold!" the guard repeats. An alarm goes up in the camp, and more people rush toward the altercation. More men and women with weapons and hastily-thrown-on clothes. "We will attack if you don't comply."

"I'm not here for fighting," Threydan says in their language. "I'm searching for my beloved. She was spotted entering this camp."

My stomach twists, and I feel the need to vomit my stolen meal. Because I know he's talking about me. Those parts of me that are missing? He has them. That's why I can feel him. We're connected. I think I might have stolen part of him, too, when I stabbed his heart. His weirdly solid heart.

Before I can look away, peacock-blue eyes fix on me. Threydan winks.

He shouts loudly, "Who's in charge here?" He keeps walking, as though nothing scares him.

A spear is thrown his way, burying itself in his back. It goes clean through until it pokes out of his chest on the other side.

He looks down at the weapon, as if it is only a minor inconvenience.

"I came to talk, not fight," Threydan says. "Last chance."

"Restrain him!" comes Dynkinar's shout as she runs to join the throng. "Don't let him—"

But it's too late. Threydan has pulled the spear all the way through. Now he has a weapon. He hurls it at the man who had been shouting at him to halt. It strikes him clean through the heart. He's dead before he even hits the ground.

Threydan's hand curls into a fist, and the dead man rises once more, his eyes now the same peacock blue, the color so vibrant, I can see it even from this distance. He turns on his own men, swinging a fist at his closest companion. Then he pulls the spear from his heart and uses it to jab at his friends. As they fall, more bodies rise with blue eyes.

Shit.

He really can raise the dead. If Threydan finishes what he started on me, will I become like that? A mindless undead puppet for him to control?

Threydan looks purposefully in my direction and makes a shooing motion with his hands.

Only then does it dawn on me.

He's *helping* me escape. He's the distraction so we can make it free.

This is so wrong, but I do the only thing I can.

I shove Kearan's arm off me and sprint for the trees. Kearan catches up with me in no time. He runs as though the very devil is on his heels, though he doesn't overtake me. His longer strides match mine through the woods. Snow-covered branches whip my face, but our tracks are lost to the mostly needle-covered floor.

I'm not entirely sure which direction we're running. I cannot orient myself, but Kearan seems to know where we're headed, so I let him lead.

My muscles are still exhausted and sore from the last two days' adventures, and I don't last as long as I should on the run. My hands go to my knees, and I heave in breaths of air.

Kearan says, "You're actually alive? How?"

And then the next thing I know, he's gripping me in the fiercest bear hug.

I have not been touched like this since I was very small.

Not since my father would grasp me to him before throwing me atop his shoulders, walking me to the library, where he would read me a story before bed.

Kearan releases me abruptly, as though just realizing what he's doing. Or perhaps it was my rigid posture that got through to him.

"I'm so sorry," he says. "I'm so relieved you're okay." He clasps his hands behind his back, as though to keep them out of my sight lest I get any ideas about cutting them off. "But *how* are you okay? I was so sure you were dead."

"It would have been preferable to what I experienced," I say.

"I was awake the whole time. They didn't knock me out as they did you. I'm too heavy to carry. They made me walk. They sailed you out on that ship, dumped you over the side bound to that iron weight. I thrashed and fought with all my strength, but it wasn't enough. I watched the water as we sailed away. I hoped you'd regain consciousness and manage to free yourself. I waited for you to surface. Minutes and minutes passed, and still you didn't."

His voice cracks on the end, and I look up.

I take in his injuries once more. The dried blood on his clothing and caked to his hands. He got himself beaten while trying to save *me*. He cried over me.

Captain, stop flattering yourself.

The reminder of those words has me stopping that line of thought immediately.

"I made it," I say. "I'm alive. You don't need to worry. Apparently I'm harder to kill now."

"Because he's changed you?" he asks.

"I guess."

"He helped us escape back there, didn't he?"

"Yes."

"Because he wants you as his mate."

My eyes close. "Don't ever say that again. He doesn't own me."

"No one could ever own you."

"I think he's going to look for me when he's done back there."

"And you don't want him to?" Kearan asks carefully.

My head whips in his direction. "Of course not!"

"Sounds to me like immortality and power are being offered to you."

I step up to him and jab a finger into his chest. "Let's get something straight. I don't *want* to live forever. I have a family waiting for me in the stars. I intend to reunite with them someday. Not be trapped on this miserable world forever. And when has power ever made anyone happy?"

Kearan doesn't flinch from my proximity. He shrugs. "Alosa seems pretty happy as a queen."

"Alosa was happy before she was a queen. It isn't the power that makes her happy."

"Okay."

I step back from him and drop my hand. "Don't you ever suggest I'm some greedy—"

"I wasn't."

"Yes, you—"

"I just wanted to know where you stood with this King of the Undersea."

"Stop interrupting me!"

"Yes, Captain." He slams his lips closed.

"No man determines my fate. Threydan may come looking for me, but he can't have me."

And then Kearan's face changes, as though he'd been forcing it to be calm. Now it morphs into a snarl. "He can look all he damn well likes; he's not taking you. I—we—the crew won't let it happen."

A moment of silence passes, where we just stare at each other. I notice his breath fogging in the air before him, while mine does no such thing.

I hold one of my bare hands out in front of me. It looks normal, a deep umber against the white backdrop of this frozen tundra. I blow a breath of air against my skin. While I feel the gust of air, I don't register any temperature with it at all. Not the cold of my surroundings or the heat that should be on my breath.

Kearan asks, "What's wrong?"

I hold my hand up to him. He pauses before reaching out with his own ungloved hand to take it.

"Can you feel that?" I ask him. "Am I tangible at all?"

"I can feel you," he says reassuringly. "You're real."

"I can feel the contact. I know you're touching me, but I can't feel warmth or cold. I just feel wrong. Does my skin even give off heat?"

He hesitates before saying, "Yes."

"Are you lying to me?"

"I would never lie to you."

"Then why did you pause?"

"I was processing how your skin felt against mine."

That ball of heat where my heart is flares at his words, and I dare to ask. "And how does it feel?"

"Electric, like storm clouds."

I stare at our joined hands, willing something—anything more—to happen. Not because I want a connection with this man, I reason. Forget that silly moment where my heart stuttered upon hearing him crying for me.

But I want to feel *something*. I want to feel normal.

"We need to fix it," I say. "I need to be put back the way I was."

"I know. We'll fix it. We'll make it right."

"How?"

"I don't know, but we're going to figure it out. Can you move again?"

I nod and stand upright.

"I don't think they meant to let me live, regardless of what that woman said," Kearan says. "They didn't blindfold me. I know right where we are."

"Good."

"Thank you," he says earnestly. "For coming back for me."

"I happened to stumble into the camp where you were being held."

"You would have come for me even if that weren't the case."

"We need to move again."

We run, flying through the forest as silently as possible. I try to slow my breathing, but I'm panting as loudly as an overworked horse. My head and limbs feel too heavy. I carry more than I ever should have to: the fate of the world if Threydan catches me, the end of my own mortality looming over me, the possibility of being kept from my family forever, and always—*always*—my past looming just around the corners of my mind, waiting to invade my thoughts should I let my walls down.

I brace myself against a tree when I need yet another break. I feel as though I could sleep for days.

"How are you?" he asks.

"I just need a moment."

"No, I mean, a lot has happened. How are you?"

"Fine."

"That can't be true. You're not a rock."

"I'm the captain, Kearan. I'm not allowed to be anything but fine."

"You could be something else right now. It's just you and me. I already know the full situation. You won't lose face or authority by being honest with me. If you wanted, just until we get back to the camp, you could tell me things and I will never repeat them to another soul."

I say nothing. All my pressing thoughts are begging to be examined, pounding at my skull. My heart feels as though it is about to burst.

"You could just be Sorinda for a moment. Not the captain. It might help," he prompts.

I'm so spent, and perhaps that is the only reason why my defenses are down. I'm helpless to refuse the release he offers me. I'm carrying too much. It's never felt like so much of a burden before.

It's never been so unbearable before.

"We tried to do a good thing," I say, rubbing at my closed eyelids. "We looked for those girls, intent on saving them. Instead, we wake up an undead being? I suppose I should just expect these kinds of things by now. Nothing in my life has been easy or gone the way I expected it to.

"Before this voyage, I had only felt truly helpless once in my life: when I was small, watching my sisters and mother be drowned one by one before my eyes." I'm breathing even more heavily than before, when it was only physical exertion tiring me out. "But then Threydan changed me. My humanity is contained in one tiny ball where my heart should be. I can feel it there, sitting in my chest, a small ember heating the rest of me. What happens when it goes out?

"And then I woke up in the abyss of the sea. I've never known darkness like that. Such fear like that. Twice in the same day. I am Sorinda Veshtas, and I do not get *afraid*. I am what men fear. I've made sure of it, but I cannot be unmovable when the being I'm fighting isn't even human and I have no means of fighting him.

"I'm not fine. I'm *furious*. He took something from me, and I want it back."

I want to scream, to growl my frustration. I feel vulnerable from exposing so much, yet relieved to have less to carry on my own.

Kearan says, "Who was he? The man who murdered your family?"

The prompt is so gentle and inviting. I didn't know Kearan could behave this way—specifically toward me. I saw him comforting Roslyn, but this is different. He's offering to take the weight of some of my rage and hurt so my shoulders can feel a little lighter.

I just faced an empty ocean.

And some undead being wants me for his mate—whatever the hell that means.

There's no more room on my shoulders unless I consciously make space.

I swallow before saying, "His name was Samvin Carroter. He wanted my father's title and was next in line to inherit it after my sisters and me. He thought to enter the house, murder us, then burn it all down, claiming it was an accident.

"He started with my father. Killed him with the slice of a knife across his throat. I was hiding under the desk, playing hide-and-chase as I liked to do. I saw it all. When Samvin left, I ran to find my mother. I got there just in time to see him strangling her in her bathtub. I screamed. That brought the servants and my sisters.

"It was dark, nighttime, and I hid in the shadows and watched as he locked the door and killed them one by one. I was paralyzed by my fear. Too scared to save my older sisters. So I just watched and held very still.

"He thought he found us all. After all, he didn't bother to count the bodies as he murdered them. He left the household and started the fire, and that's when I finally fled. I killed him not long after. He'd settled into my father's second home. Another estate in the city. I walked there, barefoot, carrying the knife he'd used to kill my father. I still savor the moment he realized who I was. Right before I slit his throat. I was five years old.

"Alosa found me several years later, feral on the streets in the pirate quarter of Charden. I had acquired more knives, learned to protect myself and kill anything I perceived as a threat. It took some coaxing, but she eventually convinced me to come with her. She gave me a family again and showed me that it wasn't too late to protect those I cared about."

Kearan is perfectly still, not interrupting. I can almost pretend I'm saying the words aloud to no one.

"I've never even told Alosa that full story," I say.

"Thank you for trusting me with it," Kearan says. "And let me make you this promise: I will die before that monster gets his hands on you and finishes whatever he started. You will not fear like that again. You will not become what he wants you to be so long as I have breath in my lungs and blood pumping through my veins. I will look out for you just as you do for me as my captain."

I straighten slowly, needing to show some semblance of strength. "I do not need looking after."

"No, you don't," he agrees, but he doesn't take back his vow.

Makes it hard to argue when he agrees with me. Especially when I still feel contentious. Contentious and angry and spent. So very, very spent.

Now I can add exposed to the list. I never meant to reveal so much about myself to this man. I don't like to think about these things. The best way to keep the fear and anger at bay is to not think on hard times at all.

"Is there anything else you want to say?" Kearan asks.

"No." Fear hums under my skin, like I just need to be prodded at the right angle and it will come bursting forth. What could he mean by the question? Surely . . .

Kearan nods and bites the inside of his cheek.

"What?" I ask.

"I want you to know that you don't need to lie to me. You don't have to edit your story or withhold anything. I would never think less of you."

"Are you calling me a liar?" I say, my voice reaching a deadly tone, the fear pounding harder against my skin.

"A man wants your father's title, and you expect me to believe he didn't count the heirs as he killed them? No, he didn't just walk away. Something happened afterward. Before he burned down your house."

My mouth floods with saliva, my stomach wanting to churn yet again. My limbs feel weak once more, and I hate that such a question can level me.

I swallow. "The details aren't important."

"Aren't they?"

"He didn't touch me, if that's what you're thinking."

"It wouldn't change the way I see you if he had."

"I don't care how you see me."

"I know."

Another moment where I want to argue but cannot because he agrees.

"You do not have to tell me, Sorinda. But my ears are always open, if you want someone who won't judge you to listen."

He says that, but he doesn't know. Not what I did. How I allowed the maid's daughter to die in my place. No one can know my greatest shame. That is a pain that only I should have to carry.

"You were five," he tacks on, as though reading my thoughts. "Children that young are blameless for anything they do. They are too young to know better."

I knew better, I think darkly. I knew better, and I let her die anyway.

"You didn't kill your family. That horrible man did. You couldn't have helped your sisters if you'd tried. You were the youngest. *You* needed protecting. There was no one to protect you except yourself. You did what you had to to survive. I know that."

"Just stop talking," I say, regretting that I shared anything at all.

"You wish you didn't survive, don't you? You wish you'd died with the rest of them, so you wouldn't harbor such guilt. Guilt that you now find magnified because you woke up this undead guy who's killing the natives as we speak."

How? How does he do that? Just pull secret thoughts straight from my mind? I slip my fingers under my clothing in an attempt to reach for a dagger, but Kearan says, "Don't bother. You need every soul you've got to get away from this horrible place."

My hand drops down to my side.

We continue walking, and I consider the matter done. Kearan, it would seem, does not.

"When I was five, I ran away from home, seeking adventure. Probably scared my mother to death. I came back after two days because I ran out of food."

I roll my eyes. Does he think his sins could ever compare to mine? He's hopeless.

"When I was seven, I stole my neighbor's cat, because I wanted to keep him, and he liked me best. So I reasoned that I hadn't done anything wrong."

I resist another eye roll.

"Never gave him back, either," Kearan continues. "He got run over by a cart only a few days later."

"What a monster you were," I say sarcastically.

"When I was ten, I beat up a boy who made fun of a friend of mine. Knocked him unconscious. That was the day I realized how strong I was and that I had to be careful.

"And when I was seventeen, the girl I thought I loved died, and I was happy for it."

At this, I pause and look at him.

"Just for a moment," he says. "Just because of how much she hurt me. And then the guilt ate at me, and I wondered if it wasn't my fault all along that something bad happened to her."

"You thought you were a bad person because you wished someone ill for the span of a few seconds?"

What would he think of me if he knew the truth? I actually did cause someone's death. A lot of someones. Bad men, mostly. But not the first one. Not little Sleina, who had swapped clothes with me earlier that day for a game of dress-up. We never switched back. That's why Samvin thought she was me, and I didn't correct him. I could have spared her, and I didn't. Instead I watched as she thrashed her limbs in my pretty dress. Clear up until the point where her lungs filled with water.

Kearan must realize that his words are making things worse, not better, so he finally, finally quiets until we reach camp.

CHAPTER 16

ROSLYN'S IS THE FIRST face I see when I enter camp. She throws herself into my arms, and I grip her to me.

"Sorinda, I thought you were gone." Tears drip from her face, and I wipe them free with a hand. I'm moved by how much she cares for me. It softens my heart in ways nothing else seems to do.

Dimella claps me on the back. "Good to see you, Captain. You must be freezing. Let's get you a spare coat."

"Unnecessary," I tell her. "I need rest, though. Kearan will fill you in on what happened. I'm afraid I'm about to drop."

"I'm tired, too," Roslyn lies, and I love her for it. She climbs into the tent with me, snuggles under the blankets, and breathes deeply. I'm out before I can kick my boots off.

IT'S DIFFICULT TO SAY how long I'm asleep before the sound of shouting rouses me, but by the heaviness in my head, it can't have been long. I'm exhausted, I'm starving again, and my head is filled with memories it would rather forget.

But I rise, and with a quick shout to Roslyn—"Stay in the tent!"—I leave.

"To arms!" Dimella shouts just as I let the flap of the tent close behind me. My rapier is already out and ready, and I cock back my pistol as I scan the area for something to shoot.

They flood into the clearing like a tidal wave. Drifta with glowing peacock-blue eyes. Bodies freshly dead. A puppeteer nearby commanding them, though I can't see Threydan yet.

How did he find us?

I leap into the fray, slicing and stabbing at anything that isn't alive.

My pistol goes off, hitting a large dead male right through the eye. He doesn't blink as the iron ball makes contact, doesn't slow, and certainly doesn't stop striding toward the tent I just exited.

I slice at his outstretched arms but still he doesn't slow, so I nick the tendons at the backs of his knees, which finally sends him to the ground, unable to walk any longer. He wriggles like a snake, but I leave him for now.

Iskirra wields an ax, and she uses it to behead the nearest undead. The body continues moving, driving forward with purpose. Its own head is not what commands it.

Shots fire, and more steel slides into flesh. I realize that not a single one of the undead carries a weapon. Threydan doesn't mean to kill anyone. My thoughts are confirmed as I witness one Drifta step behind Jadine, pull her to its chest, and hoist her into the air. It does no more than hold her in place while she wriggles uselessly.

I leap behind it, slice the back of the knees, and watch the undead go down. Jadine scuttles free, then turns and slices at the arms of the creature that is now dragging itself toward her.

Dozens upon dozens of undead swarm our campsite. It would seem the King of the Undersea put a nice dent into the armies of the Drifta. They're overwhelming my small crew.

How did this happen?

Can he sense me? Did I lead him here? First he found me among the Drifta and now with my crew. Am I like a beacon to him? The thought is horrifying.

We cannot fight off such numbers, no matter how good my crew is, but that doesn't mean they're not fighting with everything they've got.

Kearan barrels through the clearing like a bull, knocking all enemies in his path clean off their feet. The girls swoop in, dismembering and rendering the undead immobile as best they can. They're no fools. If Kearan didn't fill them in on the situation, they're quick to pick up that their quarry is nothing natural.

Visylla throws hand bombs right and left. Gooey entrails rain to the ground. Shattered bones cling to the snow. She aims for the legs, bringing the undead down to ground level in waves.

The need for sleep batters at my open eyes, begging them to close. My muscles move sluggishly, unable to perform at their best after days without proper rest.

I drop my pistol, since it's utterly useless in this fight, and grab a dagger to aid in cutting necessary tendons to stop the body from moving as it should. The undead may not feel pain, but it seems they still need intact muscles for their bodies to work.

Though, I remember those frozen skeletons in the ice leading to Threydan's coffin. Why should the sirens and Drifta bother to hide them? They don't have muscles or tendons. Why would Threydan have power over them?

The trees surrounding our clearing rustle as more undead enter the scene. The battle grows sorely bleak, as ten or more Drifta are able to surround every one of my crew. Large Drifta leap upon Kearan. He fights them off as best he can, but even he can't keep so many at bay. They pin him to the ground, holding his limbs in place with the sheer weight of their dead bodies. An undead child no older than four grabs Dimella's sword by the steel blade and pulls. Dimella is so shocked and appalled by the cut the blue-eyed girl is giving herself that she releases her hold. Two other undead get behind her and restrain her by her arms. Visylla gets her feet kicked out from underneath her. She's then hoisted into the air and restrained. I watch and fight as one by one my whole crew is rendered immobile.

Save me. Not a single undead touches me.

I stand there, taking in the scene with a ferocity that shakes away my fatigue. I can't save them. A snapped neck is all it takes to end them. I know it. My hand grips the hilt of my rapier so tightly I feel my bones grind together. I keep my weapons, but I don't move, except for my eyes, scanning the surrounding trees for *him*.

My heart beats a feverish rhythm, and I swear I go cold all over, aside from that small little bit of warmth that wriggles within my chest.

I keep my gaze away from the tent, lest anyone think to check for more bodies that may be hiding. Though if we all die and only little Roslyn is left to survive, can she really last long on her own in these temperatures? With a people who attack first and ask questions later and an undead army on the horizon?

I shake that horrifying thought from my mind and keep my gaze alert. He doesn't keep me waiting long.

Threydan strides through the trees, his eyes already on mine, as if he'd been watching me for some time. My stomach turns over at the thought.

How has the man not found a shirt yet? His tanned skin is smooth all over, except for that short cropping of hair atop his head. His eyes blaze brighter than ever, and a bit of blood is dried on his skin.

I don't want to know whose it is.

He comes to a stop when he is a mere five feet from me.

A step closer, and I'd have gutted him. I still might, depending on his next move.

The lives of my crew are what stay my hand for now.

"Sorinda," Threydan says. "Are you well?"

The question is so unexpected and jarring that a breathy laugh bordering on hysteria comes from my lips.

I say, "I'm pissed. You've attacked my crew without cause."

"Attacked? No. Not a one of them has been hurt, including the little one in the tent."

I swallow.

"I wouldn't hurt your friends," he says. "In fact, I helped you save one just a few hours ago, did I not?"

"Let them go if you mean them no harm."

"Now that is something I cannot do until we have a proper chat."

I say nothing.

He seems to find that amusing. "We did not finish the binding."

"You're not touching me again," I spit out with every bit of venom I can manage.

I hear a few outbursts from some of the crew, as though they're try-ing to agree with me, but most are silenced by undead hands covering their mouths.

"That, fortunately, is not true," Threydan says. "We must if we're to complete the binding. You are only partly mine. Resistant to only some of life's dangers, it would seem. Hot and cold cannot harm you. Water cannot drown you. But the blade is still your weakness."

"Reverse it," I breathe out. "Make me able to feel again."

"I cannot do that."

"Cannot or will not?"

He hesitates a beat before saying, "Cannot."

I don't know if I can believe him, but my desire to return to myself is too great to trust his words.

"Find some other woman to make immortal. I don't want your gifts."

"Yet you have them, and they have already saved your life once."

I say nothing to that. It is true, but I would have rather died than woken up chained to the ocean floor.

Threydan cranes his neck to the side as he observes my crew in their various forms of restraint. "Come with me, Sorinda. I wish for us to speak in private. Let me take you to my home."

"Like hell she will," Kearan says from somewhere buried among the undead.

Threydan steps in his direction, looking for the one who spoke.

Fool is going to get himself killed. I say, "If I come with you, you will leave them unharmed. That is the deal, right?"

The King of the Undersea turns back to face me. "That is the deal."

"How can I trust you?"

"You cannot afford otherwise, my love."

My nostrils flare at those words, but even I can see when I've been outmaneuvered.

"How did you find me?" I ask.

"I followed you."

"Impossible. No one is able to tail me without my notice."

"Perhaps that is true among the living."

I realize all too quickly what happened. I *was* followed. By one of the undead. A body that doesn't need to breathe or move naturally. Something I never would have thought to keep a lookout for.

So he *can't* sense me, then. That's fortunate at least.

"Come now, Sorinda. I saved you from those people who wanted you dead. All these"—he gestures to the undead bodies holding my crew hostage—"were made in your honor."

"They only wanted me dead because of what you made me."

"That's not entirely true. You woke me. They wanted you dead for that, too."

I want to scream that it's not my fault, but perhaps it is. Death has always followed me. I have always been its cause. From the time I was five years old. It is my calling and my curse.

Literally, it would seem.

I find myself with the abhorrent desire to cry.

I crack my neck to either side. "Have your dead minions release my crew, and I will follow you from this campsite."

Protests rise up from my crew, including Kearan's loud "Sorinda, no!"

"You have loyal followers," Threydan says. "I'm not surprised, but I don't know that I can trust them. You will follow me, and my minions, as you call them, will follow thereafter."

"So they can murder the crew the second I'm out of sight? I don't think so."

"Can you promise me your crew will not fight or follow when we leave?"

I keep my face clear as I look into the eyes of my crew one by one. "You will not follow. You will not fight. That is an order."

"No!"

One shout is louder than all the rest as little Roslyn finally leaves the tent. She's bundled in Dimella's coat and boots, the rapier I gifted her unsheathed and ready to skewer Threydan.

"You can't take her," Roslyn says. "I won't let you."

"Roslyn," I bite out in my most forceful voice. "Get back in the tent now!"

"She's too good to go with you," Roslyn continues. "She keeps us safe and has an important mission here that you cannot stop. If you need someone to go with you, take me instead. I'm not even supposed to be here. I disobeyed orders. Bad things keep happening, and it's all my fault. I deserve to die, not her."

Threydan turns to where Roslyn stands and kneels to her level. I take a step forward and raise my sword, but Threydan doesn't move. Doesn't even care that he's turned his back to me.

"You would die for her?" he asks.

"Yes," Roslyn answers without question.

Threydan ruffles the hair on her head, and I take the final step to reach him. He stands and turns to me before I can slice him.

"That won't be necessary," Threydan says, answering both Roslyn and my threat of violence. "No one is dying. Not Sorinda. Not you. Not the crew. The Drifta needed to be taught a lesson for threatening my plans and my beloved. But I am not here to hurt any of you. In fact, I'm here to help. Once Sorinda agrees to be mine for all eternity, I will personally find your missing crew. Then I will sail you all home on my way to finding the siren charm that cursed me. Sorinda?" Threydan holds his hand out to me, palm up. "Let's go somewhere more comfortable to talk."

I can think of a thousand things I would rather do than touch his offered hand, including hacking off my own arm.

But this crew needs me. Alosa's missing girls need me. I can't think about just myself anymore.

This is what being a captain means.

"Dimella," I say.

"Aye, Captain?"

"You're in charge until I return."

Threydan raises an eyebrow at those words but doesn't argue them.

Dimella says nothing for several seconds before finally replying with "Aye-aye."

I swallow. "Kearan."

"What?" he says in a voice filled with rage. I cannot see him through all the undead, but I know he's back there somewhere.

"You will not move a muscle when Threydan calls off his army. Not one muscle. If *anything* happens to this crew, I will hold you personally responsible. Do you understand me?"

As with Dimella, he takes a very long time to respond. Then, "Understood, Captain."

His acceptance moves something else within me, and I melt just a little, like a crying icicle.

"Philoria, keep Visylla in check."

"Yes, Captain."

"Everyone else, make the queen proud."

Then I take Threydan's hand.

The dead fade back into the trees so quickly, if it weren't for all the footprints in the snow, I might have thought I'd dreamed them.

Threydan's fingers thread through mine as he leads me away, and I feel the stares of twenty-three pairs of eyes boring into my back.

CHAPTER 17

AS SOON AS THE crew is safe and long behind us, I say, "I'm not running, but I am taking my hand back." And I pull my fingers from his.

Threydan lets me go, but he follows my retreating hand with his eyes.

"It will take time for you to get used to me," he says. "I understand that. But I am a patient man, Sorinda. I have forever."

I rest my hand on my sword hilt, drawing comfort from the hard steel, yet also disgust from the fact that I can't feel the cold of it. It should be painful to the touch until the heat of my hand transfers to the metal.

"You could draw your weapon if it would make you feel better," he suggests.

"What would make me feel better is you putting me back to normal and then releasing me."

"I already told you I can't do that."

"What *can* you do?" I snap. Exhaustion all but pulls me toward the fluffy snow at my feet. It takes far too much energy just to put one foot in front of the other.

"A great many things," he says conversationally, ignoring my tone. "I can cook, assuming such things haven't changed in a thousand years. I am rather good at playing the harp. I can win most drinking games. And . . ." He pauses to think a moment. "I also have a knack for fishing."

He turns to me and grins, his blue eyes more intense than ever.

And I can't say a single thing.

Because those words are so *normal*. It's as if he thinks he can convince me he didn't just threaten my entire crew with an army of undead. An army that appears to be strangely absent for the moment.

I stumble in my next step, and my vision goes dark for a moment.

"You're wearied," Threydan realizes. "Here." He sweeps me off my feet and holds me in his arms as though I weigh nothing. As far as I can tell, he has no supernatural strength, only the ability to not die. He's simply a rather strong man.

"Put. Me. Down."

"If you have the strength to make me, I will heed your request."

I try to push off his chest, but the action has hardly any force behind it. I'm simply too spent, and that terrifies me more than anything else that has happened so far. Threydan could do anything he wanted right now. Including finishing whatever horrible ritual he started.

"Just sleep, dear Sorinda. I've got you."

"Don't tell me what to do."

"All right, then. Don't sleep. I order you to stay alert."

He thinks he's being funny, but I find no humor in the situation. I try to hold myself away from the bare skin of his chest. To not notice the way it is still as stone, rather than moving with even breaths.

He is just as dead as those corpses he commanded earlier.

My eyes start to drift, but I slam them open. I think of Roslyn and how I have to be strong for her.

Darkness creeps at the edges of my vision, weirdly soothed by the repetitive movement of Threydan's steps.

Stay awake.

Stay awake.

Stay . . .

A DREAMLESS SLEEP IS something I haven't experienced in a long time, and when I rouse myself, I realize that I feel more rested than I have in a while.

Because you've never been so exhausted before.

The events of the last few days flood back to me, and my eyes fly wide.

I'm in a dark cavern of sorts, torchlight illuminating the space around me. A downy mattress supports my weight, a soft blanket wraps around my limbs—not that I need the warmth.

As I sit up, my eyes meet the bright, undead gaze of a Drifta man. My heart thuds painfully in my chest as I realize he's probably been waiting there the entire time I was sleeping. Watching. He stands stock-still until he sees me sit up. He points to a wooden chest on the stone floor before leaving. I look around to ensure no one else is present before opening it.

I'm not sure what I expected inside. A body part? Something taken from my crew to make me behave? Or something equally disturbing that my sleep-addled brain cannot conjure up?

Instead I find clothes. A few simple dresses in designs I've never seen before. Pants and shirts that have ties in the front. Sandals with light soles. And . . . are those bonnets?

I slam the lid closed and stand before marching from the room, stretching the sore muscles in my arms as I do so. More torches line the dark hallways, illuminating my path. I follow the lights through chambers of stone, through empty rooms without so much as a speck of dust to grace them, and then a smell hits me.

Something is cooking.

I finally step into a small kitchen. Some sort of vent in the ceiling allows smoke to be carried out of the room. An open fire sits in the middle, and Threydan is crouched in front of it, turning a few fish skewers. He's wearing a different pair of pants, and he's cleaned himself of any blood from the slaughter he wrought among the Drifta.

He looks over his shoulder as I approach. "You didn't want to change?"

"I want nothing from you."

He turns back to the fish. "So it's going to be like that, then? It makes no difference to me what you wear, but I thought you might like to cease smelling of wet campfire."

I'm sure I reek, but I've long since grown used to the smell. And I'm not about to do anything to make me seem more enticing to this man.

He pulls one of the fish from the flames and cuts into it with a knife to examine the meat. "And are you also too proud to accept my food?"

He holds the skewer out to me after deeming it fully cooked.

Saliva floods my mouth. I'm famished again, and now that my body has finally been allowed the sleep it needed, food is all I can think about. I snatch the skewer from him and tear into the fish, not needing to wait for it to cool.

I cannot be burned.

I barely taste it as I eagerly chew and swallow, needing to stop the pain that has returned to my belly.

When I'm done with the first skewer, Threydan hands me another. And then the final one.

That's when I remember he doesn't need to eat. He is truly immortal. Meanwhile, I can still die by hunger.

And thirst.

As soon as I think it, Threydan hands me a cup filled to the brim with water.

I can't even care if he's poisoning me right now. I'm too desperate to be full.

"Easy, now," he says as I chug the water. "You don't want it to come up again."

I wipe my mouth with the back of my hand, surveying the kitchen around me. "What is this place?"

"When we found this island, we knew it would take a while before we discovered the sirens and the panaceum. This was the shelter we made."

"You mean you and your crew? The ancestors of the Drifta?"

"Yes."

"How long did it take you to find it?"

"Over six months."

"That's a long time to survive in the bitter cold."

He smiles at that. "It wasn't always like this. It was cold, yes, but it wasn't so frozen. The sirens cursed the land just as they did me before they left. I suspect they thought it would deter future travelers from finding me and waking me. But nothing so silly as snow would ever deter you."

The food in my stomach starts to turn. "You keep speaking as though you know me. You don't. You don't have a claim to me. You must stop this fanciful notion of *us*."

He eyes me from head to toe in a way I do not like one bit. "But I do know you, Sora. You are Sorinda Veshtas, the pirate queen's assassin. You were born the daughter of a rich nobleman, until you lost everything when you were five. But you had your vengeance. You know much in the way of vengeance, as you've been dealing it your whole life. I need you to help me with mine next."

I choke on the next sip of water. I suspected that he was receiving my memories just as I've been getting his, but I can't believe he knows so much so soon.

"It's your doing, you know," he says. "When you stabbed my heart, you connected us. I was so entranced by what I saw, that moment when you made your first kill, that I knew we were meant to be. And while we're on the subject of your memories, we will need to talk about this Kearan lad. He can't have you, because you're mine."

I don't know which memory of mine made him delusional enough to think that *anything* is happening between Kearan and me, but he's as misguided as I once was.

"Those memories were not for you to take."

"I didn't take them. I shared them with you."

"You cannot share them! They're mine. You shouldn't have—"

"It's all right, love. I've seen your darkest secrets, and you have *nothing* to be embarrassed or ashamed of. You are extraordinary. If anything, I've only seen how short I fall compared to you."

"Stop talking to me like that."

"Intimacy scares you. I understand, but—"

I leap away from him as he tries to step closer.

"No, no," I repeat. "You don't understand. If you did, you would know how wrong all this is. You cannot keep me here. You cannot force me to be with you or to help you with whatever your ridiculous plan is. You cannot take so much from me and then expect me to thank you for it."

He's too still as he stands there. Chest unmoving. Eyes unblinking. Not so much as an itch to scratch or a muscle to stretch.

It's unsettling.

"I am sorry for how this all played out. I cannot help what I am or how our first meeting went. I—"

"That's a load of shit." I call him out on it. "You chose to be like this. To fuse with the panaceum so no one else could use it. You chose to kill and to hurt. You may not have chosen the consequences of those actions, but you are responsible for what you are."

His eyes narrow. "What I did, I did for—"

"Your sister. Yes, I know. I saw. She was in pain, and you wanted to help her. That's why you sailed this way. But it seemed to me that you lost your purpose along the way."

He glowers at me. "I *never* lost my purpose. The second Kayra was born, my life was about her instead of myself. I spent every second of my day with her, ensuring she had everything she needed. I had to witness her in pain day after day. My parents called for the most expensive physicians, but none could find the source of her agony or help to ease it.

"When rumors spread that the king was sending a crew in search of a cure to all maladies, I made sure I was hired for it. We sailed for months before reaching this island, and then we searched even longer for the mystical object that would heal our loved ones.

"I was the one who found it, and do you know what happened when I presented it to the rest of the crew?"

"They tried to take it."

"They wanted it for the king. They wanted titles and glory and money. All things that a man in power could provide. But I knew what would happen if our monarch got his hands on such a thing. An artifact that can heal any disease or ailment? He would sell cures to the highest bidders, grant longevity to the most important individuals. The rich would live forever, and people like my sister would be utterly forgotten and alone.

"So I ran. I kept it, and yes, I made it a part of myself so it would be mine to share with those who truly needed it. The poor. The desperate. Those who are in pain. Those who need relief. And do you know what happened next?"

I shake my head slowly.

"The sirens found out I had taken it. My crew was quick to lay all the blame on me, and since I could not be killed or harmed, they did the next best thing. They cursed the land to bring forth snow and ice. Then they cursed me to sleep until I was woken. Cursed me to live in an icy tomb until my sister was dead and all those I wanted to help were gone."

The siren was as beautiful as she was dangerous. Her hair was white as snow, as were her lips. She was naked as she walked toward me, rising out of the ocean, her charm trailing behind her.

I did not know true terror until that moment.

Her voice grated on my ears like a hailstorm battering the roof of a house. "You will sleep until all those you love are gone, Threydan. You will live without living until you are woken. I hope the moment does not come until the end of time."

And then there was music. The most beautiful, painful music that made me want to weep.

Then nothing.

"I'm awake now, Sorinda," Threydan says, pulling me out of the memory. "Everyone I've ever known is gone, save you. Do you know what it is to sleep for a thousand years, dreaming of the world passing you by? It was agony, but I held out hope that one day I would rise again. One day, I could claim vengeance on the sirens who did this to me, all because I wanted to help the less fortunate."

His eyes bore into mine. "You are my only hope. If I get too close to the sirens, they will only put me back to sleep. But you? You are immune to their songs as a woman. You can get me my vengeance, and then we can rule these lands however we see fit. I had one life taken from me, but I will not lose another."

My head buzzes with all the new information. Threydan waits for me to say something, but I have to tread carefully. I cannot anger this man past his point of tolerance. He holds all the power. The power to kill my crew. The power to help us off this place. The power to turn me into some deathless creature like him.

But anger simmers within me, an anger so fierce I can actually feel the heat of it within my changed body.

I say, "Bad things happened to you out of your control. I know what that is."

"I know you do," he says.

"But you are trying to take away my choices, and that is not something I can forgive."

"I'm not trying to take anything away from you. I brought you here so you could learn the truth and make the right choice. We know naught except for what this bond has shown us of each other. Let us take the time to really get to know each other. Then you can decide what you want, but I've already seen enough of you to know exactly what I want."

To his credit, he keeps his eyes on my face, but I still feel his eagerness to look me over.

I narrow my eyes. "And afterward, should I decide that I still do not want to be a part of your plans, am I to believe you will release me?"

He doesn't even give the words consideration. "You will make the right choice. I have every confidence. Let us not dwell on the alternative. You must have questions for me. Let me answer them for you."

He already did. The only answer that I needed. Threydan professes to be a good person who was wrongfully hurt. But he clearly thinks his own agenda is more important than anyone else's. He doesn't care about who he hurts. Maybe his initial intention was to save his sister and make the panaceum available to all. But he has no such motivation now. He has no one to look out for save himself.

And me. Because he needs me in order to achieve his plans.

And I need time to form a plan of my own.

"If the panaceum's powers can be shared with whomever you choose, then surely you can put me back to normal? Choose a woman who would relish in eternity and being by your side. Surely that's what you want. Someone who wants you, too?"

I don't know what nonsense I'm spouting, only that I hope it will get through to him.

"The process has already begun, Sorinda. It can only be finished."

"But you intended to use the panaceum to help lots of people. Can't you make someone else immortal to be with you?"

Threydan looks at the ground beside his bare feet. He still hasn't bothered with shoes or a shirt. Is that how the men during his time dressed? What place was he from that it was so hot he couldn't be bothered to cover up? Or does he simply prefer to wear so little? To prove that he's not afraid of anything? Not the elements and certainly not a blade.

"The full powers of the artifact could have been shared freely once. Before I had to make the difficult choice to fuse with it. It can still be used to heal whomever I wish. I've already done so with that nasty gash on your cheek." My hand involuntarily flies up to my face. I had forgotten all about the injury. "But I can only make one person immortal as I am. I intended that person to be my sister. Now that she's gone, I've chosen you. You are my savior. My resurrector. My equal. Together we can live forever and do whatever we wish."

And yet, still he says nothing of his cause to cure the sick and heal the wounded. No, he healed me because he needs me. Or perhaps he did not want my face to scar. Either way, he speaks nothing of a cause to aid those who are in need. If that was ever truly his motivation, it clearly isn't any longer.

My face doesn't alter at each new realization he gives me. If anything, I try to soften my features. But I don't know the first thing about that. I'm sure I look like I sat on something sharp.

"You said you fused with it?" I ask. "What exactly did you do? Swallow it?"

Threydan shrugs. "I knew I could not die, so I cut open my flesh and inserted the panaceum within."

My eyes rove over his body, looking for some telltale lump to suggest where it might be. When I get up to his face, I notice he's smiling at my inspection.

"Where is it?" I ask.

"If you are thinking of trying to cut it out of me, it will not work, fierce Sorinda. Many have tried and failed. I cannot be parted from it."

If I was thinking of cutting it out of him? Certainly, I was.

"How big is it?"

He brings his thumb and forefinger together to make a circle. "Like this."

"Sounds like it was painful."

"It was at first, but I cannot feel pain anymore."

No pain. What is that like?

"At all?" I question. "Not even the pain of losing your sister?"

At that, his smile drops. "No physical pain," he amends.

Ah. "So you're to live for eternity with the pain of loss. Doesn't that frighten you?"

He shrugs. "Why should it? I will live forever. I will have plenty of time to make a new family. Make new friends. I will have more people to care for me than ever before."

The more he talks, the more I realize how much my capacity for hate can grow. Everything is about him and how he feels. People are replaceable.

Has he always believed this? I felt his love and devotion to his sister when I saw his memories. Was she the exception? Or has time changed him? Or perhaps the panaceum, an item that changes you physically, is also capable of changing who you are on the inside. If so, what would long-term exposure to such a thing cause?

And since it's already made changes to me, am I in danger of losing who I am, too?

The thought is more terrifying than anything else. I am deadly as is, but what if I had no conscience? What would the panaceum have me do for the rest of my days? A killer who is unkillable?

I can't allow that to happen.

"But you will continue to lose everyone forever," I say. "You will live while everything else grows old and passes on."

"Except for you," he says, his eyes heating. "Everything except for you."

I try not to grimace at the words, but he must see it.

"You cannot fathom anything more than one life because it is all you expected, but you must learn to see the greater possibilities, Sorinda. You must imagine all the good you could do with immortality. Imagine a life where you can fulfill your every whim because no one can stop you."

My every whim?

No.

I live for others because my sins are unforgivable. I serve Alosa because she is good and will keep me on the right track.

Anything else is unthinkable.

"Good, you are considering the possibilities," he says, misinterpreting my silence. "That is all I can ask for today. That you just consider what we could do. Now then, do you have any questions about me? Not what I can do but who I am? Please, Sorinda, just get to know me. I know you'll like what you learn."

CHAPTER 18

OH NO.

Now I have to feign interest in him?

I've never done that before in my life.

I'm no actress. I'm not good at being anything other than myself or silent, which I suppose are the same thing.

I rack my brain for something to ask this man with the expectant, hopeful features. The one who holds my future and that of my crew in his hands.

"How old are you?" is what comes out first.

"I was twenty-five when I set out to find my sister's cure."

"What did you do to support yourself?"

He looks around the chamber proudly. "I apprenticed with a stone mason."

"You helped build this place?"

"Initially, it was made out of wood, but when the land changed, I decided to rebuild out of stone. Not that it mattered if I was exposed to the elements. But privacy is something that I craved dearly, and it barely took any time at all to build with the undead's help."

Delightful. Every stone has been touched by rotting fingers.

"Am I allowed to go outside?" I ask.

"That question does not tell you anything about me."

"Except it does. It will tell me how overbearing you are and what I can expect in the future."

He tilts his head back and assesses me from lowered eyes, as though trying to decide if I'm being devious or sincere. But he already knows me too well. Surely he must guess.

"When you agree to be mine, you may go outside and do whatever else you wish. Until then, we're to spend time together."

I look to the floor, as though trying to hide disappointment.

"Do not look so downcast," he says. "I have allowed you to keep your weapons. I have offered you food and clothing and shelter. I haven't harmed a single soul of your crew. These things will continue, but I expect something in return, Sorinda. Your time and patience."

I let my hand drift toward the hilt of my sword and clench the comforting leather around the handle.

Manipulation.

It's such an ugly tool men use to get what they want. I saw it time and again with the pirate king. The fact that Threydan is trying it with me makes my blood boil. And in that rich anger that fuels my desire to kill, I realize something very, very important.

"Stop," I say, my voice barely above a whisper.

"Hmm?"

"Stop thinking of yourself as some benevolent person. You let me keep my weapons because I cannot harm you with them. You have offered me clothing that was already here when we arrived and made sure to feed me because you need me alive to accept your offer. You didn't hurt my crew because, as you said, it would ruin your chances with me. But all these choices? All these things you have done? They're still about you. You, Threydan, are selfish. You do not think of anyone but yourself. And do you know what I think?

"I think you cannot complete the ritual until I am willing to complete it. Otherwise you would have done it by now. You were able to start it because I was distracted by the onslaught of your memories. But to finish, you need me to agree to it. How close am I?"

His lips tighten; his jaw clenches.

"You're stuck with me, but I am an unwilling partner. So now what will you do? Hurt me? Hurt my crew? How will that convince me to your side? It won't.

"You should know by everything you've seen of me that I am too clever to believe your lies and omissions. So I'm going to leave now. You've given me a lot to think about, and now it's time to give me some space. We can talk again later."

I have no intention of speaking with him again, but he can't know that. He needs to be convinced this is the best way to get him what he wants.

"Which way to the exit?" I ask him.

Threydan says nothing for so long that I worry he's contemplating horrible ways to punish me for my outburst. But finally, he points. "Through that door. Down the hallway. Make a left."

I take one step.

"Sorinda."

My body freezes in place.

"I will let you leave on one condition. The man, Kearan—you must make it perfectly clear that anything he hopes for between you two is not possible. Break his spirit if you must, but he needs to accept that you're mine now. And should you fail to do this, *I* will make it clear in a way he will never recover from. Do you understand me?"

I try to swallow past the tightness in my throat. "I understand."

"Good. I will seek you out in three days' time. Your crew's camp is to the south."

I take another step toward the exit.

"Do not let it be said that I cannot be kind. You want your time? I'm giving it to you. Remember that, dearest."

"I will," I say in what I hope is an encouraging tone. I will say anything to get away from this man now.

"You will, of course, wish to move your crew to a location where you think I can't find you. Don't bother. You're always being watched."

I spin in place. "Do not have your undead follow me."

"I will do as I wish."

I turn back around. Take another step toward the exit.

But he speaks again, and I wonder if I will ever make it out of this stone prison.

"As a further show of good faith and my devotion to you, I have a present for you. You'll find it on your way back to camp."

"What will I find?" I ask.

"Go before I change my mind."

I leave, slowly at first, but once I clear the stone shelter, I take off at a run. My muscles are still sore from days of misuse, but they're about to loosen up from the workout I intend to put them through.

It was too much to hope that he wouldn't send his undead to follow me, so I take roundabout paths, hide in the trees, move like a cat to lose anything Threydan might have tailing me. He knows where my crew is camped, but with any luck they've moved.

What I want—what I need—is to be alone. Truly alone where nothing and no one is watching me. I need time to think. Time to process. To understand. To plan my next move.

And I need to do it without the undead breathing down my neck.

I scale down some sort of ravine, run across a frozen stream, and race back up the next side. I try to control my breathing, in case Threydan can hear it through his undead. I've long suspected he can see through their eyes, but I don't know how else he's able to use them.

At a noise behind me, I duck into some thick bushes, scrabbling under them and holding my breath as an undead walks by, his head tilting in every direction. When he passes, I scurry out and take off toward my crew's camp, but of course the undead are all headed that way. They're keeping eyes on me. I can hide and duck all I like, but it's useless. If they don't run into me, I'll run into them.

For once in my life, I give up being stealthy. It will get me nowhere.

The thought is terrifying.

I'm so very afraid of the turn my life has taken. I thought my ship sinking in a strange land was as bad as it could get.

How very wrong I was.

Though I miss the way my body used to be, it still reacts the way it should to strong emotions. My skin feels ready to burst from the internal pressure. From thoughts of Threydan's hand on me to the threats he made against those I'm supposed to protect.

I'm dealing with forces far greater than I thought possible. After Alosa reconciled with her mother, I thought we were done having troubles with sirens. But of course there is more than one charm in the world. Just as there is more than one school of fish or community of humans.

These northern sirens have caused quite a fuss, and then they left so they wouldn't have to deal with the consequences. Not that they're still around. Sirens live longer than humans, but not a thousand years, as far as I know. Threydan likely wants to hunt down all sirens, for they are all that pose a threat to him.

Them and Kearan, apparently.

I scoff.

He wants me to break Kearan's heart. As if he were smitten with me. He's made it very clear how he feels. How I gave too much credence to things he'd said and done while drunk. He's a new man now, one who wants nothing between us. Whatever memory Threydan saw, it must have been outdated, and any protests I make or efforts to set the record straight would only appear as if I'm trying to spare Kearan because I return those feelings.

So he's forcing me to do this.

My blood begins to boil the more I think about the King of the Undersea and all his plans for me.

I pull a dagger from the confines of my clothing and throw it at the nearest tree trunk.

Thwack.

It imbeds in the wood with a satisfying sound. I pull another dagger, imagine Threydan's face and throw.

Thwack.

My breathing comes quicker as I reach for more knives, giving my sore arms a workout and my mind something to focus on. A healthy outlet for all the nervous energy I'm dealing with.

A way to attack all the negative thoughts that permeate my mind.

Can't feel anything. *Thwack.*

Can't die by cold or heat. *Thwack.*

Stuck on this island. *Thwack.*

Still have no hope of finding Alosa's missing girls. *Thwack.*

I was the wrong woman for this job. *Thwack.*

I've failed everyone. *Thwack.*

And now Threydan thinks I can break Kearan? Ha! *Thwack.*

He gives me too much power. I am powerless. I can do nothing. *Thwack.*

On and on I throw. When my remaining twelve daggers are imbedded in the wood, I retrieve them before wreaking havoc on the trunk again.

Soon I see Kearan's face and his wicked grin. *Throw until you miss.*

Danger excites him. I excite him because I'm dangerous. And he clearly doesn't care about getting hurt. He didn't even flinch when that last knife cut him. No, he smiled.

Because he's mad.

And unpredictable, which is why he unsettles me so. What will he do when I tell him the King of the Undersea wants him to back off?

Doesn't matter. It was the agreement for letting me go, so I'll follow up in case the undead are spying on me. If Kearan's life weren't hanging in the balance, I wouldn't bother. But he's under my protection. I just have to figure out how to broach such a ridiculous topic once again.

Captain, stop flattering yourself.

Ugh.

I fling all my knives for a third time.

A fourth.

A fifth.

At a rustling behind me, I duck behind the tree I'm using for target practice, but when a snowy fox darts past, I relax. Then I remember I'm not bothering to be quiet because Threydan will find me regardless of what I do. Still, old habits are hard to break.

I retrieve my knives and sheathe them one by one inside my clothing as the world finally feels more manageable.

There is much that is out of my control.

My own body.

Threydan's intentions.

The Drifta's threats.

But I need to focus on what is within my power to change.

This very second?

My current location.

I continue south, keeping my eyes straight ahead so as not to glimpse the undead hiding behind the trees. I've no reason to think Threydan will change his mind and drag me back prematurely. If he wanted me to do something, he would have kept me in that stone house he built so many years ago. It's hard to imagine it still would have been standing all these years later. With dozens of undead at his command, I imagine he simply had everyone refortify and clean the place in a matter of hours.

The thought of sleeping in a bed made up by undead fingers has me gagging.

It must be midafternoon, and for the first time, I wonder just how long I slept. I do not think it was only one night. I had been pushed past the threshold of exhaustion again and again. My body quit on its own. Fell asleep in that immortal man's arms. I never would have allowed that otherwise.

And how long did he carry me before reaching this place? We could be days away from my crew's camp for all I know.

But there is nothing to do except keep walking.

So I keep on.

THE TERRAIN ALL LOOKS the same.

White everywhere.

Though, I do pause when I find a frozen waterfall, the water turned to icicles clinging to the cliffside. When the sun hits it, I have to blink for the brightness.

It's a single image of beauty. A reminder that not everything is dark and forlorn right now.

I scale the cliffside, taking a route to the right of the waterfall. It is harder than it looks, but I don't fall. Only slip a few times. Good thing the cold doesn't affect my grip on the rocks.

When I reach the top, I see something through a break in the trees. Someone standing just as still as any trunk.

I have a present for you.

Oh, what has he made his undead do now?

I try to decide the best approach to take. Head-on? Roundabout? Nothing matters anymore, though it feels that it should.

When a sound cuts through the trees, I halt in place.

Shouting.

Shouting in Islander.

I can't make out the words, but I'm certain of the accent. I can't have reached my crew already. This terrain isn't familiar yet . . . unless they've happened to move camp closer to Threydan?

I move closer.

From within the cover of the trees, I spot a clearing, where the shouting grows the loudest.

I do not recognize the people before me.

I note fifteen of them, wrapped in furs and deprived of weapons. Some are in bad shape with arms in slings or bandages on their heads. Too thin and haggard from not enough nourishment. I recognize not a soul among them, but I know immediately who they must be.

The crew of the *Wanderer*.

And they're being herded by the undead, forced to come straight in my direction.

CHAPTER 19

THERE'S AT LEAST TEN undead for every single Islander. They surround the crew of the *Wanderer*, blocking them in a fence made of undead clutching one another's arms. They move as one unit, seamlessly forcing the living to keep pace or be trampled underfoot.

I watch one of the larger men try to punch the closest undead. It does nothing, of course, just results in more shouting from his crew.

"Dammit, Nydus, stop hitting them!" one of the women says. "You've as much brains as they do."

"I suppose you'd rather I wait until they force us off a cliff, then?"

"Quiet," another man says.

"Have you a plan, *Captain*?" The woman says his title like it's an insult.

"No, Shura. I just don't want to hear your bickering any longer."

When I finally make my presence known, the undead halt their march, and the Islanders within the circle of arms stop, too.

No one says anything for a full minute. Then, "Who the hell are you?" This comes from Nydus, the man who's supposedly all brawn and no brains.

"Quiet," Shura snaps. "You know the natives can't understand us!" She's a tall woman, probably nearing six feet, and her figure has all the support to bear such an impressive height. Her cheeks have a rosy tint to them, which contrasts beautifully with her onyx-colored skin.

She is not the only woman among them. There are six in total, and I pray each of them is one of the women Alosa sent me to find. I'd hate for any of them to have been lost because I took too long to reach this cursed place. Since the *Wanderer* was a large ship, I can tell they've already lost two-thirds of their crew as it is.

"My name is Captain Sorinda Veshtas. I was sent by Queen Alosa Kalligan to find what became of the crew of the *Wanderer* and bring any survivors home."

One man steps in front of the others, coming as close as he can to me before reaching the wall of undead bodies. He's older than the others, perhaps in his forties. A stern chin sits beneath chapped lips. "I am Toras Warran, captain of the *Wanderer*. Neither I nor my crew have any need of being saved by pirate filth." He spits on the ground before stepping back toward the rest of the survivors.

The rest of the crew exchange looks between themselves.

"Speak for yourself!" Nydus says. He's about the same height and build as Shura, and he rubs his hands together before blowing warmth into them. "I would very much like to be saved, and I'll kiss the pirate queen's boots if that's what it takes. I've had it with this stars-forsaken place."

Another man asks, "Why should the pirate queen take an interest in the crew of one of the land king's ships?"

I meet the eyes of Shura, and she winks at me.

"Do not trust any offer made by pirates," Captain Warran says. "If they offer food with one hand, the other is sure to hold something sharp. Obviously the Kalligan girl means for us to serve her or die. That is always the way things go."

I manage to withhold an eye roll. "I'm to drop you off at the Seventeen Isles. What you choose to do after that is up to you. The only thing I expect in return is more sea hands for the return trip."

"Sounds pretty good to me," Nydus says. "I'm an excellent sea hand."

"Count me in," Shura says. The rest of the girls nod or voice their assent.

In fact, the only person *not* in agreement appears to be the captain himself. The rest of the crew is perfectly happy to be saved, by pirates or not. He stands behind the others, arms crossed and face turned away.

"This is the best crew His Royal Majesty could bequeath me with? Defiant arselings is what you all are. You think you know best, gallivanting off with pirates?" He zeroes in on me with his hateful gaze. "Do you have an army behind you in those woods somewhere?"

"No, my crew lies to the south. We will rendezvous with them."

Warran looks victorious. "Then how, pray tell, are you supposed to free us from these cursed individuals?"

Threydan said it was a present, but I can't believe he wouldn't want to be here to witness this. To see my gratitude—not that I would give him the satisfaction. But I note with horror that every single pair of blue eyes is pointed right at me.

He is *watching my reaction.*

I say, "Release them."

At first, I think nothing will happen and I will look the fool. Then the undead drop their arms and cross into the woods without a sound, leaving only me and the crew of the *Wanderer* behind.

"Neat trick!" Nydus says.

"You fool," Warran says. "She's obviously controlling them! This is no pirate, but some scheming enchantress sent to put us under the same spell that lot is clearly under."

"Warran, for just once will you shut the hell up?" Shura says.

The captain looks mortified by her words. "It'll be prison for you when we return. I'll have you—"

"Surely even you have heard of Sorinda Veshtas, the pirate queen's assassin? She's notorious, if not recognizable, given she wouldn't be a very good assassin if everyone knew what she looked like."

"I don't know what you—"

Oh, but Shura loves cutting him off. "You need more convincing? Fine. I serve Alosa Kalligan, and I have for months before I ever stepped foot on your ship."

At that, Nydus's gaze cuts to her so quickly his neck cracks.

"Pirate filth!" Warran says, pointing to her.

"You're unbelievable," Shura says, stepping up to my side. "Thank you for the rescue, Captain. It's a pleasure to make your acquaintance." She extends her hand, and I take it.

When done, Shura turns back around. "Have my eyes changed color? No? Can we please get the hell out of here, then?"

The rest of the girls step to my side of the clearing.

"Not you lot, too?" the captain asks.

"We were sent to keep eyes on the land king's endeavors," Shura says, "and you should be grateful for it. I don't see King Ladell sending forces to rescue you lot, do you? You ought to praise Alosa's name for extending an invitation of rescue to you as well, even though you don't serve her. And don't deserve it, in my opinion. Where to, Captain?" The last sentence is directed to me.

"This way." The girls fall into step with me.

Nydus is the first to join us, stepping up to Shura's side and taking side glances at her when he thinks she's not looking. More men quickly follow, until it is only Captain Warran and another man left behind, likely his first mate.

But soon, even they follow. Just at a distance.

"So . . . ," Nydus says after a minute, "am I really the only person who wants answers about the folks with the creepy blue eyes? What do you know about it, Captain Veshtas?"

"That is a question without a simple answer."

"Well, Nydus isn't about to understand it, then," Shura says.

Nydus glares at her.

"I will say this," I say. "There is a being on this island with the power to control the dead. He is not on our side, and we should be wary of him and his army."

"If he isn't friendly to us, then why did the Blue-Eyes listen to you?" Nydus asks.

Shura smacks him. "If the captain wants you to know something, she'll let you know. Stop asking questions about the natives."

I silently thank her for that.

"Apologies, Captain," Nydus says. "You have our deepest thanks for the rescue. Tell us about your ship. Is she large? Enough room for us all?"

"If not, we can always put Nydus in the brig," Shura offers.

I say, "There will be room for everyone when we leave. No one is getting left behind, though surely the most annoying among you will be the first on my list for staying should that change."

That finally shuts up the lad.

I AM CONFLICTED WHEN I find that my crew has remained in the same location since Threydan carried me off. On the one hand, I should be furious they did not seek a new hiding spot when this one had clearly been compromised. On the other, I am touched that they would remain so I could easily find them again. As though they didn't doubt for a second that I would find a way back to them. I don't know that I deserve such faith after the turns this journey has taken.

Once we're spotted, a shout goes up from the treetops. I hate that this is becoming far too familiar. Me being gone and then showing up unexpectedly when some of the crew must surely expect I'm already dead.

Dimella is there first. She sees me, shakes her head in astonishment, then grabs me gently by the bicep. She looks me up and down, as though barely daring to assume I'm alive.

"How?" she asks.

"Believe it or not, I talked my way out of this one."

"Impressive. And am I correct in assuming this is the missing crew of the *Wanderer*?"

"Aye."

"Damn, Captain. Is there anything you can't do?"

"Don't be too impressed. That dead arsehole is the one who told me where to find them."

"Why would he help us?"

I clench my teeth. "Because he wants me to like him. Turns out he can't complete the ritual unless I'm willing."

"That's messed up."

"You don't need to tell me. How's the little one?"

"Sorinda!"

As though I summoned her, Roslyn barrels toward me. She jumps at the last second so I have no choice but to catch her. She presses her cheek against mine and squeezes her little arms around my neck.

"You need to stop leaving," she says between tears.

"I'm hopeful that was the last time."

I let my hand slide down the back of her hair, comforting her in the way I've seen Wallov do before. It seems to do the trick.

"Dimella, can you see to our new crew members?"

"Aye."

Still holding Roslyn, I step closer to my first mate and say, "Keep a sharp eye on the two in the rear."

"You've got it."

"Sorinda?"

At the deep voice, I turn my head toward the direction we just came from. Kearan stands wrapped in furs. He's got an ax hanging off his belt and a load of wood held in his arms. His hair sticks to his forehead in an unruly mess from the exertion.

We stare at each other.

That single ball of warmth within my chest flares so violently, it's a wonder that I do not catch flame and go up in smoke.

Kearan drops his load of wood on the ground and takes the remaining steps to reach me. I think I lost my breath sometime right after he dropped the wood.

"Right, now if you'll all just follow me," Dimella says with an awkward lilt to her voice, "I'll introduce you to the rest of the crew and get you all settled."

They pass us by, and I barely even notice. And wasn't I holding Roslyn a second ago? How did she manage to shimmy out of my arms without me realizing?

"You're alive," Kearan says, his voice lower than I've ever heard it before.

"For now."

"What does that mean?"

"He gave me three days. After that, he's coming for me."

Kearan looks over my shoulder. "You found Alosa's missing girls. We'll figure out a way off this island before he comes."

I wince.

"What is it?" he asks.

"I need to talk to you." I look around at the crew, practically bouncing on their feet, wanting to have their turn to welcome me back. Again. "Alone."

I grab his arm and haul him off a ways from camp. Only when we are out of sight of everyone do I realize I'm touching him and quickly release his arm.

My eyes do a sweep of the area, slower than usual. "We don't know who might be listening. I've long suspected that he can see as well as hear through the dead."

Kearan tilts his head down toward me so his lips nearly brush my ear. "Then perhaps we should whisper?"

A shiver goes through my whole body, and there's no masking it as a reaction to the cold when we both know I no longer feel it.

I take a step back. "Not for this part."

He cocks his head to the side. "What part is that?"

I swallow. Discomfort swirls within my gut. I swear it's more pronounced than anything else since there's literally nothing else to feel down there.

There's nothing for it except to get the stupid words out.

"The King of the Undersea let me go on one condition," I say in a slightly louder than usual tone so any undead who might be listening can hear clearly.

Kearan looks worried. "And what was that?"

"I'm to inform you that there is no hope for a future relationship between the two of us. Threydan will not suffer any competition for my affections. He made it very clear that you would not be long for this world should I refuse this stipulation or should you not agree to it."

I pause there, waiting for Kearan's reaction. His face doesn't change at all. In fact, he's gone rather still.

"I tried to assure him that you have no interest in me," I continue. "You've made it clear many times, and I find it ridiculous that Threydan can't see that for himself since he's been privy to some of my memories."

At that, Kearan blinks. "What?"

"I know, I thought it ridiculous, too, but—"

"No, I mean what is this nonsense about him seeing your memories?"

I look down to the ground, unable to bear his scrutiny while I share this part. "When I stabbed him, I . . . formed a connection between us. It flares up randomly, or rather when something jogs a certain memory. He's seen parts of my past, and clearly some of the parts with you in it."

"I see," Kearan says quietly, his voice growing dark.

"I don't. As I said, if he were smart, he would know that you have no interest in me. He would know that we are nothing more to each other than captain and crewman. He would leave you entirely out of this horrid obsession he has with me." I laugh once without humor. "He wanted me to break your spirit. Your *heart*. But I'm telling you plainly, because there is no need for such deterrents. First of all, because no man controls who or what I pursue. Secondly, because—"

"I have no interest in you," Kearan deadpans.

"Precisely."

A silence falls between us, one that seems to hold millions of words unsaid. Kearan's eyes never leave my face, and his face never changes. I can't tell if he's angry beyond words or shocked? Indifferent? He's giving me nothing. He's always been such a mystery.

"Will you please agree to it?" I ask.

"Agree to what?"

"I have told you his terms. Now you must agree to them. For the undead listening in the trees. Do you agree that you will not pursue anything with me and that I am nothing more to you than your captain?"

At that, his eyes draw into slivers. He leans down so that there is only a breath of space between us.

"There is no way in hell I am agreeing to that."

My eyes widen, and I find my hand going to my sword hilt for comfort. For comfort, or because I worry any nearby undead may start attacking him if they managed to catch his words?

"Why not?" I ask, anger seeping into my voice, but I keep my tone at a whisper to match his.

"Because no man, immortal or not, tells me what to do. I only take orders from one person, and she's standing right in front of me."

"And should I order you to agree to his terms?"

"Can't, Captain. I made you a promise that I would never lie to you."

I try to swallow, but my mouth has gone dry. Does he mean—

What does he mean?

"Then don't lie to me," I find myself whispering. "Lie to him. Right now for all the undead to hear."

Kearan's head tilts slightly, and I lose my breath when his eyes dip down to my lips.

He blinks once, slowly. Before stepping back and laughing.

"Aye, Captain," he says loudly. "I'll be keeping these hands to myself. Just as I've always intended. You just do the same so this fool doesn't come after me, aye?"

I glare at him to make the ruse more believable. "That won't be a problem."

"Thought not." He scoffs dramatically before walking back toward camp.

I stare after him, taking in the shape of his strong shoulders, which are bunched tighter than I've ever seen them. He walks with a slight hunch, as though he feels defeated, but his steps never waver.

What. Just. Happened?

And what does it mean?

CHAPTER 20

AS I STAGGER BACK into camp, I can't look away from Kearan. He retrieves the wood he dropped, places it near the closest fire, and brushes wood chips from his gloves and clothes. He lays the ax to the side methodically, as though he's being extra careful with his movements. As if he knows I'm watching him.

And not just me.

But Threydan, too, through the eyes of the undead.

After a moment of stillness, Kearan takes off toward the other end of camp.

"Kearan?" Enwen asks. "What's wrong?"

Kearan doesn't answer as he leaves, barreling into the woods and out of sight. Enwen follows after him, calling his name as he goes.

Is he angry? Is he angry with me?

What is happening?

I'm torn between following and staying right where I am. I want to follow, to demand answers of him, but if Threydan is watching, that is the last thing I should do.

I try to distract myself by focusing on what's in front of me. The girls are integrating with the crew of the *Wanderer*, getting to know them.

Shura hugs Visylla. They must have known each other before, and the two are immediately swept into conversation. Dimella tries to get a word out of Captain Warran, but he won't even look at her. He stands by another one of the fires to warm his hands, glowering at anyone who dares come near.

"Captain Warran, you will be civil to my crew, or I will ensure that you remain on this island forever," I snap, showing a burst of anger that is uncommon for me. "Is that understood?"

His eyes land on me, and something he sees there has his posture relaxing. "Aye, Captain."

"Good."

Now where did Roslyn go off to? I need someone who isn't confusing as hell to be around.

I RISE IN THE wee hours of dawn, having gone to bed supremely early. I gather snow into a pot and set it by one of the fires. Once it's melted, I wash myself as best I can with a rag and don fresh clothes. I stay close to the flames, watching them flicker. I may not feel the heat or cold, but I have no interest in letting my wet hair freeze to my skin again. I keep my damp locks positioned near the fire while I wait for everyone else to wake.

I need to have a plan ready for them. My return, as well as the presence of the missing crew we were sent to find, has bolstered their spirits. But my victories feel . . . cheapened.

For it wasn't me who found Alosa's crew. Threydan did with his undead. He only handed them over to me because he wants something from me. It was a show of good faith. Something that he can retract at any moment with his hordes of undead. In fact, I wouldn't be surprised if he was in the process of growing his numbers by causing fights with the Drifta. What else has he to occupy himself with in that lonely stone house? Thoughts of revenge do not keep a body idle. They demand movement. Preparation. I well know this.

We need to leave before we're even more outnumbered. Otherwise, we won't last until Alosa arrives. Not without me agreeing to Threydan's terms. And if Alosa arrives, some of her pirates will surely die and join the undead before we manage to put Threydan back to sleep. Her voice alone will not be enough. She is but half siren. We need a full siren to keep him asleep for a significant amount of time. She will have to call on aid from her mother, and who knows how long that will take?

I cannot allow us to wait. It is not enough to constantly move camp and do nothing. Besides, we cannot stay hidden long. Not with hundreds of undead able to scour the wilderness without need of food or rest. Threydan will catch me.

Yet what other choice do we have? We have no ship. A large crew. Angry Drifta. Untiring undead. And one immortal man with powers over life and death.

I feel so small. So . . . insufficient.

And then I remember—

At the barest sound of movement behind me, I turn, expecting the worst.

And it is the worst. Kearan stomps into camp. He makes it clear to the fire I'm occupying before he notices me. Normally, I swear he senses me, but he is clearly distracted right now.

"Were you out all night?" I ask him.

"Aye."

"Where's Enwen?"

"He turned in with everyone else. I wanted time alone."

I flip my braids to the right, letting the underside catch the heat of the fire better. "Now you will be unfit for today's activities."

"And what would those be?"

I lower my voice so any listening undead cannot hear.

"Stealing a ship."

"The Drifta's galleon? The one that sank us? You mean to take it?"

"Aye. We've now enough crew to man it. If necessary, I will of course stay behind so everyone can escape. But if it's possible for us all to get away together, I would prefer that."

"We won't leave without our captain."

"You will if I command it."

"Aye," he says, his voice growing husky. "I will, and when I get everyone to safety, I'll come right back for you. Even if I have to do it in a rowboat all by myself."

"Don't be ridiculous."

"I am utterly serious."

"You're fatigued, Kearan. You best get some sleep while you can."

"I have never been more awake."

"Well—good, then. We will need all hands for the task ahead."

He doesn't move any closer to the tents, and I don't leave my seat by the fire. His breath fogs into the air, while mine remains invisible. I'm glad for it. He can't tell just how much faster I'm breathing.

You can't be afraid of the dark when you're the monster lurking in the shadows.

I am no such thing right now. Not with him. Not for some time.

And I don't know why or what that means.

"You've thought yourself a poor captain for this journey," Kearan says, pulling me from my thoughts. "Let me point out that time and time again, you've put the crew before yourself. Even me. You've put me above you when you never should have. Do you still think of everything that's happened as your failings? Is that why you are out here alone?"

I cannot speak for a moment. "That is what you think I'm stuck on? My failings as a captain? Kearan, there is no doubt in my mind that another captain could have done a better job, but that is not what keeps me up at night."

"Then what is it? What troubles can I ease?"

My heart picks up like it does before I'm about to make the kill. Only this time, that is not what is happening.

I do not fear this man in the usual way. I do not fear his height or his bearing. I do not fear his mind or his words. It is his heart that terrifies me, and the few times that I have been afraid of something, it has always been remedied with some quick knifework so it can trouble me no more.

But blades are not the only way to kill something. Sharp words can make feelings die.

"What you said to me yesterday," I say, keeping my face neutral. I am in control of this conversation. It will not go anywhere that I do not allow, and I am sick of fearing it.

"Mmmm" is the only response he makes.

"Well?" I demand.

"What?" he asks, exasperation tingeing his tone.

I lower my voice again. "You said you would never lie to me. You said you didn't want anything between us. You said that by agreeing to Threydan's terms, you *would* be lying. All three can't be true."

"Can't they?"

At that, my look turns chilling. "Kearan Erroth, stop talking in questions and speak plainly."

"What's the point of that? No good will come of it."

"The point is that I cannot make sense of you, and I want to understand what you meant."

"No, you don't."

My hand goes for a knife. I pull it from a sheath in my boot and twirl it between my fingers. I need a means to occupy myself. And perhaps he'll be more forthcoming if I have something sharp in my hands.

"You don't want the truth, Sorinda," he continues, moving closer so I can hear his lowered words. "You want what will make you feel in control. Believing I want nothing from you makes you feel in control. Unthreatened. It doesn't force you to make decisions or think about me the way I want you to think about me. You want what's easy. You need it. Because what you're doing, all these external pressures of being stranded in a foreign land and looking after so many individuals— these trials would be difficult for anyone. You don't need my feelings and thoughts making things harder. Besides, if I showed you exactly how much I want you, you would only distance yourself further from me. This way, I could help. This way, I could be your sailing master for the voyage. Your confidant. Your friend. I couldn't have become any of those things if you thought I wanted even more."

My knuckles turn white on the knife. "So you did lie to me."

"I said I didn't want anything from you. And that's true. I don't want just anything. Sorinda, I want *everything* with you."

My gaze leaves the knife I'm holding and latches on to his face.

Everything? "What does that entail?"

"Does it matter?" he asks. He looks furious.

"If it didn't, I wouldn't ask."

"Fine. Everything entails trust, honesty, friendship, love. A lifetime of all of it."

"Oh, is that all?" I ask to be difficult. My fury rises to match his, but I refuse to raise my voice. Not when his life still hangs in the balance.

He has wanted me from the beginning and led me to believe otherwise. For my own good, no less, he proclaims.

So I would let down my guard. So I wouldn't push him away so readily.

"You tried to trick me into liking you, is that it?" I ask, my voice going deadly.

"I wasn't trying to trick you into anything. I was making this journey better for the both of us."

"By playing with your words. Lying but not lying? You think you're clever?"

"I think that, even now, you'd rather fight than be truthful with me. You'd rather stick that knife through my gut than tell me that you like me the smallest bit, even if it's true."

I toss the knife to my left hand, let my right index finger trace the indent of the fuller. "Truth? That's what you want from me? You think if I tell you the truth we'll live happily ever after?"

"Ever after is uncertain, but it looks a lot more hopeful when you have someone to share it with."

Hope. Is that what he wants? Then I'll just dash his hopes right now so he'll finally see me for what I really am.

"All right," I say quietly, twirling the knife in the air and catching it. "I'll tell you the truth."

And then he'll leave me be, and I can focus on the problems at hand without his constant attention and nagging.

"You were right," I say. "I did lie to you about what happened the night I lost my family."

Kearan shakes his head abruptly. "No. We don't need to do this now."

"We do," I disagree. Clearly he needs to see me as I really am.

"Sorinda—"

"Be quiet."

He slams his lips closed.

"The beginning happened as I said. Samvin Carroter killed my family one by one. I did hide in the shadows as it happened, too overcome by fear to do anything more than watch and be still." I shut my eyes as those images, forever burned into my memory, try to come to the surface. "He drowned my mother and sisters in that tub. And he knew there was one daughter left. Some of the servants were in the room with us. One, a maid, had a daughter my age. She was there. We'd been playing dress-up earlier that day and switched clothes. She was in my fine dress while I wore servant's garb."

I turn the knife in my hand around so I'm gripping the blade instead of the hilt. It's the only way to keep my muscles from tensing. "She screamed so much louder than my sisters. She tried to say she wasn't me. She begged for her life. And what did I do? I stayed right where I was. Hiding. I watched as he drowned that little girl in my stead. I let her die for me. I did nothing." Tears slide down my cheeks silently, and

I brush them away with closed fists. The knife I'm holding pinches my skin, and I drop it before I can do myself any damage.

I look back up at Kearan, who is back to his unmoving self. "Now you see. It was one thing to stand by and silently watch as my sisters died. It is as you said. There's nothing I could have done to save them. I was too small. Too powerless. But the other girl? Sleina? I could have saved her. All I had to do was tell the truth. Reveal my hiding place. I would have died, and she would have lived. Then I would shine in the night sky with my family, and she would have been able to live the life she was meant to lead."

I feel hollow as that memory finally breaks free. I've carried it for so long, never telling a single soul. Threydan stole it from me, but Kearan—I gave it to Kearan.

I swallow down the ache in my throat. "There. You're set free."

"Set free?" he asks.

"Yes. This delusion you have that you want anything from me. You don't have to carry it anymore."

He blinks. "Why is that?"

"Because I'm not who you thought I was. I may be a lot of things. I'm fierce. I'm talented. I'm smart. I'm capable. But my sins are so much greater than my strengths. They are a shadow that follows me wherever I go. I do my best by serving Alosa and doing good, but I know I can never make up for taking the life of that little girl. The only innocent I ever killed. She is a stain that will never wash free from my hands."

Kearan moves then; he marches right up to where I sit on the snow-covered log by the fire. He kneels on the ground in front of me, heedless of the cold that must be seeping in through his pants.

"You listen to me, Sorinda Veshtas, and you listen well," he says. He places his hands on either side of the log where I sit. "You were a child.

Children are blameless. Children cannot sin. You were *five*. You were in shock. You were traumatized by the horrors you had witnessed. You were acting on instinct, driven to mere impulses, no longer in control. You are no more responsible for that little girl's death than I am. That man? That murdering bastard? He killed her just as he did your family. You did not do any of it."

How is he still not listening to me? "But I could have stopped it! I could have saved her. I could have, and I chose not to."

"You could not have stopped any of it. Tell me, did any of the servants make it out alive?"

I shake my head frantically. Though it's the correct response to his question, I think it might be a response to the way he's reacting.

"That girl would have died whether you came forward or not. Do you think he would have spared her? Do you think he wouldn't have killed you both just to be sure he got the right heir? Do you think he wanted any soul in that building alive to tell the tale of what happened? Justice happened because you survived. You lived to make it right."

"It doesn't matter. What matters is the choice I made."

"It doesn't matter to me."

"How can it not?" I nigh scream the words before I remember myself. "Look at little Roslyn. She was ready to give her life for me when Threydan came for me. She's seven, and she was prepared to die. She wanted to save me. You can't tell me children aren't capable of making difficult choices."

Kearan leans forward. "And would you have had her die for you?"

"Never."

"Your life was not any less important than little Sleina, who died in your stead. You must see that. And is it the right choice for Roslyn to throw her life away like that?"

"You're trying to talk me into a corner."

"I'm trying to show you." He reaches forward, places his large hands on either side of my face, and I go utterly still. "You are worthy of saving. You are worthy of life. You are not that little girl anymore. You have given your life time and time again for this crew. You have risked that precious life a hundred times over for Alosa. For others. You are good. You are capable. You are worthy of love, Sorinda. You are worthy of my love."

I'm crying again. I *hate* crying. And Kearan is there to wipe away my tears before I can.

"I expect nothing from you," he continues. "But do not ask that I stop caring for you because of this sin you think you have committed. It won't work."

I am so raw and exposed, yet his words are just what I need to hear. I feel myself leaning into his touch. I place my hands over his as I cry.

Because if the person in front of me can see good within me, then maybe it's okay for me to see it, too. Maybe every day doesn't have to feel like I'm making up for past crimes.

Maybe I can just live.

"I'm sorry, Sleina," I say as I turn my face toward the sky. "I'm so sorry." I cry for her. I cry for me. I cry for everything that should have been.

Kearan moves to the log to sit beside me and enfolds me in his arms. It is a touch I have not welcomed in thirteen years. But today I am desperate for it.

Even if I cannot feel the warmth of that touch.

Because I know what it means.

It means someone cares.

And that is what is most important.

CHAPTER 21

"YOU SHOULDN'T TOUCH ME like this," I say when I get my tears under control. "He might be watching."

"To hell with him," Kearan says.

"He can't be sent to hell. Only back to sleep."

"Then I hope he has nightmares of me every night."

I laugh.

This isn't natural for me. Not the crying. Not the embracing. But it's what I need nonetheless. I have never had another soul make me feel so light. I can't help but want to be physically close to him.

When the first tent flap slides back, Kearan scoots away from me. I know it's not because he doesn't want to be seen with me, but because he knows I can't be seen leaning on someone else. Not as the captain, and certainly not in front of newcomers, who still don't really know my character. I'm glad my tears are dried. We can appear as though we are merely sharing the warmth of the fire. But the truth is, we shared so much more.

A precious moment. One that I feel might just change the course of my life.

If we make it off this island.

Jadine and her helpers start on breakfast. Kearan adds more wood to the fires.

I add more hope to my soul.

I thought all I had to do was reveal my secret truths and then I would be rejected. People would hate me. Kearan would hate me, and the choice would be made for me. I wouldn't have to decide if I like this thing that has blossomed between us. This feeling I get whenever he is near.

But now? Now I do have choices to make.

Just not until I get this crew safely out of here. Not until I know whether I live or die.

Otherwise, it's a moot point.

I feel myself stealing glances at Kearan as the morning goes by. The crew eats and the women on watch are switched out with fresh eyes. Dimella takes roll, and Captain Warran tries to hide his disdain.

Yet I cherish every time Kearan's eyes meet mine. I relish in those brief connections until it is time to go to work.

"Listen up, you lot," I say. "It's time we got off this island."

"Has the queen been spotted on the horizon?" Dimella asks.

"No, but we're not going to wait around for her."

"Why should we need to wait for your queen to arrive before leaving?" Captain Warran interrupts.

There's no dancing around this issue any longer. What's Warran going to do at this point? Leave?

"Our ship sank same as yours, but it is of no matter. There's—"

"You don't have a ship!" the captain thunders. "All that talk of rescue and your noble pursuits, and you don't even have a way to get us off this bloody island? Bloody pirates! You lot—"

Kearan steps in front of the man, blocking him from my view. I can't see the look he gives the other captain, but it finally shuts the man right up.

"The Drifta have a ship," I say. "We're going to steal it. We know the general direction of where it struck from. We'll find it, we'll take it, and we'll never look back."

"We're going to *steal* something?" Nydus asks, the prospect clearly exciting him.

"Pirates," Shura reminds him. "Besides, the natives stranded us here in the first place. It's only right they be our means of returning home."

"Indeed," I say. "Pack up camp at once. We won't be returning. Be ready to move out within the hour."

Everyone leaps into movement, letting down tents, packing up the food, dousing the fires. Even amidst the flurry of movement, I catch something out of the corner of my eye. I turn, seeing a figure stride away.

Though I'm not perfectly familiar with the crew of the *Wanderer* yet, I'm certain that man isn't one of theirs. No, it was one of the undead, and he's been called away elsewhere.

Threydan surely knows of our plans.

We don't have much time.

Roslyn reloads pistols while the adults do the packing. We make quick work of it, getting everything loaded up in under thirty minutes.

And then we move. Dimella takes the front with her compass, leading us back the way we came. Roslyn stays at my side, holding my hand. Kearan stands on the other side of her. Near me, yet not so near as to mean anything by it.

"I really want my papa," Roslyn says.

"Of course you do," I say.

"But he was so overbearing, Sorinda. I thought I would want a break from him for years and years after the way he treated me. But I don't. I wish I could see him this very moment."

I squeeze her hand. "You will see him again. I'll make sure of it."

"Do you think he will be immediately cross with me? Or do you suppose he'd let me hug him first?"

Kearan takes her free hand, shifting the load he carries to his other arm. "He'll be so happy to see you, he'll forget there was ever a reason to be cross."

"How can you be so sure?"

"It's what I would do if I were missing a daughter."

"His happiness over seeing me returned won't last forever. He'll do something afterward."

"Probably skin your hide," I offer.

Roslyn shrugs at that. "It was worth it."

"What was?"

"This adventure. It's worth whatever punishment Papa has for me."

"This was an adventure I could have—" I cut myself off. I was going to add *done without*, but I realize that's not true. How can it be? When this journey gave me hope for my own future and clarity on the past. When this journey drew me closer to a man I otherwise would have been able to ignore.

"You'll have to work hard to earn back his trust, though," I say instead.

"Probably, but at least I won't have to listen to him forever!"

"What do you mean by that?" Kearan asks.

"Alosa says I'll be old enough to fight with her crews when I'm thirteen."

"Yes, I'm sure your papa will let up then," Kearan says sarcastically. Roslyn doesn't seem to notice.

THE DRIFTA'S VESSEL IS easier to find than I anticipated. The natives dock her not far from where we sank, between a jutting cliff side and an iceberg bigger than any building built by Islanders. From the inside of the island, looking outward, it's not hard to see how we missed her.

Thick ice has formed between the cliff and the iceberg, creating a ceiling over the docked ship. The sea must have shown the reflection of the ice, making the structure look solid. But from land, looking outward, I can see the stern peeking out from the ice tunnel.

I can also see the Drifta on watch. They stand atop towers hidden in the ice surrounding the island, always watching for approaching vessels so they know to attack. Dozens upon dozens of them up there with spyglasses. They'll have hours' notice before any ships arrive. Plenty of time to assemble a crew to attack.

Let's see how many they leave on board when they're not expecting a skirmish.

From the tree line looking to the sea, it's a several-hundred-yard dash. There's no cover. No way to mask almost forty people approaching. The ship ahead is mostly in shadow. Impossible to tell who might be looking this way.

"What are you thinking?" Dimella asks me.

"I don't want to run for it. If they're alerted to our presence, they could shoot us down before we ever reach the sea. There's no cover on the shoreline. We need to get someone aboard that galleon to cause a distraction."

Dimella sizes up the distance and looks to the surrounding lookout towers. "That's not going to be easy. Even if we could camouflage someone sufficiently, those lookouts will surely notice the movement against this flat expanse of white."

"I'd try it, Captain," Roslyn offers. "I can be stealthy, just like you taught me."

"I know you can," I say to her, "but this is different."

"We could wait for the cover of nightfall," Kearan suggests.

"We don't have the time," I say. "Even now, Threydan is on his way. We need to be long gone."

"I thought you said he gave you three days to decide," Roslyn says.

"That was before I made plans to leave the island." A pause. "Roslyn, lesson number three of being an assassin is always assume everyone is lying."

"What if someone caused a distraction inland?" Visylla asks. "We could draw them away from the ship."

"We've already done that once," I say. "They won't fall for the same trick twice."

Everyone falls silent, and no more ideas are forthcoming. I simply stare out at the ocean, watching those ice-cold waves crash onto the shore.

Cold to everyone except me.

I wince as I remember my time alone on the ocean floor. It was horrifying, something I never want to experience again. But I know what I must do if I'm to save everyone.

"I need to go around," I say.

"Around what?" Kearan asks.

I point to the west. "The tree line meets up with the ocean over there. I could slip into the water, swim to the ship, then board her."

No one says anything for a moment.

"How would you manage that without dying?" Shura asks, speaking up for the first time.

"Cold doesn't affect the captain anymore," Enwen says. "She's half undead. 'Twas an unfortunate accident."

"*What?*" Captain Warran bellows.

Kearan silences him with another look.

To Dimella, I say, "I know you don't like me going off alone, but this might be our only chance off the island."

She nods. "I think you have the right of it. We can't risk waiting for nightfall with everything that's hunting us."

"We don't have time for me to silently kill the whole crew," I say, more to myself than everyone else. "I'll be the distraction so you can approach the ship. When you hear them sound the alarm, you'll know they're sufficiently occupied and it's safe to board."

"Just don't get yourself killed."

"I'll do my best." I point over my shoulder. "Fill in the crew of the *Wanderer* on everything that's happened. They need to be prepared for the worst."

"Aye-aye," she says.

"I'll walk you to the beach," Kearan says.

I don't argue with him. I leave Roslyn in Enwen's care before following the edge of the tree line toward my destination. Kearan is silent at my side, matching my strides.

"He knows what we're planning," I say. "I saw one of the undead at the camp. It overheard my orders to the crew. He's definitely coming."

"He won't catch up," Kearan reassures me. "We'll be on that ship sailing away before he gets here."

"He will catch up eventually. Even if we get away today, even if this is the only ship on this island—which I doubt it is—then he will swim after us. He doesn't need food. I don't even know if he needs rest. Nothing can harm him. It may take months or years, but he'll make the swim to the Seventeen Isles."

"By then, Alosa can be prepared to handle him. She'll have her mother and the charm ready. He won't be able to hurt anyone else."

"If he gets me—"

"He won't."

"If he gets me, do I have your word that you will help Dimella get everyone safely home and warn Alosa?"

"I already told you—"

"Swear to me," I say, my voice rising. "I need to hear it right now. Roslyn needs to get home to her papa."

Kearan doesn't slow or skip a beat. "I swear it."

"Thank you." His vow makes me want to reach out and touch him. I hesitate for several seconds, before reminding myself that I'm not afraid of anything.

I reach for his hand, despite how unnatural the gesture is for me. But my forwardness is rewarded by him threading his fingers through mine.

It feels incredible, even if it doesn't feel the way it should. There's a humming in my chest, a nervous flutter that is delicious and unlike anything I have ever felt before. It is nice to touch him. To be touched by him. Even though I cannot feel the heat of his body.

Kearan must read my thoughts because he says, "We'll find a way to put you back to normal."

"Threydan said it can't be done."

"Since when do we trust that bastard?"

"We don't."

"Then don't lose hope. You said it was a siren artifact that made you this way. Maybe Ava-lee knows a way to fix it."

I hadn't considered that the siren queen might have answers for me. It is a possibility, if a small one. But that's all one needs to hope.

"Thank you," I say. "For last night. For the hope you bring. For the promises you keep. I won't forget any of it. Ever."

"You are my captain. You do not need to thank me for such things."

"And if I weren't your captain?" I ask.

He turns his head to face me. "I would still do them for you, Sorinda."

I want to ask him why. What does he see in me? The same things I see in myself? Or new ones that I never even noticed? Does he know about the things I see in him? His kindness and bravery and thoughtfulness and fierceness. There are other things, too, things that cannot be explained.

They can only be felt.

And I do feel them for this man. This kind soul who's never demanded anything of me. Done nothing but be there for me, even when I did not deserve it. He's always been what I needed. He's always done what I needed, including hiding his feelings until I was ready to know about them.

How could I have kept him at a distance forever?

When we reach the beach, I stare out at the dark blue water and shudder.

"It's not like before," Kearan says. "You're in control. You can change your mind if you don't want to do this."

"I can't," I say. "Not if I'm to be a good captain."

"Then you admit you're a good captain?" he asks.

I smile, and Kearan's lips part.

He swallows. "Your smiles are rarer than diamonds and infinitely more precious."

I frown. "Don't quit piracy to become a poet."

"Ha." He nudges me with a shoulder. "I'm serious. It is a lovely smile."

"Thank you, but watch what you say else Enwen will never let you hear the end of it."

"Don't I know it."

I'm glad for the banter. It lessens my nerves and helps me see my task more clearly. I'm doing this for all of them. If we pull this off, we'll have completed the task set out for us—despite all the complications that have come up along the way.

"It will be hard to move about the ship when I'm sopping wet," I say, thinking of this for the first time.

"You could always undress and carry your clothes above you in the water."

"That won't exactly help in the area of stealth now, will it? Besides, it would slow me down."

"Aye, but I'd have a nice image to reminisce on as I returned to the crew."

My mouth drops open, and Kearan flashes his teeth in a smile.

"We're fighting for our survival, and you want to be flirty now?"

He shrugs. "I haven't had the chance to before now, and we might die."

Truer words were never spoken. "Don't expect me to reciprocate. I don't know how to flirt."

"Yes, you do. You just don't do it with words." He eyes my side, where he knows I have at least a couple of knives tucked away.

"You're a strange man."

"Aye."

There's no more delaying what I have to do next. No matter how much I may want to stand right here and take the time to actually enjoy being around him. Now that I know I am allowed to. Because he doesn't hate me for what I did.

"Watch for my signal," I say.

"We will. Give 'em hell."

"You can count on it."

And without another word, I dive into the water.

It is so strange to feel the water but not the temperature. It is unnatural to breathe when I know I should not be able to. I feel a momentary panic at being underwater like this again. A feeling of being trapped and surrounded by the unknown.

There could still be dangers about, but it's easier to fight when I know I'm not just doing it for me. I've got thirty-eight people on this island counting on me for their survival. It is a humbling feeling. It focuses me, keeps my eyes straight ahead, straining to make out anything dangerous in the water. I don't stray too far from shore. Where the water is more shallow, fewer creatures can be hiding. And I can't get turned about that way.

Light cuts through the surface of the water, but it doesn't travel far. That's why this plan will work. The enemy won't see me through the water.

It takes me fifteen minutes to make the swim to the ship. When I catch the darkness of the hull underwater, I slow my approach, looking for the best place to breach the surface. The closer the better.

How does Alosa do this? I try to remind myself that she has perfect vision underwater, whereas I don't. She's half siren; I'm not. Still, I feel entirely out of my element below the water. But on land with a knife in my hand, I am the most dangerous of predators.

I pop my head above the surface just far enough to have my eyes out of the water. The side of the ship is massive. I don't think I've ever been on so large a vessel. That bone-white wood has been patched over time and time again, and I wonder if this is the original ship that Threydan's crew sailed over on, updated and rebuilt as time went on.

There's no rope ladder extending down the side of the ship. Any handholds I might make use of are too spread apart for me to get all the way up the side. I swim for the fore of the ship. The bowsprit extends like a knifepoint some forty or fifty feet above the water. That's not going to be helpful.

But the figurehead extends straight down into the water, and I'm able to get a handhold, then a foothold. Whatever the figure used to be, it has long faded with time. Not sure what the paint or wood once depicted. Something humanoid, I think.

Whatever it is, I thank the stars that it's still intact enough for me to climb.

My muscles strain as I pull my legs out of the water. My wet clothes are unbelievably heavy and noisy, water dripping into the ocean as I climb. I move slowly, listening for any movement through the gunport above me. When I don't hear so much as a rustle of clothing, I find another handhold and pull myself up another arm's-length. Pause. Repeat.

When I'm just below the gunport, I carefully peer over the top of the opening. There's very little light within the enemy's ship, and the tunnel the ship is docked in certainly isn't helping matters. I take that as a good sign, since I would hope that no one is bumbling around below-decks without light to guide their way.

As I try to get a leg up, my foot slips, and I nearly plummet back into the ocean. I take a deep breath before trying again, finally pulling myself into the gunport and collapsing on the floor.

I do nothing but breathe for a full minute as I try to collect myself. Then I stand.

I can still hear the water dripping from my clothes. That will never do. I can't very well walk around the ship like this. I wring out my braids as best I can. Then I pull off my shirt and quietly squeeze all the water from it. My eyes dart around the dark area for any sign of movement, but there is none, so I continue with my pants and boots.

In that time, my eyes adjust to the darkness, and I can begin to make out shapes, like the barrel of gunpowder next to the cannons. I open it and help myself, putting dry grit into my pistol so it'll actually be of some use should I need it. There's even cloth for cleaning out the cannons. I use it to dry the soles of my boots as well as my weapons.

Then I start to explore.

The fore cannons are located in a small room of their own. I crack open the door at the end—soundlessly, thankfully—and peer through the other side. Water storage. And on the other side of that, the gun deck. Stars, but whoever built this vessel intended on it being put through a ton of sea battles. That'll be fortunate for us once she's in our possession.

When I have a choice to go above deck or below, I head down first. Above, I'll lose my cover. I'll be visible to all who pay attention. And anyone on the main deck is more likely to be alert.

No one expects an attack from within.

Besides, I need to make a scene, not get killed before I can sufficiently distract the crew.

I take the steps lightly. Only one manages to creak, but since ships creak and groan all on their own, either no one hears or no one makes anything of it.

When I reach the lower level, which houses the crew's quarters, I find six individuals in the bunks. The majority are sleeping, likely before their shifts on watch tonight. But two converse quietly. I pick up only a couple of words. Something to do with fishing at high tide.

Six is more than enough to raise an alarm. I'll thin their numbers a bit first, but I need to be quick.

The Drifta nearest me is fast asleep, and I creep through the shadows until I'm level with his hammock. My knife cuts across his throat silently, and his gasp is barely a breath of air, easily masked by the whispering at the end of the room.

The next sleeping body is on the top bunk: too high for me to reach without climbing up and waking him. So I swing myself onto the middle hammock, take aim, and thrust my knife point through where I judge his neck must be resting. Blood drips down my blade and onto my hands. The choking sound is less capable of being masked this time.

The whispering couple cut off and look toward my end of the ship.

I stay where I am in the hammock, blood dripping on my clothing in a steady rhythm.

"Anderrin?" one of the two asks, standing from their bunk. She pads this way on sock-covered feet. I hold absolutely still, pretending to be another sleeping person.

The approaching woman pays me no mind as she strides right up to her crewman, climbs the ladder next to the bunk, and peers into his hammock. It begins to sway, so I assume she must be trying to rouse him.

Quick as a snake, I lash out, slicing into her gut, which is now on level with me. She cries out, before falling to the ground. I manage to keep hold of my knife as she lands.

That wakes the other two who were sleeping and alerts the one who had been conversing with the woman I just killed. I fling my dagger in the direction of the nearest one, who tries to get out of his hammock. He's not at the right angle for me to cause serious damage, so I aim for the rope holding up his bunk instead. He starts to tumble downward and tangle in the sheets, which buys me time with the two still trying to get their bearings.

When my feet hit the ground, the first newly awakened woman already has her sword raised and pistol cocked. I throw another knife at the hand with the pistol, and it sinks into her flesh, resulting in the firearm dropping to the floor. She screams.

There we go.

I pounce before she has a chance to recover. My rapier sneaks past her guard, piercing her heart. Before I can pull the blade out, another sword swings for me, and I flatten myself to the floor to miss it. I pull out a second dagger as I roll and come up on my feet so I can hold one in each hand.

I have two opponents now: the man who finally freed himself from the sheets, and the woman who just took a swipe at me. They charge together.

I duck under the first swing, catch the second between crossed daggers, and kick out at the man. My blow lands right between his legs, and he goes down with a groan.

The woman holds her blade in two hands and starts swinging left and right, trying to hit me from all angles. I'm no more than a blur as I leap and dodge and deflect. She's relentless with her attacks, and she even flings insults at me that require too much of my attention to translate.

After ducking her latest swing, I shove a dagger through the thickest part of her foot, effectively pinning her in place. She shrieks and slashes downward. I shuffle out of the way and place my remaining dagger through her other foot.

I race for my rapier. I sight the corpse and get my hands on my sword, when something painful connects with my back. I turn to find the upright woman's sword on the ground next to me. It hit hilt first, effectively bruising me, but nothing more. I can't believe she would try to throw it.

The man is still trying to work through the pain between his legs, and he's rolling back and forth on the floor. Meanwhile, I rush at the woman I've left with my daggers.

Seeing me approaching, she grits her teeth and reaches for both daggers simultaneously. With another scream, she frees herself and tries to fend me off. But her wounded feet make her slow. I get under her guard in no time and send my sword point through her midsection.

I retrieve my daggers and approach the final man. He's finally gotten his feet underneath him again, though he walks with a sort of limp. He flings a word at me. One I *do* translate, but it doesn't merit repeating.

A bell clangs above deck. *Finally*. I was starting to think the rest of the Drifta couldn't hear all the screaming coming from down here.

The remaining man sneers at me, looking rather proud at the sound of that bell.

"What makes you think they'll arrive in time to save you?" I ask him in his language.

His face falls as I charge.

CHAPTER 22

NOT A SECOND AFTER I kill him, the room fills with more Drifta. There are ten or so of them, each looking angrier than the last. I don't recognize any of them. It's impossible to tell if they know who I am, though I have a hard time imagining that they'd want to kill me any more than they already do either way.

There is the briefest moment of stillness, where I size up the newcomers. They look me over before turning to survey the six dead surrounding me. Hard to look innocent when blood covers my hands and clothes and blade.

I don't give them the chance to move first. I pull out my pistol and fire, taking out the closest Drifta to me. Since I've no time to reload, I throw the weapon at another man. It clonks him square in the nose, halting his advance.

Then I run.

I bolt through the doors at the far end of the room and slam them closed. I slide one of my longer daggers through the handles of both doors to buy me some time.

Shots fire through the door, and I have to leap aside to avoid wayward bullets. I'm in the galley, and I land between two benches bolted to the floor. As I rise and race the length of the room, I hear bodies being thrown against the door.

They're trying to break in.

I reach the kitchens, which is the last room on this level of the ship. There's a cooking stove at the far end, washing basins surrounding it. Between it and me, there's a kitchen island, a chopping center for the cooks to use. I manage to launch myself to the other side of it as the galley doors finally snap under the barrage of Drifta breaking through.

The island is what saves me. It forces them to come at me two at a time, one on each side of the island with me in the middle. I've got my rapier in one hand and a knife in the other, as I prepare to fight them two at a time.

The first man who runs at me on the left skewers himself on my knife. The man behind him practically shoved him onto the sword in his haste to reach the fighting. I let go of the knife and drop down to grab his cutlass instead so I can have a longer reach with my left hand.

I angle myself back a foot to keep everyone within my sights. I dodge and thrust simultaneously, stabbing one man through the gut while fending off the other's blow. Flicking my wrist, I send the enemy's cutlass flying across the island and slice the empty-handed pirate to ribbons.

The men waiting their turns push harder and harder, desperate to join the fight. One leaps atop the island, thinking to overpower me from above. I dodge a strike from the right, and that pirate's sword goes charging between the legs of the man on the island, who then stumbles and land flat on his back. I stab at the first man's now-exposed back.

They keep coming, each man thinking he'll be the one to finally beat me. It's truly astonishing the number of fights I've won because of male arrogance.

After another thrust into meaty flesh, I've no time to withdraw the sword before veering to the side to avoid an ax swinging downward. Above my head, pots and pans hang down from the ceiling. I grab a large cast-iron skillet, yank it off the hook, and swing. It clonks the ax wielder in the head, sending him sprawling atop the pile of bodies.

And then I hear a sound.

The clicking of a pistol.

The man atop the island regains his feet. I reach up for his shirt and pull him downward. He screams when the iron ball makes contact with his back instead of me, and I drop him with the rest of the corpses growing around me.

Blood gathers in puddles on the floor, smears under my boots, flecks on my clothing and skin, runs down my sword, and coats my hands.

A man charges me, dodging under my rapier and sending the breath from my lungs as I fall. He might have made some progress if we'd landed on solid ground. Instead, a dead body takes the impact, and with the leverage, I'm able to roll the pirate off me. I drop the skillet and go for another dagger now that we're in closer quarters, raking it across his neck before I stand. Blood flies into my face with the movement.

They're getting smarter as they watch me kill. More men climb atop the island at once. I throw a knife. It has just enough space to make one arc before embedding into one man's eye. Then I'm forced back against the washbasin as five cutlasses shove at me at once.

I turn in a half circle, my rapier touching blade after blade, but there are too many. I knew this was a possibility, of course. That this mission might be the equivalent of me sacrificing myself.

This is it, I think. The moment when I meet my end. It's how I always wanted to go. Dying for the sake of someone else. Dying for Alosa's crew. Risking my neck so they have a chance of making it home.

But, for the first time in as long as I can remember, something is different about this.

It takes me far too long to realize that *I don't want to die.*

It's terrifying as those words form in my head.

I've always been eager to reunite with my family. To do as much good as I could in the meantime and gladly go when it's my time.

But I don't want it to be my time.

Not when there's still more that I can do. Not when I'm just beginning to realize that I might be worthy of having a life that is my own. Not that I'd ever abandon Alosa and her cause, but maybe there's something I can do for myself. Maybe I can train more girls like I'm starting to do with Roslyn. Maybe I don't have to hide. Maybe I can just be where I want, when I want.

And maybe I want a large brute by my side while I do it.

Terror lances through me in a way that makes me feel more alive than ever. For I do fear death, and I do have something to lose now.

This can't be the end.

I hear a loud grinding sound bounce off the walls of the ship. The enemy freezes in place, even looks around, as though trying to determine the meaning of the sound.

"Is that—" one starts.

"The capstan!" another shouts.

Some of the men and women around me turn about, racing from the kitchen to stop the anchor from being raised, it sounds like.

No sooner have I started to hope, to think that I might survive this after all, when—

Those closest to me attack.

There are too many sharp blades. I cannot dodge them all.

I sidestep the one aimed for my heart, fend one off with my knife and rapier. But the third—

It slides into my stomach. The shock of pain has me just standing there, looking at the point of entry. A moment later, I hack into the one who delivered the blow. As he falls, he pulls his cutlass back out of me.

I scream.

Any Drifta remaining in the room leave to investigate what's happening with the anchor.

Now that I'm hurt.

I stumble forward from the pain. My hand goes to my stomach, to keep in the blood.

I fall to my knees.

Stars, but it hurts. I have had many an injury over the years, but not like this. Never like this.

This one is serious.

I need a healer. Immediately.

There's a shot from somewhere above, and the sounds of battle commence. I focus on my breathing, trying to find a way to do so without causing more pain, when a voice cuts across the fighting.

"Give them hell, lasses!"

Dimella.

They're on board.

I look about me at the bodies and blood, looking for some answer to a question I haven't fully formed. Some way to make sense of what I must do next.

There.

A skinny lad with his gun belt about his waist. He looks about my size.

I scoot along to him, get my fingers around that buckle, and loosen it. It slips free from his person, and I drag it over to me.

I grit my teeth. This is going to sting.

I place the belt over my injury, effectively covering the entrance and exit wounds, and cinch it tight.

A horrible sound escapes my lips, and I nearly black out as I fasten the buckle. I lie still on the floor, waiting for the pain to become bearable, but that doesn't happen.

Nothing for it but to fight through it, then.

Getting to my feet takes an age, but once I do so, things get a bit easier. I'm not sure if I finally grow accustomed to the pain or if the belt is holding it in or something else altogether, but I'm able to gather my weapons, clean them off, and leave the room. Slowly.

What I find above deck is heartening.

My crew.

They fight off the measly remains of the Drifta aboard the vessel. It doesn't take long at all, and it ends with the last two of the enemy surrendering. They drop their weapons and raise their hands into the air.

Kearan and Enwen dump them over the side of the ship.

They'll probably make it, if they can get to a fire soon.

"Captain," Dimella says by way of greeting when she sees me.

"Get us going," I order.

"Aye-aye!" She barks out orders to the crew, and they get to it with an enthusiasm I've yet to see from the crew of the *Wanderer*, including Captain Warran, who takes it upon himself to go to the helm.

Kearan steps up to me, eyes me. The belt must be doing a good job, because he doesn't find anything to point out. "How did it go?"

"Swimmingly."

"You're covered in blood."

I worry he's noticed the injury, until I realize of course I'm covered in blood. Drifta blood. "Makes me look more fierce."

"It makes you look a great many things."

His tone is flirty, and I can't even fathom what I'm supposed to infer from his words. I say, "Get your arse to the helm. I don't trust Warran with it."

"Now you're thinking about my arse?" he asks.

"I'm thinking about where I could stick my blades if you don't get moving."

He gives me my favorite grin, the one that says he knows he's trouble, before heading up to the aftercastle. I would follow, but I don't think I can manage more stairs right now. It's taking everything I have just to act as though everything is fine.

As if I won't die today.

Iskirra's a fine healer, but I'm not so foolish as to think that blade didn't hit something vital as it went clean through my stomach. I can spend the day having her fuss over me or I can captain this crew.

I choose the latter.

The lines keeping us close to shore are cut, the anchor is raised the rest of the way, and a steady breeze takes us away from land. Away from these cursed shores.

We haven't gone far at all when a clamor steals our attention back on land.

Dozens of people race toward the boat. They clear the tree line, waving their arms in our direction. Screaming at the top of their lungs.

"Help!"

"Wait!"

"Please!"

These aren't the undead. They're the remaining Drifta.

There are children and livestock among them. Women and men of all ages.

"What are they saying?" Dimella asks.

"They're asking for help. They want to go with us."

"Pfft," Enwen says. "That's rich. They try to kill us. Try to kill our captain three times over. Now they think they're in a position to ask for anything. Show us yer gold!" Enwen shouts the last sentence. "Then we'll be more likely to open our ears."

Obviously they can't understand him, but it doesn't stop him from yelling at them.

"Stop the boat," I order.

"What?" a handful of people ask simultaneously.

Dimella does no more than raise a brow.

"They didn't ask for any of this. It isn't their fault. Those are civilians. Not warriors out there. Lower the rowboats and bring them ashore."

"Can we even fit so many?" Captain Warran asks.

"We'll make room."

"And how do you intend to feed them?"

"The sea will provide."

"But—"

"Lads, to the rowboats! Bring the Drifta aboard!" Dimella shouts, cutting off the captain's further protests. When no one moves right away, Dimella says, "Pull your weight or we'll make you weightless in the depths of the sea!"

That does the trick.

Kearan is already by the railing, working on lowering the lifeboats. Enwen, Nydus, and Taydyn quickly join him. It's not long at all before the boats are in the water and sailing for the shore.

I watch as the lads row closer and closer. I brace myself for some sort of trickery, but just as I suspected, there is none. The natives board gratefully, and the lads row them back, handing families onto the ship before rowing out for one more load of people.

Dynkinar is among those aboard. She is with her little translator. I hear her say, "Ask for who's in charge here."

"That would be me," I say, sidling up to the pair.

The speaker looks me up and down. Since I understood her just fine, she doesn't have to guess my identity. "You didn't die."

"No thanks to your people."

"And yet you still let us board."

"I would have aided you from the beginning, had you not tried to kill me."

"You are the only thing stopping him from becoming truly invincible."

"Or maybe I'm the only way to truly stopping him. Kearan told you of our queen. He wasn't lying."

Dynkinar holds herself up as tall as she can manage. She is silent for a moment. "I've misjudged your people, Captain Veshtas."

"You were only looking out for your own, just as I would have done. Let us start fresh."

Apparently, I'm feeling a lot more forgiving now that I know I'm dying.

Dynkinar nods.

"What happened?" I ask. "Why were you fleeing to the sea?"

"The undead attacked in full force. They were killing everything in sight. We are all that made it out alive. The King of the Undersea must be stopped."

"We'll stop him. When we regroup with my queen, we will form a plan of attack immediately."

Dynkinar bows her head. "It is our only hope now."

"See to your people, and I will see to mine."

She nods before helping to locate space for people below and above deck.

And I eye my sailors, who are rowing like mad for the ship, and I see immediately why.

The undead have arrived.

They pour out of the trees by the hundreds, their movements jerky and unnatural. Their eyes glow that peacock blue, even from here, and they move as one force.

One mind behind them all.

"Hurry it up, Kearan!" I scream at him.

"Thought I'd take in the sights first," he fires back petulantly.

The undead reach the shoreline, but they do not stop. They plunge right into the water, sending it foaming and frothing upward. They march in over their heads, disappearing into the unknown depths.

"Damn," I say.

Are they swimming? Are they walking the distance? How long

will that take? Obviously the boats will reach us first, but will there be enough time to help everyone aboard?

The crew moves as quickly as possible. We haul all the newcomers aboard, and then the lads bring up the rowboats.

"Get us moving, now!"

They don't need telling twice.

Captain Warran takes the helm again, and he gets us going while Kearan assists the smaller children about the ship. If anyone has noticed that I haven't moved since coming up top, they don't say anything.

That bundle of heat within my chest flickers slightly.

"Fighters to the starboard and port of the ship," I call out. "Keep an eye on that water. If anything tries to climb aboard, slice it!"

As the ship begins to move, the crew takes position at the edges of the railing, peering into the water.

There's a silence, as though everyone is holding their breaths, waiting to see if we've made it. I manage to walk myself to the side of the ship and look into the water below.

Nothing but a smooth surface.

And then I hear screaming belowdecks.

CHAPTER 23

I LEAP FOR THE stairs leading belowdecks before I remember I'm injured. Maybe I pass off my scream of pain as a battle cry. Luckily, Kearan beats me to the stairs, so he doesn't see the way I lean against one of the walls when I make it to the bottom. The way I have to pause to catch my breath. To process what has happened.

I killed all those Drifta belowdecks after first boarding the ship.

Threydan has risen them again.

He must be close.

The undead are swiping at mothers holding children, charging at the elderly, pinning men in place. Each has Threydan's bright blue gaze. I lock eyes with one, holding that glowing stare, and I swear I see those eyes move down to the belt keeping my insides together.

I take out that undead first.

He doesn't even move as I get within range with my rapier, slicing him to ribbons. He stares at my face, then down to the belt again. I realize then that blood is seeping out from under my makeshift tourniquet.

I'm going to lose energy fast, so I have to be quick.

I slice through muscle and tendon, rendering the undead useless.

There's only a handful of them in this room, and I can't imagine what Threydan plans to do with so few. Perhaps slow us down, even if it's just a little.

Kearan is right beside me, fighting off his own undead. Many of my girls have followed us, and they join the fight without question, making me proud.

And then the floor moves, and I'm jerked off my feet.

I realize a moment later that the floor didn't move. Rather it *stopped* moving. The undead lowered the anchor.

Oh no.

The fall jostles my belt, and I can't move for a moment, so I just yell weakly, "Capstan!"

A combined group of Drifta, my girls, and the crew of the *Wanderer* all rush for the stern of the ship, where the mechanism that controls the anchor is housed.

"Are you okay?" It's Kearan's voice, but I don't seem to have the energy to move my head in his direction.

"I'm fine," I say from the floor. My torso throbs unbearably, and I try to calm my breathing.

And then a shadow is thrown over my form as Kearan kneels before me.

"What is that?" he asks, his voice almost too low for me to hear. He points toward where the blood is escaping from my body.

"Stab wound," I answer.

His large hands hover over the belt, but he dares not touch me. "How bad is it?"

"Goes in one side and comes out the other."

"And you're still fighting?"

"I'm not dead yet."

"Of all the stubborn—" He adjusts the belt, cinching it tight over the wound once more and ignoring my scream of pain. Kearan hauls me into his arms, and I gasp as the wound is jostled again. "Iskirra! Captain down! Iskirra!"

His voice has turned desperate, haunted. I don't like the sound of it.

"I'm okay. We just need to get the anchor up and then we can flee. We can still make it. Put all our efforts into getting the ship running again."

"Save your breath," he says to me as he takes the stairs at a near run.

"Just help me stand. I can keep going."

He glares at me. *Glares*. Like I've said something incredibly stupid. "You've given enough. Now let your crew take care of you."

"I'm the captain, and I order you to put me down."

"You're injured, Captain. That means I take orders from Dimella now. Iskirra!"

"Enemy behind us!" comes a shout from a little voice high up in the crow's nest. Roslyn has clearly taken the liberty of keeping a lookout for us.

Kearan turns toward the stern with me in his arms. There's a churning in the water now, as though the undead are gathering together, and they're moving closer.

"Get the ship moving again!" I try to shout, but the words don't come out as strongly as I intend. "He's coming."

Kearan swears.

More than half the crew has gone below to help fight against the dead, yet— "Why is it taking so long?" I say, more to myself than anyone else.

Dimella must hear Roslyn's call, because she races up top to get a look at the oncoming enemy for herself. She sees Kearan holding me.

"Captain down," he says to her. "You're in charge now, and we need a healer immediately."

"I can still captain this ship," I argue.

"You can't even stand," he bites back.

"Because you won't put me down!" I want to stick him with a knife, but I haven't the energy to reach for one right now.

"I'll get Iskirra," Dimella says, returning to the hatch.

"Find out what the holdup is!" I shout after her.

Kearan looks about the ship desperately, as though the next course of action will come to him if he can just find it. All around us are the terrified faces of the Drifta civilians. Members of my crew are dispersed between them, watching the water, waiting for the fight approaching. Captain Warran remains at the helm, ready for the moment we get the anchor up again.

"You could put me down and help everyone below," I suggest.

"That's not going to happen. There's too many people down there as it is."

He finds the nearest crate and perches atop it, keeping me close. Now that he's not holding so much of my weight, he uses one hand to cup the side of my face.

"Don't be scared. You're going to be okay," he says.

"Dying isn't so scary. It's living that's hard."

"But you're going to do it. You're too tough to die."

I look up into his face, and only then do I see the fear in his eyes. I'm not the one who is most scared right now.

I place a hand against the one he has pressed to my face. "Don't be afraid."

"But I am. I haven't had enough time with you. You can't go yet."

"Will you promise me something?" I don't think the end is too far off for me. My wound doesn't hurt as much anymore.

"Anything."

"When—if I die, don't turn back to the bottle. You can't—"

He moves his thumb to cover my lips. "I wouldn't dream of it. I don't want to forget a single moment that I shared with you. Not your smiles or your viciousness or that deadly aim you possess with those knives. But that doesn't matter because you're not going anywhere."

"Just remember," I say. "You're too good to throw your life away by not really living it. I'm sorry it took me so long to see it. I'm sorry I pushed you away again and again. I'm sorry we didn't have any time to really be together."

"We were together in the ways that mattered," he counters.

"Fighting?"

"Fighting. Talking. Working together. That's all I ever wanted. Just to be near you."

A tear slides out the side of my eye and catches in my hair. "Would you do something for me?"

"What is it?"

"Kiss me."

Kearan swallows, and his eyes tilt down toward my mouth. "This isn't the right moment. Not now when you're hurt."

"It might be the only moment."

He still hesitates.

"If I had the strength, I would reach up and initiate it, assuming you want—"

"I want," he growls, the two words forming a complete sentence of their own. He leans down and presses his lips to mine.

I learn then that there is a difference between physical heat and the electricity of being touched by someone you care for. While I can't feel the former, I can certainly feel the latter. My skin tingles at all the places we are connected, and while I cannot forget the horrible numbness of my limbs, it is nice to have something else to focus on.

The soft scratchiness of his beard against my cheeks. The texture of his lips placed so gently over mine. The way his thumb moves up and down my neck while he still cradles my face with one hand.

I never would have guessed such a precious moment in time would be possible for me. My tears come more quickly now, because I realize that one moment is not enough. I need more. I need a lifetime of moments like this.

Moments with him.

A shout has Kearan drawing his head back. We look over in time to see Enwen and Taydyn hauling one of the undead up the stairs. It's moving like a beached fish while Enwen holds the arms and Taydyn grasps the legs. It takes some maneuvering, but they finally get the body thrown over the side of the ship.

"What's that about?" Kearan asks them.

"They're not staying dead," Enwen says. "Rendering the muscles useless isn't working anymore. Their very bones are being moved for them. We can't clear them out of the room with the capstan. Miss Dimella says to toss them over and keep watch so they don't reboard."

They both disappear back below. Another two men come up top carrying another wriggling undead.

"They're not staying dead?" I repeat aloud. "But that would mean—"

"He's been playing with us this whole time," Kearan says. "Making us feel like we had hope and a sense of control. But we can't render his armies useless. It's never been possible."

And that's why all those skeletons were encased in ice. All he needs are bones.

"You need to go help them," I say. "He's getting too close. Please. Just set me down."

Kearan isn't happy about it, but he listens, as he's always done. "I'll find out what's holding up Iskirra." He sets me against the crate in a sitting position so I have a view of the deck and the sea. He gives me one last, longing look before running downstairs.

I wonder if he suspects, as I do, that perhaps Iskirra isn't with us anymore. If the undead cannot be rendered useless, then there's no way I have a full crew still alive downstairs. My heart falls at the thought, and I curse this wound that's preventing me from moving.

I watch the churning water grow ever closer. A musket shot away now. They'll be upon us within the minute. But as I count my breaths and try not to think on the pain in my torso, the ship doesn't move. I don't hear chains rising out of the water or the cranking of the capstan.

And though the remaining fighters on the main deck do their best to keep the bodies that have been thrown over from resurfacing, they can do nothing when a tower of bodies lunges out of the sea. Threydan climbs a ladder made from undead bodies and hauls himself over the ship.

King of the Undersea, indeed.

The dead follow him aboard.

They sweep through the ship like a tide, grabbing all in their path, holding them immobile, just as they did at our camp.

Threydan's eyes move over the boat, and I know he's seeing with more than just his own vision. He's also taking in all that the dead see and hear. When his eyes land on me, I stiffen, but I don't move. If I'm going to expend any energy, it has to be at the right moment.

Still barefoot, Threydan approaches me, despite my crew trying to reach me first. I admire their efforts, but now is the time to stand down. The dead keep them held in place, clearing a path for Threydan to reach me.

I feel for the buckle at my chest, not sure yet if I mean to undo it and speed up my end or reinforce it so I can be here for whatever comes next. It is a futile attempt. My fingers cannot grip anything properly at the moment.

Threydan stares down at me, eyeing the injury and my fumbling fingers. "Beloved, you are dying," he says.

"I am not your beloved, and it is my right to die as I choose."

"And what of your crew? What will you choose for them?"

The undead spill out from belowdecks, carrying members of my crew, of Warran's crew, and even Dynkinar's people. There's not enough room for everyone up here, but Threydan makes sure the people I care about most are within my sight.

Dimella eyes me from between the grasp of two undead. Enwen has his eyes shut tight, trying to pretend he's in a better place, no doubt. And then there's Kearan. Held back by no less than five undead, all of them enormous and putting their full weight into him. I try not to stare at him for fear that Threydan will notice.

He notices anyway, his rigid gaze fixing on the man I care for most.

I try to get his attention back on me. "You said you'd give me three days."

He scoffs. "And you said you would end things with him." He points to Kearan, as though I don't know who he's talking about.

"No, I said I would *tell* him things were ended between us. And I did that."

"And then you tried to flee from me."

"An eternity of servitude didn't sound like fun."

Threydan looks as though he wants to hit something. "Are you completely stupid? Did you not hear anything I've said to you?" He switches to another language, perhaps his native tongue? His next words are for my ears only. "The panaceum doesn't make you a slave. You still have your mind and will. You'll only be invulnerable. Invincible. A queen at my side. The world ours for the taking. All I asked in return was help dealing with the horrible creatures who took so much from me. Is that really so much?

"I have been patient," he continues. "I have tried kindness and love to persuade you. I wanted you to choose this of your own free will, but that's clearly not going to happen. So we're going to jump ahead to the part where you're like me. And in your gratitude for me freeing you from mortality, you will finally see me as you should." He takes another step in my direction.

"Don't come near me," I say, though I can barely move.

He looks heavenward. "I leave you to your own devices for mere hours, and you get yourself stabbed. You're dying, Sorinda. I will not let my chances at revenge die with you."

I cough, and the motion causes unbelievable pain. I fumble with the buckle some more, as though that'll help anything. "You said it had to be my choice. The panaceum can't influence me any longer. I have to want it."

"You don't have to want it. You only have to accept it. And now your choices are death or eternity with me."

I laugh, even though it's agony. "I choose death."

Threydan stares me down, as though waiting for me to finish the joke. It takes him far too long to realize I'm serious.

"You'd rather die than be with me," he deadpans. "Even though I can offer you power and forever?"

"I don't want any of it. Not power. Not forever. And especially not you."

We're back to speaking in Islander now, and I don't care who can hear. What's he going to do? Kill me? I'm already dying.

And he thinks I'd damn myself for eternity to save myself.

Fool.

Threydan's gaze lowers to my rapier. He strides forward to protests from my crew and unsheathes the weapon. Alosa's gift sparkles in the sunlight, and Threydan admires the sword for a few seconds. What's he going to do now? Speed up my end?

My heart rate picks up, because I have a feeling that's not what he's about to do at all.

He turns away from me, strides off in Kearan's direction with the sword extended.

"Wait," I say, my voice growing weak. "Stop." I try to stand, but all I manage to do is topple fully onto the deck. As a sharp pain lances through me, I manage to raise my head just in time to meet Kearan's eyes. They are unafraid, and he doesn't take them off me.

I scramble to rise, to stand, to do anything except watch what is about to happen.

The King of the Undersea stabs him through the gut. In and out so quickly I can barely follow the motion. It is only the hordes of undead that keep Kearan standing.

"No!"

It hurts so bad, but I scoot along the deck, trying to get as close to Kearan as possible. He has a wound that matches mine, though his isn't stanched. He'll bleed out much quicker than I am.

"Now you have a choice to make, Sorinda," Threydan says. "You can watch him die and know that I will have his body join my ranks of undead forever. Or you can accept my offer, gain the power of the panaceum, and heal him with it."

The breath stutters out of me as two horrible choices are laid before me. I want neither; neither can happen. Why can't I just die so the choice is made for me?

I cease my struggling and fall still.

Death for me will not stop whatever happens here. Am I foolish enough to think Threydan will cease terrorizing my crew once I'm gone? No, he'll likely slaughter everyone I ever knew for what I took from him.

He says, "Make the choice now, Sorinda, or I will speed this along. Where is the little pirate? She's who I'll maim for you next."

Roslyn.

"All right," I croak. "I'll do it."

"No!" comes too many shouts for me to count. One from a wounded Kearan, one from little Roslyn up top. One from Dimella and countless others. They are a good crew.

If I'm to remain a good captain, I need to do this one last thing for them. Then this nightmare of a journey will finally be over for them. I'll worry about my forever after that.

"Good girl," Threydan says demeaningly. He returns to me, scoops me up in his arms—and I close my eyes, pretending it's only Kearan holding me again.

Threydan turns his back to the majority of the crew, as though to give us a semblance of privacy. Then, without hesitation, he lowers his lips to mine again.

I can't pretend it's Kearan any longer. Not now that I know how his lips feel and taste. But Threydan doesn't seem to mind that I'm not reciprocating the kiss. This is a ritual. I'd imagine this is the only way he can share eternity with me now that the panaceum is a part of him.

What is a kiss but a meeting of two souls?

That place inside me where all my heat is contained around my heart—it throbs, swirling like an angry mass within me. I feel a tug, something trying to coax it upward.

And I resist. Violently. Because that is my essence. My mortality. That is me all condensed into one place. I grab ahold of my heart with clawed fingertips, keeping it right where it is.

Threydan says against my lips, "Give in to me, Sorinda. He doesn't have long. You must give it to me now."

One by one, I loose those fingers. I force myself to hold absolutely still. Do nothing as my mortality is pulled from my chest. Up higher and higher. Until it reaches Threydan.

Or perhaps it is the other way around. Perhaps immortality is invading me, snuffing out my light. Building me anew.

It takes but a moment, and then—

Everything changes.

CHAPTER 24

EVERYTHING FEELS DIFFERENT.

If I thought I was empty before, when it was only temperature I could no longer feel, it is nothing compared to what I am now.

A husk.

No pain.

But also no spark of life.

There is a breeze on my face, but I feel removed from it somehow, as though it hardly registers to me. I cannot smell the briny water of the sea or feel the tight braids in my hair. Though I can see the bodies around me, I feel no particular connection to them. I know that I care for them. But the actual sensation within my heart? It's missing.

I'm missing.

I'm a mind full of thoughts but no feelings.

Once mortality is ripped from a soul, what meaning does anything have? One cannot enjoy happiness if there is no sorrow. There is no joy without pain. No love without hate. No feeling of being rested when one cannot feel restless. How can the days matter when they are innumerable? How can one enjoy life when it is endless?

This is what Threydan gave up everything for? A half-life?

For power.

And yes, I can certainly feel that. I have a connection to all the undead surrounding me. All I need to do is think a phrase, and they will carry it out. I can see through their eyes if I concentrate. It is an instinct as familiar to me as breathing once was.

I look down, note that my chest no longer rises and falls. It doesn't need to. Breath no longer sustains me. The panaceum is what gives me life now. I can sense it from Threydan's chest—

I couldn't risk them taking it. Not when I was so close to saving Kayra.

If I hid it, then I wouldn't be able to use its power and survive off this island. Perhaps I should swallow it? Or would my body only work it through my system given time?

I was running out of time and ideas.

And then a new thought struck me. Something that would hide the panaceum from the world and make it accessible only to me.

I sharpened the knife for hours, then spent another mustering up the courage. When I finally put the blade to my chest, I screamed and screamed as I cut into my own flesh, reached inside, and removed my heart.

With the panaceum firmly grasped in my other hand, I couldn't die, but I could still feel the pain. Every second of it. I sliced into my heart, thrust the artifact within, then placed my heart back into my chest.

The moment my hands let go, something remarkable happened.

The pain vanished. The power overwhelmed. The possibilities were endless.

Let them come for me now.

With steady fingers, I remove the belt around my waist. I don't need it any longer. My skin has knit itself back together, but I barely have a thought to spare for my own well-being, for there is a sense of urgency within my mind. One I cannot feel throughout my limbs, but I still heed it. I walk with purpose toward the dying man on the ship. The one who was hurt because of me. The undead move away from his side at my silent order. Kearan slumps to the ground, and I don't have the strength to catch him. But I join him on the floor.

"Your eyes," he says, and I know they're glowing a peacock blue. "Are you all right?"

"No."

"You shouldn't have done it."

"Quiet. I need to concentrate." I place my hand over the wound, and Kearan gasps. I pull on the power of the panaceum. I can access it freely, because Threydan has shared its full powers with me. He chose me to be his equal.

I should be horrified.

I should feel disgusted.

I'm never going to die.

Instead, I am empty, driven by the strong impulses that remained when I was still human. But they are a memory more than anything that I feel now. Human Sorinda would be distraught that Kearan is hurt. But the new me holds all our memories together yet feels cut off from them, as though I wasn't the one who felt all the emotions that went with those memories.

It is not difficult at all to imagine how the years ahead will change me. More time means more distance from my humanity and the things I'll remember about it. Those human feelings will fade until I hardly remember them at all. No wonder Threydan is as he is now.

When the skin has fully healed, I step away from Kearan and tread back to Threydan's side. Kearan rises on steady feet, and the undead surround him once more by Threydan's will.

"Now you see," Threydan says with a smile. "They are nothing. We are everything. Soon, even your feeble feelings will fade, and you will become so much more. You will build a life as you are now, and that will be all that ever truly existed."

He takes my hand in his, and I don't resist.

"What now?" I ask.

"Now we sail for the Seventeen Isles. Did I not promise to return the humans to their own lands? Unless, of course, you wish for them to serve you now in death?"

If there was any fidgeting among my crew, it quickly halts. Everyone goes perfectly still.

"No. Let's return them home."

"And then we can search for the sirens."

"Yes," I agree. Turns out acting is a lot easier when you're lifeless.

"Good. Now why don't we put all the prisoners belowdecks for now? I think it's time you and I had some real privacy."

I don't say anything in response. I can't. I'm concentrating too hard.

"Sorinda?" he asks.

Still nothing.

"What are you doing? Let go of them. I need to put the prisoners below."

Instead, the undead do not move, for I am giving them one order while Threydan is giving them another. They can do nothing more than hold absolutely still until one of us wins.

I turn to Threydan, King of the Undersea, terror of these lands for a thousand years.

"What am I doing?" I repeat his words back to him. "I thought you said you knew me. You should know exactly what I'm doing."

Were I still human, sweat would dot my brow from the struggle Threydan and I are pursuing. It feels like an arm wrestle, but with the mind. Each of us trying to get the better of the other one.

Threydan clenches his teeth from the strain of it. "You're adjusting. Give yourself a moment to acclimate to immortality. Let me handle things right now."

"Do you know what happens to men who try to tell me what to do?" I ask him.

Threydan raises my rapier, which he still holds from stabbing Kearan. He advances toward me. "Let them go!" he bellows. "I'd hate to restrain you, but I will if I must, dearest."

"Sorinda!" A tiny shout rings from above, and I look up at the crow's nest just in time to see little Roslyn drop my old rapier, the one I gifted to her. It lands point first into the wood not far from me.

I dart for it, and Threydan races after me, hot on my heels. My fingers clench around the hilt, and I pull the blade from the deck in one smooth motion. Threydan halts at the end of my sword point.

"This is ridiculous," he says. "What are you hoping to accomplish?"

It's a fair question. I have no idea where this is about to lead. I just know I have to act now. While I still have a little bit of myself left in me.

"I was told to rescue this crew. That includes saving it from the likes of you."

"Told to? You don't have to take orders from mortals! You are a god compared to them now."

"I'm sick of hearing your voice."

I take a stab at him.

He smacks my sword away with his own, the movement clunky, as though he were a bit out of practice, which I'm sure he is.

I attack a second time. He blocks it quicker this time. Smoother.

Then, as I prepare to attack a third time, he narrows his gaze at me and doesn't even bother to parry. My blade slides into his flesh. Threydan stares at me; I stare at him. He takes a step backward, drawing himself off the sword length. His skin slides back together, and the blood clears.

"Again, what are you hoping to accomplish?" he asks. "I can't be killed, and neither can you."

"Then I suppose we'll find out who tires first."

Threydan leaps backward as I slash at him, and now he's smiling. "If you wanted to see what your new body could do, all you had to do was ask."

He thrusts forward with his own strike, and I divert the attack before scratching at his shoulder. A line of red appears for only seconds before the body heals itself once again. Threydan holds himself up higher.

"It's been a while since I've done this," he says, "but as I recall, I was actually quite good at it."

And then he moves. *Really* moves this time.

Before I can blink, he's under my guard, and his sword is embedded in my gut. It is the oddest sensation. I can feel the sword against my innards. The steel caresses my intestines and severs my skin. Yet there is no pain. No fear. Because I am not in danger.

That knowledge is heady.

Threydan withdraws his sword, and I watch as my skin heals itself. I could get used to that. No pain. But I cling to the reminder that I didn't want this. It was forced upon me by this man. He means to control me, and I cannot allow it.

I leap at Threydan, slashing right and left. He dodges both, but he can't go far. The undead only leave a small ten-by-ten-foot section of deck surrounding the mainmast for us to occupy, my crew still held within their grasps.

With his next attack, our swords meet in the middle, and Threydan uses his full weight to shove me backward. I collide with wet dead bodies, but they might as well be a brick wall for how much give they have. Threydan's will still pushes against mine in an attempt to control them.

I bounce off the undead and hit the floor. Normally, I'd ache from the bruising I'd take after such a fall, but of course, there is nothing.

I've had many lifetimes' worth of pain, and I can't deny that there's a part of me that thrills at never having to experience it again.

But when I look up, I find Kearan staring down at me from where he's pinned in place. He's a reminder that I haven't had a lifetime's worth of love yet. His eyes say everything. They encourage me, show me that I hold meaning for him, show me that I have his trust and confidence.

A deep pressure streaks across my face, and my vision goes dark. I blink my eyes furiously as liquid fills them.

"Stop looking at him," Threydan says, and I realize that he just slashed me across my open eyes. When the blood finally clears and my vision returns, Threydan is standing before me. "You're with me now. Don't forget it. I made you this way. I'm what's healing you. You're *mine*." He holds out a hand to me, thinking to help me to my feet, and I swipe at it with my rapier.

Three of his fingers fall to the deck in a heap of blood. Threydan sighs as he turns the empty sockets toward his face for examination. No sooner has he done so than fresh fingers sprout in their proper places.

He wiggles his new digits in my direction.

I rise slowly, rubbing at my eyes, even though there's no need. It is a reflex more than anything else.

"Done yet?" Threydan asks.

"I've barely started."

I launch myself at him.

Time ceases to be measured by seconds and minutes. It is counted by drops of blood and slashes of the sword. By the tiring of muscles. The encouragement and gasps from my crew.

We carry on for the better part of an hour.

Threydan is not in as good of physical condition as I am, having slept for a thousand years, but the panaceum sustains us both far longer than mortal muscles should allow.

My advantages have counted for naught.

I've sliced the arteries in both his legs. He's lost an ear, the tip of his nose, and more fingers—each of which grew back shortly after they were separated from the rest of his body. It doesn't matter what I do or how I cut him. That beating artifact in his heart keeps us both alive.

But tire, we eventually do.

We both collapse to the ground, arms like liquid, legs like rocks. The undead don't move an inch, not while we both try to take control of them. Threydan has not stopped his mental assault once and neither have I.

"Shall we call it a tie?" Threydan asks, his voice slowed considerably from the exertion.

"No. This is only a respite."

He manages to laugh. "And how long will you keep fighting?"

"Forever. That's how long I'll protect those I'm sworn to defend."

"Not likely. The panaceum will make you forget them soon enough."

From the deck of the ship, I stare up at the sky. Sweat should drain from every pore in my body. Instead, my muscles simply feel out of my reach, and I can hardly find the words to speak amidst the concentration I must maintain.

As I lie there, waiting for strength to return to my limbs, I listen to the panaceum beating away in Threydan's chest. It is agonizing to be so aware of it yet separated by layers of meat and bone. This is the object that could be the answer to Threydan's end, but he has made himself one with it, so he cannot be parted from it.

Unless . . .

It wasn't Threydan's heart I stabbed when he was in that ice coffin.

It was the *panaceum*. That is how I bonded us. That is how the transformation started. I'd chipped at it. And once he started to hear my memories, he let me in. Let me start to become as he is . . .

Threydan is not the only one the panaceum obeys now. I am just as bound to it.

Do the undead not attempt to listen to me just as they do Threydan? Am I not capable of sharing *all* his powers now? He said no one could take the panaceum from him.

But that was back when I was human.

I'm not human anymore.

No, he made it perfectly clear that I was to be exactly as he is. The only one who could share the panaceum's powers with him.

Let's put that to the test.

It takes several tries, but eventually I find my feet.

"Can't I have a few more minutes, dearest?" Threydan asks as he tries to roll up first onto his knees and then his feet. He nearly falls twice. When he does manage to stand, he hunches considerably.

I tighten my grip on my rapier before charging at him. Threydan doesn't seem to have the energy to do anything at all but let me ram him through the center. I drive him backward with every bit of strength left in me. Eventually the tip of my sword connects with the mainmast, skewering Threydan thoroughly to it.

"Thanks for that," he says cheekily. "Nice to have something else holding me up for a bit."

I reach in my clothing for a knife. I slam Threydan's right hand against the wood, force his fingers open, and drive the point through his open palm.

My second knife is in my hands before he can react to the first. It impales his left hand to the mast on his other side.

He laughs. "You can't kill me, so now you mean to trap me? I've dug myself out of cave-ins and bodies and more. I will free myself from this, too, Sorinda. Your mind will tire eventually. The undead will free me."

He kicks me, sending me back several feet. I reach into my boot for a third knife and throw it. It slides through his right leg at the ankle, pinning him place.

Throw until you miss.

I grab another knife and hurl it with the practiced ease of one who has thrown knives every day of her life for thirteen years. My aim rarely fails me, especially when I'm desperate.

"Sorinda, stop this foolishness."

I throw another knife, first through his right shoulder, then another through his left. When he tries to get leverage with his thighs, I pin them in place with knives around the edges of the limbs.

I throw and throw until he's plastered against that mast with no hope of moving.

Until I have only one knife left.

Threydan laughs as I approach him. Using the tip, I draw an X right over his heart.

That silences him.

"What are you doing?" Threydan asks.

Before his skin can heal itself, I shove my hand into his chest. I place my knife between two of his ribs and use the leverage to crack the top one.

Threydan cannot feel the pain of it, but he screams anyway. "Stop it! Whatever you're doing, stop it right now!"

"Why? I thought you said I couldn't kill you."

He says nothing, only tries to fight against the firm grip of all my knives.

I pry his heart from his chest.

"Please! Dearest, I didn't mean to put this on you so quickly. You just need time to see. You must understand—"

"I understand plenty," I say as I stare at his purple heart. The red of the organ mixes with the blue of the panaceum, resulting in a violet glow. I cut into the unmoving flesh, until I see the first signs of the panaceum. It is hardly bigger than a walnut, and it shines like a star in the night sky. Peacock blue.

"Revenge was the first real emotion you ever felt as an immortal," I explain to him. "It consumed you, because it was all you *could* feel. It made you desperate, desperate enough to make me like you. But I am your undoing. Because I control the panaceum as much as you do."

The moment I pry it from his heart, Threydan thrashes so much, he tears part of his skin from my knives, gaining an inch.

Though the skin of his chest now starts to repair itself, the panaceum is already clasped within my hand.

"It belongs to both of us!" he shouts, spittle flying from his lips. "We control it together. We are invincible together. I saw you, bits of your life. I know you're the perfect match to take on the world with me!"

"It's your will against mine, Threydan. I fight for my crew and the lives of all the world. You fight only for yourself. Whose will do you think will win in the end?"

It begins in earnest then, that mental battle between the two of us. I close my eyes and see him, both our metaphorical hands clasped upon the panaceum. Each trying to be the one to wrest it from the other.

Except Threydan is all alone. A black void stretches out behind him. It is only his own strength that he uses to try to claim control of the panaceum.

I, however, have help. Countless individuals line up behind me: Kearan, Dimella, Jadine, Roslyn, Enwen, Taydyn, Philoria, Visylla, Dynkinar, and so many more. They add their strength to mine.

Threydan puts up the best fight he possibly can, but in the end, the battle finishes in the only way it could.

The panaceum is mine. I cut off his access to it, and I recall the powers that it granted him. He falls alone into darkness.

When I open my eyes, Threydan's head is slumped against his chest. He doesn't breathe or move. It isn't the stillness of an immortal, but the stillness of the dead.

I close his brown eyes with my fingertips.

CHAPTER 25

I STAND WITH THE panaceum in hand and survey my crew.

There is a tense moment where we stare each other down. I can only imagine how I must look: my eyes an eerie blue, blood raining from my hands, my body extra still.

I see the fear in their eyes. I am physically changed. So why shouldn't my mind be changed as well?

My eyes drift down to the panaceum, clasped gently between my fingers. It is mine to control now, not Threydan's. I close my eyes to concentrate. I can feel my essence encased within that small orb, thrumming excitedly.

I seize it like a parent does a lost child. I put my lips to the swirling blue, and for the first time in a long time, I *feel*.

Warmth spreads across my lips as I make contact. I feel that writhing mass of *me* reenter my body, settle within my heart, then disperse throughout the rest of my limbs.

The cold of this frozen land slams back into me. More so than usual since I recently went for a swim in the freezing ocean and am still damp with both salt water and newly shed blood. But I welcome that biting cold like an old friend. I missed it. I missed feeling.

I missed being alive.

When the physical changes are done, I try to cut myself off mentally from the panaceum. I hear the undead slump to the deck, lifeless once more. Within my mind's eye, I imagine a pair of scissors aiming for that tether between me and the panaceum, except as I look at it, I realize it's not alone.

There is the smallest bit of my essence contained within the orb.

And I realize that if I were to completely sever that tie, I would die. Because the object was still corrupted—still encased within Threydan's flesh when he changed me—I, too, suffer the consequences of that corruption. If I were to cut ties with it, that healing would be undone.

It has to stay with me always. I can't hand it off to Alosa and be done with it. My hand tightens in a vise around the cursed object.

When my eyes reopen, I know they are brown once more by the way all the occupants on the ship suddenly relax their postures.

I say with a slight chatter, "What do the lot of you think? Is it not time we put this place behind us for good?"

Then the cheering starts.

Drifta and Islanders embrace. Dimella whistles in a way that splits the ears. Philoria and Visylla jump into the air with arms clasped around each other. Roslyn slides down from the crow's nest and clamps herself around me, uncaring that I'm covered in blood.

Kearan meets my eyes over all the celebrating people, but his widen before they roam frantically over the crowd.

"Wait!" he shouts. "Where's Enwen? Has anyone seen Enwen?"

All sounds stop, and no one answers his question.

"Enwen!" Kearan bellows. He weaves through the dead bodies, rolling them over and checking their faces. When it becomes impossible to tell how many he's sorted through, he starts tossing over the dead and previously undead. The rest of the crew doesn't need my order to help. The lads help carry all the bodies overboard. Some of the girls go below to search. The injured are brought to me, and I heal them all in quick succession. Dimella begins roll call and takes down the names of the Drifta who have joined us.

When done, I aid in the search, finding Kearan near a pile of bodies at the front of the ship. One at a time, he rolls them off the heap with the strength of a bear.

Enwen's still form lies beneath them all.

The panaceum can do many things, but it cannot bring people back from the dead.

Kearan falls to his knees beside the body. His face is distraught. He gathers Enwen up in his arms and—

Drops him.

"You bloody bastard!" Kearan says. "I could feel you breathing, you half-wit."

Enwen cracks one eye open as he rubs the back of his head. "Maybe I lost consciousness."

"You were faking dead!"

"I wouldn't have to if you just told me how much you cared!"

Kearan looks ready to punch him. He stands, turns around, and meets my eyes. I cross my arms and look pointedly between the two of them. It takes a while, but eventually he gathers control of his temper. He reaches out a hand to Enwen and helps him to his feet. I observe as he draws Enwen close, whispers something in his ear, then releases him.

The crew goes back to cheering, and it's as though nothing happened at all.

Enwen steps back from Kearan with the biggest grin I've ever seen. "Don't worry," he says. "Your secret is safe with me. Now, go on." He pushes Kearan in my direction, not that Enwen could make him move if he didn't want to.

All the screaming and laughter of the crew fades to the background as that big, brutish man approaches me. He enfolds me in his arms, covering my poorly clothed limbs with his warmth.

"You're freezing," he says.

"I know. Isn't it exciting?"

He smiles.

"What did you say to Enwen?"

He rolls his eyes. "I told him he was my best friend."

"Was it really so hard to say?"

"I'll never hear the end of it now."

"Nor would you want to."

"Suppose not."

Then I pull his head down to mine.

There may be onlookers, but I doubt they can see anything around Kearan's form. Besides, I'm too thrilled to care. When our lips touch, a jolt of heat spreads through me. This, *this*, is how it is supposed to be. How could anyone be content with less?

Heat and soft lips, rough facial hair scratching along my palm. My limbs infusing with his body heat at every point where we touch. It is thrilling and terrifying all at once.

He tilts his head slightly, so our foreheads touch, our lips now a breath apart.

"I like this," he says.

"Then why did you stop?"

"Perhaps we should get the ship moving?"

"Perhaps you're right." I peer around his shoulder. "Dimella! Get us going."

"Aye-aye, Captain! Kearan to the helm, riggers—"

"Captain Warran can take the helm," I tell her.

"Indeed he can. Warran, take the helm! The rest of you lot, get moving! We've a long sail ahead of us."

I take Kearan's hand and pull him after me into the captain's quarters. Not a second after I get the door closed, a fist pounds against it.

My eyes slam shut, and I barely contain my sigh of frustration. I'm cold and tired and covered in blood. I want nothing more than a moment. Just one moment! Is that so much to ask for?

I slip the panaceum into my boot with my knives until I can fashion something else to carry it in, then wrench open the door and find Dynkinar on the other side.

I say nothing, just stare at her, waiting.

Dynkinar says something in Driftan, and I'm excited to find I can still translate. After all, the panaceum is still mine.

"That was well done, Captain Veshtas. I thank you for your courage and strength in doing the right thing back there. I beg another favor of you. Please return my people and the panaceum to the island."

Thoughts of kissing Kearan slip from my mind as I focus on her words. "Is that truly what you and your people want? To return to that frozen place and guard a relic that was foisted upon you so long ago?"

"It is our sacred charge."

"Last I checked, sirens weren't gods. Why don't instead you come with us, and we can discuss the artifact with the sirens. We can free your people from its influence forever."

She stares me down for some time. When she speaks again, her tone is only curious. "What kind of life would my people have?"

"My queen is good and generous. She can always use more helping hands. I will plead on your behalf for a settlement. Or you're welcome to join us. We're always looking to expand our ranks. Your crew did a fair amount of pirating while protecting that cursed place."

"We have little ones. Most of those left among us aren't fighters."

"That's not a problem. We have little ones at the queen's hideout and those who perform duties other than fighting."

Dynkinar thinks for but a moment. "And the panaceum?"

I hesitate. Do I say that I have to keep it? Won't she think that I'm being selfish and wanting it for the immortality and infinite power?

I don't. I wish with all my heart I didn't have to be dependent upon it for life, but that was the cost for using its power.

I say, "I would like to discuss it with my queen and the sirens so we can decide how best to keep it safe."

But I know Alosa, and she would trust me to keep it safe. She wouldn't even entertain the notion of letting me part from it once she knows I have to keep it close to stay alive. To keep everyone I use it on alive.

Kearan shifts slightly behind me, just a gentle movement, but I sense it. It's impossible to forget he is behind me. And I *desperately* want to speed this up.

Finally, she says, "We will go with you. It is high time we started living our own lives. We must integrate with your crew so we can begin to learn each other's language."

"I agree."

"In the meantime, I trust you will keep a close eye on the panaceum?"

"I will have it on me always."

"I thank you."

She leaves, and the door closes once more.

Though there is a fire going in the room, I am not near enough to it to feel its heat. My teeth begin to chatter, and I wrap my arms about myself.

Kearan shrugs out of his coat and throws it over my shoulders. His hands come down to rest on either side of my neck. Then there's a rapping at the door again.

Stars, but this is getting old.

Kearan strides past me and opens the door. "What?"

Jadine's voice comes from the other side. "Don't you use that barbaric tone with me, you great brute. The captain has to be freezing after everything that happened. I've had the girls boil water so she can properly bathe and heat her bones back up. Unless of course you mean to let her freeze and remain coated in blood while the two of you do whatever it is you had planned?"

Kearan turns to me. "It's for you." He strides past Jadine, exiting the room and leaving me alone.

I don't say a word as they bring in the water, filling a wooden basin. It's one of the few things that looks new in the room. The captain's quarters resemble all the others I've been in before. There's an elaborate bed piled with furs. A desk that looks like it hasn't been used in quite some time. In fact, I believe there's some sort of storage underneath where the captain's legs are meant to go. Most of the walls are covered in firewood and kindling. For what else is really necessary for survival out here?

Distantly, I wonder if I killed the captain of this ship, or if the Drifta don't really bother with such positions, since this vessel was only used to attack newcomers.

I certainly hope it's up for the voyage ahead.

The water is heavenly. After time spent truly embracing the cold once again, it is a delight to feel the comfort of being warm. Warm and surrounded by water that is not dangerous or full of the unknown. I wash the grime and blood from my body. The stink of smoke and brine and everything else is whisked away.

When done, I simply soak in the water. Only then do the events of the day really sink in. We're okay. We're going home. And Kearan . . . left.

He left without so much as a good-bye. Why?

I ponder that until I'm wrinkly and the water has run out of warmth. Then I quickly dry and dress in layers and layers of clothing. Then I turn to the fireplace. I promise myself I'll stay just until my braids dry. They've grown during the voyage, and I'll need to have them rebraided when I return home.

When I resurface again, Kearan is at the helm. Only the bare minimum of necessary crew are present on the main deck, and I hear singing coming from below.

I meet Kearan's eyes. His reveal nothing, so I leave him be and tread down to carry out my duties.

What I find below is sheer revelry.

Hands clap, voices sing, and the folks dance or laugh together. Bottles are passed around, and a Drifta I don't recognize offers me one. I take it to be polite but then pass it along when she's not looking. Even now, I always want to stay sharp.

When I spot Dimella, I find her in Taydyn's lap, one arm thrown around his neck and the other swaying to the melody of the singing Taydyn is leading. When she sees me, she straightens right away.

"Captain! I haven't been imbibing, just observing the festivities. I swear on my honor!"

"I believe you. Relax, I thought only to come down and address the crew. I thought they might need bolstering."

"Ahh, well, the little one has already seen to that."

"Roslyn?"

"Aye, she's the one who organized this. Said it's tradition after a victory among the pirate queen's crew."

"That it is." Roslyn's always eager to have a party. She loves music and dancing. I also suspect she enjoys watching the crew drink a little too much and turn into bumbling versions of themselves.

"I think it might be good for the crew to see their captain celebrating with us. Stay a while, won't you?"

"I'm not sure I know how to do that," I admit.

"It's easy, Captain!" comes another voice from behind me.

Enwen shows up wearing a new hat that he must have stolen or salvaged somewhere. He holds out a hand to me. In the past, I would have stabbed any hand presumptuous enough to assume I'd want to take it. But with Enwen, I let it slide. I wave him off.

"You'll have far much more fun without me stepping on your feet," I say.

"Suit yourself. How about you, little lass?"

Roslyn giggles as Enwen tosses her into the air before returning her to her feet and spinning her about. I tap my foot gently to the music, which is really the only thing I'm comfortable doing in such a situation.

I'm not like other people. My emotions aren't so easily visible on my face, nor am I comfortable showing them most of the time. I don't know how to be a part of things, because I never thought I was worthy of happiness.

And now things have . . . changed. It's confusing, but all is well for now.

I stay at the party for several hours, just to observe how everyone is integrating. Those from the Seventeen Isles may not know the language of the Drifta, but that doesn't stop them from dancing together. Threydan's shadow has been cast over them since the day they were born. While they don't know us well, we freed them from being prisoners to that island forever. That's a cause worth celebrating over.

Even old Warran smiles now and again and claps along when he thinks no one is looking. Jadine, who must be the closest to his age among all my crew, pulls him into a swinging dance that he doesn't refuse.

When I've judged that I've stayed long enough, I return to my quarters. Neither Warran nor Dynkinar has tried to fight me for them, so I take that as a good sign that they've decided I've earned them. Thank goodness, because I desperately need some time alone.

With the undead following me for who knows how long, I need to be somewhere I can breathe and be unobserved for once.

And then someone is at the door, yet again.

"I wish to sleep," I say, "so unless it's urgent, you can return another time."

The footsteps retreat.

But I recognize that gait, so I rush to the door and open it.

Kearan halts at the sound with his back to me.

"You can come in," I say. "I thought you were someone else."

"Are you expecting someone else?" he asks as he turns.

"Only people who need things from me."

"What makes you think I don't need anything?"

I am not used to this. There is a charge in the air, something building that will eventually reach its limit and then ... something will happen.

I don't know how to answer that, so I just step aside, a silent invitation for him to enter.

He takes it.

I shut the door before going to the fireplace, striding right past him. "Having gone only a few days without it, I suddenly find myself addicted to the heat."

"That'll pass once we're back in the tropics, I imagine."

"Perhaps."

At the silence that fills the room, I ask, "Why did you leave earlier?"

"You needed to heat up."

Yes, and I thought he'd intended to help with that.

"You were covered in blood from head to foot," he adds.

Ah, I suppose I was rather filthy. "That's all?" I ask.

"No, but that's all you need to know of it."

I glance over my shoulder, find his heated stare on my face. Any thoughts I might have had about his intentions quickly fall away.

"Why?" I ask.

"The rest of it doesn't paint me in a very kind light."

I laugh lightly. "I showed you all of my dark spaces. Do you really think you could say anything to scare me?"

"Aye, I do. But since you asked—" He approaches the fire until he stands beside me. He raises his hands to touch the heat with his fingertips.

"I also left so I wouldn't do something stupid. You were shivering and covered in so much blood, but I wanted you all the same. Would have taken whatever you offered right in that moment and relished in it. Then Jadine appeared and reminded me what a brute I was being, taking no heed of your own well-being. I left to collect my head."

I swallow. "I see you cleaned up yourself."

"Nothing like cold water to clear a man's head and turn his mind to better thoughts."

"I see."

He's not so close to me that our shoulders brush. But I could reach out and touch him if I wanted to.

"Why did you think I left?" he asks.

"I honestly had no idea. You might have guessed that I have no experience when it comes to these kinds of things."

He turns, rotating his body to face me. "What kinds of things are those?"

"You know all too well," I say, keeping my face on the fire.

"Aye, but I want to hear you say it."

"You're not going to."

"That's a shame."

I take a deep breath and let it out. "I don't know how to do this."

"You're doing it right now. You're talking to me. Though I admit it might be better for the both of us if you'd deign to look at me, too."

I turn only my head to meet his eyes.

"There's no right or wrong way to do this. Just talk to me, and I'll talk to you. That's all we need. Honesty and communication. The rest we can figure out along the way."

I feel restless, so I reach for a knife and start twirling it about. "I've spent my whole life hating men. I don't know how to suddenly start liking one."

"That can't be true. What about Wallov?"

"Wallov is the exception, and only because I've observed him so closely with his daughter. You have to understand, aside from my father, my experiences with men have been limited to the man who slaughtered my family, the boys on the streets who preyed on little girls, and the pirate king—who abused Alosa beyond my comprehension."

There's also what happened to Niridia, but that's not my story to tell.

"My point is," I continue, "that I'm used to seeing evil in men. I looked high and low for it in you, but I couldn't find it. So I thought to scare you off by showing you the evil in me. That didn't work, either."

He smiles softly. "You gave it your best effort to prevent us from happening. I commend you for it."

I fight off a laugh. Kearan's eyes trace my lips, taking in my smiles like they're sunshine.

"I don't like that it was you who made me see I shouldn't be so hard on myself," I say. "Alosa tried to tell me. Mandsy and Niridia both tried. But I never told them the full story. I don't think I *could* believe it until someone knew the whole truth of it. I don't like that it was finally you. A man. I don't need a man to prove anything to me."

He takes some time to process that. "The thing is that you love Alosa and those girls you fought with. Their good opinions mean the world to you. I was expendable. My good opinion wasn't something you wanted. You lost nothing by telling me."

"No, instead I gained everything, including a desire for you to think well of me."

And more importantly, a reason to think well of myself.

"It's all right to need a little help sometimes," he says. "You must realize that you helped me long before I helped you. Or have you forgotten? If anything, I owed you one."

The drinking. I was what made him finally stop and take back his life.

I *had* forgotten. I'd been too caught up in accepting so much from him. But I saved him just as much as he ever saved me.

That's what a partnership looks like.

That's what *love* looks like.

That word still makes me uncomfortable. I can't say that I'm ready for it yet. But I am ready to see where this goes. To try. To open myself to someone who will not think less of me for being me.

"Almost forgot," Kearan says. He goes to the floor where I discarded his coat before climbing into the bath. He reaches into one of the many pockets and pulls out the last thing I'd expected to see.

It's the tricorne he gifted me our first day at sea.

"How did you . . . ?"

"I snagged it before *Vengeance* went down. I hoped you might accept it eventually."

"Where have you been keeping it all this time?"

"Close to my heart."

The answer is ridiculous, but I adore it anyway. He reaches his hand out and puts the tricorne on my head. It gets caught on my ponytail, so I undo it and regather my hair closer to my neck.

"I like you," I say, even though the words are as sharp to my consciousness as any blade is to my body.

"I like you more," he says.

"That may have been true once. I don't think so anymore."

"No?"

I step closer, so we're sharing the same breath.

"No."

And I finally take the kiss I want.

Or rather, we share it.

CHAPTER 26

IT'S NOT AT ALL like the last few times.

Then I was changed by the panaceum or weakened with an injury or high off the thrill of victory and covered in blood.

But now? Now I'm fully myself.

And he kisses me in the way a pirate assassin ought to be kissed.

With fervor.

His arms wrap around me, trapping me against him. One lands on the small of my back while the other presses between my shoulder blades. At first, I worry about what to do with my arms, but they find the most natural position around his neck. All the better to keep his mouth fused to mine.

He smells of salt and leather and soap. He tastes like water. He feels like death.

Yes, death. That sweet, sweet moment just before I end someone. When I know I'm relishing in vengeance yet again. He is that feeling magnified by a hundred. A sense of accomplishment and rightness and *mine*.

He is mine just as much as those lives I take.

But he burns with life. I feel the heat of him from my head to my toes. It's more effective than any fire. Makes me feel alive in a way temperature can only hint at.

This is a dance I enthusiastically take part in. The dance of our lips to the music of our rapid breathing.

I know how to issue out threats with the merest of gestures, but I didn't realize how my blood could pump faster when he moves his hands to my waist, moves his thumbs along the straight line of my stomach.

And when he lifts me onto the desk, I suck in a breath of air before he captures my lips again. His hands are on my legs now, widening them so he can slip between and press our bodies together once more.

That's when I finally uncoil my arms from around him so I can do some exploring of my own. I wrap my hands around his biceps to feel the strength of his arms from atop his clothes. I clasp my ankles together behind his back, pull him flush against me, let my fingers roam up and down his back.

That night, no more knocks come to the door. No, everyone lets their captain get her rest.

Except that night, I get none.

I'm too busy kissing the man who loves me.

THE DRIFTA LOWER NETS into the water to catch food for everyone during the journey. The Islanders crew the ship. Everyone does their part to help us reach home.

The below-freezing temperatures drift away until it's only the normal cold of the north. We are close to reaching the Seventeen Isles. Perhaps only a day or two's sail now.

The entire journey has been smooth and quick. Not a single skirmish to be found on or off the ship.

And then, "Ships on the horizon!" Roslyn's shout rouses the whole crew to full alertness.

I join her up in the crow's nest, Dimella's spyglass in tow.

What I find brings a smile to my lips.

"Who is it?" Roslyn asks.

"It's the queen. She came for us."

"Looks like we didn't need her help after all."

"Nope. We saved ourselves in the end, but it'll be nice to explain the situation to her sooner rather than later."

Roslyn nods. "Do you think my papa is with her?"

"Only death would have stopped him from being on that ship."

Roslyn thinks on this. "Suppose I best work on my apology, then."

"You've had months to do so," I point out.

"Aye, and I haven't thought of anything yet."

"Just try for honesty and sincerity."

"Sincerity?"

"Don't fake anything."

"Oh."

I leave her to think on that and slide back down to the deck.

"It's Alosa," I say to Dimella and those near her. "The *Ava-lee* leads five ships toward us."

"Thank the stars!" Enwen says.

"Aye. You might be meeting them soon if we can't find a way to let her know it's us. Don't forget, we're on a foreign ship now."

Dimella says, "We haven't our colors. They went down with the ship."

"We'll need something the queen will recognize," Kearan puts in.

And as I eye him, I know just what to do.

"Your coat," I say, gesturing to Kearan. Alosa is all too familiar with it. "Off with it, and we'll hoist it high."

By the time we're close enough to the pirate queen's fleet to make out the flags on all her ships, Kearan's coat is strung high, flapping in the breeze. We've explained the situation to the Drifta, and they grow slightly on edge. I don't blame them. They're about to meet a foreign monarch. No one would expect the likes of Alosa.

A few hours pass before we're finally upon each other. Alosa surrounds us with her ships before lining up the *Ava-lee* with our vessel. A gangplank is lowered, and the queen treads across the distance between the two ships with all the grace and beauty one would expect from a half siren. Two men walk just behind her. The first is, of course, the frantic Wallov, whose eyes scan the ship in search of his daughter. The other is Riden, the queen's consort.

Alosa's crew follows after them. They fan out along the edges of the ship, as is protocol when boarding a captured vessel.

Alosa scans the entirety of the ship, taking the measure of all the unfamiliar faces. When her gaze lands on me, she strides forward and embraces me. In my ear, she asks, "Roslyn?"

"Alive and well. She's at her usual post."

Alosa claps me on the back before turning to Wallov. "I think you'll find your daughter up in the crow's nest."

He takes off toward the mainmast. I look up at the top, where just Roslyn's eyes are peeking over, watching her papa advance with a desperation that almost tears at my heart.

To me, the queen says, "I see you've brought back with you more than I sent you out for."

"Aye, Captain. There were lots of folks that needed saving."

"From?"

"A siren artifact and a man's greed."

At that, Dynkinar steps forward, her little translator in tow. It makes sense that she would rather one of her own speak for her than have me be the go-between. She bows her head in a sign of respect, and Alosa does the same.

"I am Dynkinar, last surviving Speaker for my people," the boy translates. "We are blessed to meet you, Queen Alosa. Captain Sorinda has told us much about you and your greatness."

"Greetings, Dynkinar. Perhaps we'd better find a place to talk so you can both tell me the whole story?"

We all nod.

"Riden?" Alosa says.

"Aye?"

"Assess the crew aboard this vessel. Have the healers tend to any wounded and make sure all their bellies are filled."

"Aye-aye."

Alosa won't know yet that I've already healed the injured, and I don't correct her. The time for that is not yet.

Alosa takes my arm and leads me across the gangplank toward her captain's quarters. Dynkinar follows behind us. Alosa says, "Have I mentioned how much I love having him as my new first mate? Bossing him around is such a delight, and he's so good at following orders."

I look over my shoulder. Riden has gripped Enwen in a fierce hug. Kearan stands not far off, arms crossed, as he waits his turn.

"He might like it more than you do," I point out.

"Then we're both lucky, eh?"

"Aye."

When we're behind closed doors, the whole story comes out of me. Dynkinar offers her side of things, sharing a brief history of her people and their sacred charge. I don't stop until I get to the part where we set sail for the journey home.

Though Alosa looks perfectly perplexed, I know she believes every word. "My mother has never once mentioned the existence of siren artifacts, but then again, she's not good at offering up information unless I ask for it. Just doesn't occur to her the things I might want to know. I'll set up a meeting with her straightaway when we return. We need to know if there could be any more of these artifacts lying in wait about the seas. What did you do with the panaceum?"

I procure it from my boot so she can look at it. She tries to reach for it, but I say, "There was a cost. I can't let it be parted from me, else I will die. Maybe Kearan, too." The object was still in Threydan's heart when I used its power to heal Kearan. The rest of the injured were healed after I freed the object and killed Threydan, but Kearan and I will depend on it for as long as we both live.

Zarian translates for Dynkinar, and she narrows her eyes slightly.

So I explain in detail what I know to be true about my connection to the object.

I finish with "I don't want it, but it's what's keeping me alive. I have to have it on me at all times."

Alosa turns to Dynkinar. "I can imagine how you feel about that, but the four of us in this room are the only ones who know where the panaceum is. If we keep it that way, it will remain safe. I trust Sorinda with my life, and it would seem she has already preserved yours once. Is this going to be a problem for you?"

Dynkinar listens to Zarian's translation carefully. She meets my eyes.

In Driftan, Dynkinar says directly to me, "Let no more blood be spilled between our peoples. You have saved us from Threydan after we tried to kill you. You have proven yourself to be trustworthy when he offered you immortality. For that, I will allow the artifact to remain in your safekeeping. But if word should get out about it, we will need to revisit this discussion."

"Understood," I say.

Alosa looks at me curiously.

"Another perk of having the artifact."

"Very nice."

"Dynkinar agrees."

"Excellent. You've done well, Captain."

I wince.

"You disagree?" she asks.

"Only at being called Captain. I don't care for the position or the title."

She sighs wistfully. "I hoped a journey like this would change your mind. I do so need more captains I can trust. But I understand. You are who you are, and I shall not ask you to captain a vessel again unless I grow desperate once more."

My relief is palpable. I want nothing more than to return to my duties as assassin.

"Do you have a new job for me?" I ask.

"Oh, no. You haven't even finished this one yet. That vessel and all those upon it are in your charge until we return home."

I try not to cringe. A month still of captaining.

"And then, when we return to Queen's Keep," Alosa continues, "you're to rest from your travels and recuperate. We'll also have to see about acquiring a new ship for you." At the face I make, she adds, "Purely for emergencies, mind you."

My lips twitch. "Then I won't object if it's only for emergencies. I'll try not to sink this one."

"Technically, my people sank it," Zarian says. "You did the best you could."

"Aye," Alosa says. "That she did, and it was more than enough. Sounds to me like she stopped a threat to the entire world before it could even leave the island."

"That she did," the translator says on Dynkinar's behalf. "I am eager to learn more about the incredible individuals within your ranks, Captain Kalligan. If any of them are half as talented as Sorinda, then I don't think the King of the Undersea stood a chance in the first place."

Embarrassment heats my cheeks, and I look away so the pair don't notice.

"I have only the finest working for me." I can hear Alosa's smile in the words. "As for you and the Drifta, we would be happy to have you join us at the keep. We are still building our fortifications there. Perhaps you could occupy another section of the island and build the first town?"

"I'll take my leave of you for now and discuss this with my people." Dynkinar and the boy leave, leaving me and Alosa alone in her captain's quarters.

It is a comfort to be in such a familiar setting. I've spent years of my life sailing on this ship. She is more familiar to me than any other place in the world. I have hidden in her shadows and found every nook and cranny there is for secreting stuff away. This ship was the first place that felt like home again after I lost my family.

"You look like you wish to say something," Alosa prompts.

Where to begin? "I . . . changed while on the island," I start.

"Yes, you mentioned how the panaceum made you temporarily immortal."

"No, I mean, me. In here." I point first to my head and then to my heart. "I don't know how to say this, but I think I might . . . *be* with Kearan."

Alosa blinks twice. "What do you mean *be* with Kearan?"

I take a deep breath. This is Alosa. I can tell her anything. Her good opinion of me won't change. I have to trust that. So I tell her my story. The full story of what happened to my family. What happened with Kearan. Where we're at now. I end with "So now we're together, and it's strange, but I'm just trying to take it one day at a time."

Alosa shifts slightly, but she doesn't break eye contact. "That's a lot of information you just threw at me, but let me see if I've got this right. You've lived your life at a distance because you didn't think you were worthy of anything more. Because of that little girl who died in your stead. But you've had a change of heart, thanks to Kearan. Also, you are *with* him. As in there's kissing and stuff happening. Have I got that right?"

"More or less."

She takes a moment to let it all sink in. "I'm sorry I didn't make you feel as though you could trust me with the story of your childhood. I should have done better—"

"No, it wasn't anything you did. I cared too much about your good opinion. I didn't think what I did was forgivable. I was stuck for a long time. And then you forced me and Kearan together on this voyage, and it was the best thing that's happened to me since the day you found me and convinced me to join your crew."

Alosa smiles. "If that's the case, then I'm happy for you. I'm happy for you both."

"Thank you."

"And of course I don't hold your past against you or think less of you for it. If anything, I'm more astonished by you than ever. You're a rare soul, Sorinda. I'm proud to know you and call you a friend."

I feel my face softening, so I turn it toward the floorboards. "There is one more thing I wanted to discuss. I think that perhaps I might like to train some of the girls."

"Train? As pirates?"

"Assassins."

"Stars," Alosa says. "I'm just trying to imagine more than one of you at the keep. The land king will shat his royal britches once he hears of it."

"I have your permission, then?"

"Of course. I think it's a wonderful idea. I'll spread the word and get you recruits. Besides, if this means you'll spend more time at the keep, then I'm all for it."

We return to the Drifta's ship, where Alosa's crew is catching up with friends who've been apart during our journey. Riden finds us and takes position at Alosa's other side.

"There aren't any injured, but the crew seemed grateful for a change in food options. I understand there was quite a lot of fish being eaten. The Drifta didn't know what to make of the bread we had with us. Do they not grow wheat? Just how cold was it up there?"

"Cold enough to freeze the blood in your veins," I answer.

Riden makes a face before throwing his arm over Alosa. He pulls her in close and kisses the side of her head.

"How is the situation with your brother?" I ask him. "What of Mandsy and Niridia?"

Alosa answers for him. "I'm expecting an update on the situation very soon. Last I heard, they were close to apprehending Draxen. It's taken an unusually long time. I'm not sure what to make of that, but I trust that Niridia will get the job done, especially with Mandsy watching her back."

"Aye," Riden says. "Draxen doesn't stand a chance."

DURING THE NEXT LEG of the voyage, Kearan and I have a talk about the panaceum and how our lives now depend on its proximity to me at all times. We're in agreement that we won't use it to prolong our lives. We only need the one to share together. That's plenty.

A lot has changed at Queen's Keep since I last saw it. Half the fortifications are done. There are barracks housing different crews, a dock has been furnished out to sea for the ships to anchor off of, and the kitchens and queen's quarters are fully done.

The builders are still working on the training grounds, where Alosa says she'll have them make a special section just for me and my group of aspiring assassins. Just yesterday, she sent me the sign-ups for the hopefuls.

Twelve girls and one lad, that translator Zarian.

As I go over the names again, Kearan looks over my shoulder.

"Naturally, Roslyn managed to sign up first," I say.

"She's learning from the best. Of course she's excited. What will you start them with? Knifework?"

"Footwork. If you can't get close enough for the kill, there's no need to bother with a blade."

"Hmm." Kearan leaps behind me and tries to wrap an arm around my neck, but I sensed the move before he made it. I duck, and his arm brushes nothing but air. I have a knife out and pressed against his side before he can do anything else.

"You're quicker than lightning," he says, with that full grin that makes me want to return it. I don't usually, though. Kearan prefers to coax them from me anyway.

"Maybe you're slower than mud."

"That tongue is quick, too. Maybe you should teach them that as well."

"An assassin's job should be done without any talking."

"Then what else will you teach them?"

"How to be fearless."

He cocks his head to one side. "How does one teach that?"

"You find a way to conquer what you're afraid of. You face it over and over again until it doesn't affect you anymore. As a small child, I used to fear the dark, but I have a mantra that helped me stay strong. *You can't be afraid of the dark when you're the monster lurking in the shadows.*"

"Bloody hell, Sorinda."

"I know, but I think I'll amend it now. I've learned more about myself, and I don't think I need to be a monster anymore."

He wraps his arms around me, and this time I let him as he pulls me in for an embrace. "You were never a monster."

"No, but I liked to think of myself that way. It helped me to feel strong. Made everything all right as long as I was taking down worse monsters."

"Perhaps that is what we should call your new trainees. Sorinda's monsters."

I smile. "I've no doubt I'll think of them as such by the end of each session."

"Whatever you think of them, I promise it's nothing compared to what they'll think of you. You will give them hell every day and make them work for it. As well you should."

He leans in for a kiss, and I return it.

"Shall we go down to dinner?" he asks.

I nod and turn to blow out the candle of our shared rooms. He finds my hand in the dark and leads me into the hallway.

I've learned it's okay to lean on others for strength, but it's even more important to find your own strength from within. I discovered mine once I realized it was okay for me to exist without guilt any longer. It's okay for me to share myself and my knowledge with others.

And that's when it comes to me.

You can't be afraid of the dark when you're the light keeping the shadows at bay.

ACKNOWLEDGMENTS

I ALWAYS MEANT TO come back to this world to tell Sorinda and Kearan's story. I'm so thankful to the team at Feiwel and Friends for allowing me to write this book. Thank you especially to Holly and Brittany for fighting so hard for my pirate books. My gratitude also goes out to Jean, Gaby, Leigh Ann, Dawn, Celeste, Morgan, Kristin, Kaitlin, Ebony, Jordan, Samira, Tovah, the audio team, and everyone else behind the scenes who I didn't work with directly.

Thank you to the team at BookEnds Literary, especially my agent, Rachel Brooks. I can't tell you how much it meant to me that you read this book so fast and showed excitement about it before anyone else did!

Thank you to Caitlyn McFarland and Mikki Helmer for brainstorming ideas with me in the early stages of this book. I had a hard time organizing my thoughts, and your feedback was instrumental in helping me cement the plot structure. Caitlyn, I especially appreciated the reminder that people are thirsty for Imhotep.

Thank you to Grace Wynter and others who wished to remain anonymous, for your early reading of this book.

Thank you to BookTok. You guys are what made it possible for me to write this new book so soon. Your enthusiasm for this series was contagious, and it spread word of Alosa faster than anything else could.

Thank you to all the other social media folks on Instagram and Twitter and everywhere else for talking about my books, reviewing, and spreading your love of reading.

Thank you to Alisa and Johnny, who watch Rosy for me so I can travel and do book events. Thank you to the rest of my family for your continued support and encouragement.

Thank you to Bridget for helping me put more time into my writing. I appreciate all that you do!

Thank you to bookstores and booksellers, libraries and librarians, who do so much to get my books into the hands of readers.

Thank you to you, dear reader, for picking this one up.

On to the next manuscript!

BONUS CONTENT

Turn the page to read a chapter with handwritten
annotations from author Tricia Levenseller,
sharing insight and inspiration for the opening
scene of *Vengeance of the Pirate Queen*.

At first, I was worried I'd have trouble finding Sorinda's voice, but the moment I sat down to write, this first sentence popped out.

CHAPTER 1

first sentence popped out.

↓

YOU CAN'T BE AFRAID of the dark when you're the monster lurking in the shadows.

she had a rough childhood

I've lived by these words since I was five years old. They've served me well through many cold nights spent alone. They're doubly useful when I find myself killing, which is more often than not. The pirate queen has many enemies, and I'm the one she sends to take care of them.

Remember this guy!

Tonight's target is the pirate lord Vordan Serad.

This is the first time in my career I've had to track down the same target twice. I don't like it. Would have been far better if we'd gutted Vordan the last time we caught him, but the late pirate king had wanted him alive.

Vordan's been busy since he escaped. He commissioned a ship under a false name, hired himself a new crew, and slowly began to grow his prestige, starting on the island of Butana. I have no doubt he hoped to raise enough forces to eventually usurp Alosa's throne.

He should have known better. He should have kept running after he

for me, the only thing cooler than a pirate is an assassin pirate.

managed to free himself during the scuffle between the land king and for-mer pirate king. Might have had a nice, long life that way.

Instead, he has no idea that I'm curled up under his bed.

He prepares for the evening by lantern light. With my limited view from the ground, I watch him kick off his boots and throw them in the direction of the closet. A white bit of clothing joins them. His shirt, I think. Thankfully, he keeps his britches on. He riffles through one of his pockets, and a soft *chink* sounds a moment later. He must have pulled out that coin he likes to fiddle with and placed it on the bedside table.

Vordan seats himself on the floor, leaning his back against the edge of the bed, mere feet from where I hide. My heart pounds out a too-fast rhythm at the threat of discovery.

I could do it now, I suppose. Just roll over, grab my dagger from its sheath at my side, and slice his throat.

But Alosa wants him to know on whose orders he's being killed, and I'll be in a better position to keep him quiet if I can attack from above rather than below.

Killing is easy. The tricky part is being quiet. Being patient. Waiting for the right moment. That's what makes me good at my job. Being an assassin is not always about the easy kill. It's about the best kill.

I hold perfectly still and watch as Vordan stretches out his bad leg. Alosa once used her siren song to force him to jump from a two-story height. I'll bet he thinks about her every time it stiffens from the cold. He leans over to rub at the muscles near his knee before standing. He takes a drink from something at his nightstand, puts out the lantern, then sits on the bed.

I extend my arm until it is only inches from Vordan's left ankle. My fingers tiptoe ever closer, until my pointer finger is directly behind his

Handwritten margin notes:

Remember him now?

how creepy she is.

I just adore

yeah, Alosa's not letting him live after all he did to her & Riden

So, so creepy.

heel. It would be so easy to slice his Achilles tendon. He'd never walk again. Instead, I draw circles against the wood slats on the floor, allowing Vordan to think the last thoughts he will ever have. Eventually, he sighs, pulls his legs onto the bed, and fidgets with the covers.

When he finally goes still, I listen to his breathing, waiting for it to slow. Then I wait some more. If I stay my hand until my marks are deeply asleep, they're less likely to rouse from any soft sounds I might make in the room. I don't want them to wake until I'm in position. Until it's too late to fight back. Not to mention, the longer I wait, the more likely it is that everyone else in the estate will be asleep.

I slide out from under the bed and stand, watching Vordan's sleeping form for any movement. When his breathing doesn't change, I draw a dagger and tread to the bed. Scant light from the moon slants through the window. I stand on the opposite side of the bed so my shadow isn't cast upon Vordan. He sleeps on his back, hands at his sides atop the covers, face pointed at the ceiling.

He's unremarkable in appearance, with a medium height and build. Brown hair and beard. No distinguishing features. It's how he stays hidden. Stays alive, really. We pirates don't typically have long life spans. At least not under the former king's rule.

As I let my dagger drift closer to his throat, I replace the face before me with one from my memories. One with lighter skin, a beauty mark on the left side of his forehead, a single gold hoop high up on one ear. Straw-colored hair and a clean-shaven face. A cleft in the middle of the chin.

My first kill.

I pretend they all are so I can savor it over and over again.

As instructed, I let my dagger rest on the skin of Vordan's neck. His eyelids twitch twice before shooting open. Without moving his neck, his eyes veer to the right so he can take me in. "You," he says. "You're one of hers."

"The pirate queen sends her best wishes. You'll need them where you're going."

"Wai—"

Before he can finish the request, I slice deeply, nicking the carotid artery. Blood drenches the sheets, drips quietly on the floor.

And I watch as the life leaves Samvin Carroter for the eighty-ninth time.

I clean my dagger on an unmarred section of blanket and sheathe it. Then I retrieve my rapier from under the bed and reattach it to my waist. Most pirates carry cutlasses, but I prefer the speed and dexterity of the rapier. Besides, I am noble-born, and I like to retain that remembrance of my family.

I exit Vordan's room, letting myself into one of the hallways of the exquisite mansion he'd been living in. He killed the family who owned it. Bribed or threatened all the staff. Set up what few men he has in the comfy rooms. It was the pattern I had to look for while tracking him down.

He learned the first time that if he stayed in one place, Alosa was sure to find him, so he'd take up residence in some fancy estate, stay there a month at most, frequenting the big cities and rallying supporters. Then he'd move to a new city on a new island within the Seventeen Isles and do it all over again.

Unfortunately for him, a discernible pattern is just as bad as staying in one place.

The door makes the softest of clicks as I shut it behind me before treading down the carpet-clad floor. I round the hallway and take the

It's a book rule. Things never go according to plan, but Sorinda's weirdly okay with it.

main staircase, stepping toward the outside of the steps, where they're

less likely to creak. Three levels down and I reach the main floor.

Thinking to leave the same way I entered, I pass through the kitchens.

"Hello?" a voice calls out, and I drop into a crouch.

Everyone is supposed to be asleep, but someone must have grown hungry in the night.

I might not be done killing. The thought sends a delightful shot of warmth to my sword arm, my fingers itching to reach for a weapon. As I crawl behind the nearest table, my heart races again. It's a wild percussion that I've grown used to, even craved at times. The thrill of the hunt.

Tell me you're an adrenaline junkie without telling me you're an adrenaline junkie.

"Did you hear something?" the same voice says.

"No, but it was probably Miss Nyles coming by the kitchens. Probably turned tail the second she spotted us."

The first man grunts. "We gave her a good beating last night, didn't we?"

"Not so good as the tupping we gave her the night before that."

Don't like your sentence ou

Their laughter fills the corners of the room like a disease infecting a body. I peer over the edge of the table to get a look at them. Two brutes, mostly dark silhouettes next to the meager candle they have on the table between them. They're spearing cold meats with a knife before filling their gobs and passing a flask back and forth.

I could creep past them silently, leave the mansion with no one the wiser.

But I'm not about to do that after the conversation I just overheard. It's a risk to attack with two of them fully alert, but it's one I'm willing to take.

I move under the table and push between two chairs. I am no more than a shadow as I waltz behind the pair and draw my sword. I strike the

Sorinda doesn't tolerate bad men living.

•• 5 ••

bigger one first, smacking him on the back of the head with the pommel of my rapier. The second turns and manages the first note of a yell as I slam his head down onto the counter. Both don't rise again after slumping to the floor, unconscious.

Footsteps pound above my head, roused from the short-lived sound, and I have a choice to make. I can still slip away, lose them in the winding city streets.

Or . . .

I stare at the duo on the floor.

Or I can see vengeance done.

It isn't really a choice.

I just love it when she thinks things like this.

I slip back into the dark entryway once I ascertain no one has reached this level yet. A banister lines the stairs, with rails connecting it to each step. I reach out to see if my hands will fit into the spaces between each rail.

They do.

GH is fit as hell

As the men race down the winding stairs, lanterns held aloft, I climb them from the side with my arms, hauling myself up rail after rail. Reach, grip, pull. Repeat.

My legs are too high off the ground by the time the men hit the main floor for them to notice me. Four individuals cross underneath me to reach the kitchens. I let myself drop when the last one is in just the right position. He collapses to the ground under my weight, and I snap his neck before he can rise.

Poor guy; never had a chance.

The first two men are already in the kitchens, but the third turns at the sound of his crewman falling. I slice his throat with the tip of my sword before he can make sense of the scene in front of him. I flick the

Don't worry; she's not done with them yet.

blood from my rapier as I race for the doorway, placing my back against the wall just beside it. I sheathe my sword and draw my dagger.

"Two knocked out cold in here," one of the men says. "Sound the alarm."

The one following orders dashes out of the kitchens. I grip his arm, throw him against the wall, and rake the blade across his throat.

"Hello?" the remaining man calls out, likely having seen his crewman pulled from out of his line of sight before the doors closed.

Why do people call out a greeting when something highly suspicious happens? Do they expect us monsters to announce ourselves?

He follows up with "Who's there?"

I adjust the grip on my dagger as I wait to see what he'll do.

He shouts for help, cluing me in to his approximate location in the kitchens.

I throw the doors open wide, sight my mark, and fling my blade. The dagger lands true, embedding in his throat. I don't retrieve it just yet. Time is precious now.

I veer to the right, where the hidden servants' stairs rest. Meanwhile, men rouse from their beds and burst out into the hallways. I see them on each landing as I make my way back to the top level. The dark works to my advantage. I'm used to being in its caress. I doubt there's a soul alive who has better night vision than I do. While I can see the outlines of Vordan's men, they haven't a clue I'm a handful of feet away.

Not a soul even looks in my direction. No one thinks to use the servants' stairs. They might not even know they're tucked away here. These are murderers, thieves, and all other manner of foul scum. They're not used to the layout of fancy accommodations such as these. And since

Handwritten margin notes:

Honestly though.

This was a fun trait I decided to give her.

Oh, also don't mess with girls with knives.

But Sorinda did her homework and scouted the building ahead of time like a smart assassin.

Vordan kept the staff on hand, his men would never have had occasion to use this route.

I reach the third floor, where Vordan's corpse has started rotting, and peek through bedroom doors one by one.

When I find a man who wasn't roused by the shouting, I enter, tread to the bed, and slice open his neck. It's not the most creative way to end a life, but it is the most efficient with the least amount of effort. And I have many more throats to slit, so I've got to reserve my energy.

Pacing herself. So smart! (And creepy)

"Six down!" someone from below shouts. "Spread out and search the mansion, and you there, go rouse the captain."

"Let's tell the assassin about what we're about to do it!" everything we're about to do it!"

I bolt back for Vordan's rooms and slip under the bed. The blood has stopped trickling. It's partially congealed on the floor at the opposite side of the bed.

The door sways open, and boot-clad feet reach Vordan's resting place. "Captain, there's an intruder." He steps back, likely because his hand has come away sticky.

I pull his feet out from under him, climb atop his wriggling body, and prepare to go for the throat.

At the last moment, I turn my hand to the side and land a punch with my knuckles still wrapped around the dagger, right where Mandsy taught me to if the intent was to render someone unconscious.

The lad can't be more than twelve. He's all height with no muscles to his limbs. He's fallen in with a bad crowd, but even I don't murder children.

Back out in the hallway, I creep through the house, quieter than a ghost. I hear doors slamming beneath me, swords coming out of their sheaths, and men murmuring to one another. I search the rest of the

She has lines she won't cross, even as a killer.

bedrooms on this floor, slitting three more throats, before returning to the servants' stairs and taking them down to the next level.

With just my head peering down the hallway, I watch a pirate enter into a bedroom to secure it. I follow after him, sneak up behind him, and cover his mouth with one hand while my dagger rakes across his throat. Back out in the hallway, I note that only some of Vordan's crew are holding lanterns. Should they see my silhouette, I will merely look like another pirate searching through the mansion just like everyone else.

I follow another man into another room, employing the same tactic as before. This one gets down on his knees to look under the bed and doesn't hear me as I come up behind him. Blood trickles onto my fingers from the knife as I right myself, so I take the time to wipe it and my hands off on the bedsheets before exiting again.

Two figures come toward me down the hall without their own light sources, so I flatten myself against the wall to let them pass.

I pull a second knife from my person as I follow them into another room. The first man gets a dagger thrown to the back where his heart rests beneath the skin and muscle. The second turns, but I'm already launching myself at him, slitting his throat with the second knife.

As I rise, I try to remember the last time I killed so many men in a single night. In fact, I don't think it's happened before.

I'm making new memories.

Some men continue up to the third floor, where they're about to find more dead. Others leave for the first floor. I follow the men upstairs first.

I reach the last one in line, covering his mouth as I kill him and catching him before he can land on the floor with a thud. The next one

I cannot even express how fun this chapter was to write.

They've got to be wondering how many knives she has...

She's basically Batman.

is too heavy for me to catch as he lands, so I flatten myself into one of the closed doorways as a couple of men look behind them.

"Shit!" someone says. "Find 'em."

I'm not sure if he said *Find him* or *Find them*. Should I be insulted or flattered? I launch from my hiding place when someone passes by and slam his head against the opposite wall. I hear the hammer of a pistol being cocked back, so I turn the man, letting him take the shot.

Tee hee!

I reach for another dagger before I let the body drop and throw it at the person holding the lantern. The light sputters out as they fall.

More footsteps pound up the stairs, bringing more lanterns with them, and I drop to the ground, as though I'm just another dead body among the mess.

"Where is he?" one of the newcomers asks.

"He vanishes like smoke," someone from the first party says.

Definitely offended.

The men tread past me, and I hold perfectly still. One of my arms is looped over my head, concealing my long ponytail from discovery if anyone tries to look down.

A boot knocks into me, but I hold back a grunt as I wait for the newcomers to pass me by.

When they do, I descend upon them one at a time. Slitting throats. Bashing heads. Catching bodies. Kill. Repeat. Kill.

She deals death the way dancers perform a routine.

My hands are slippery with blood again. My front is covered with it from all the blood spatter. I dodge a swinging cutlass on my way to deliver an attack to another pirate. He blocks my first strike but doesn't expect me to deliver a second one so quickly. It pierces his heart.

I spin as the man I dodged comes charging at me with his sword raised; I leap aside but land atop one of the fallen bodies, and my ankle

Bound to happen.

I just love how resourceful she is.

rolls. When I land on my good leg, I pivot in place, ducking a slash and stabbing the man in the gut. I finish him with another slice to the throat.

Then the mansion is perfectly silent.

I rise, take a look around at the carnage. A throbbing pain lances up my leg when I try to put my full weight on my ankle. It slows me down as I retrieve all my daggers and find unmarred cloth to wipe them clean on. I scrub at my hands, though they're still red when I'm done. Dried blood has worked its way into the creases of my skin. I sheathe my rapier and daggers into their respective holsters. I pull my braided hair out of its loose ponytail and redo it.

Then I search through the mansion until I find the servants' quarters. Most have barricaded themselves in their rooms or hidden under their beds.

It takes some time, but I finally locate Miss Nyles's room.

"These are for you," I say, and I drag the two unconscious men from the kitchens inside, one at a time, ignoring the shooting pain in my ankle. Thankfully, the servants sleep downstairs; otherwise I wouldn't have managed transporting them.

I pull out one of my daggers and hand it to Miss Nyles, hilt first.

The young woman looks between my dagger and the two unconscious brutes tied up on the floor of her bedroom. She takes the weapon offered to her.

"I suggest waiting until they're awake," I offer. "It'll be better that way."

Then I put the mansion behind me and sail home.